ESTRID

A CRAE ROMANCE

ADDISON JAMES

ADDISON JAMES

To endings, and beginnings, and the things we create in between.

CONTENTS

CONTENT NOTES

*On page violence/fighting

*On page harm to and kidnapping of a minor (not involving the main characters, no permanent damage). Harm includes captivity and medical trauma.

*References to/vague threats of sexual assault of the minor (not carried out and not made by the main characters)

*References to a past sexual assault (not involving the main characters)

*Kidnapping/imprisonment between our main characters

*Family loss (off-page, not recent)

*Strained family dynamics, including disowning

*Light use of restraints during sex

*On page explicit sex scenes

BEFORE YOU BEGIN...

Welcome to the end of our journey with the Craes and those who hang around them. I am honored to be here with you all; these books have meant so much to me.

This is the first book to take place chronologically after *Callum*. As such, it is the first book that would be improved by a working knowledge of what happens in the prior five books. In addition, Ryder and Hannah are characters in this book, and while you don't need to have read it, I have released a short story about them to newsletter subscribers if you want to know more about them and their relationship.

The Crae Romance Series has always been about found family, and Estrid and Clay might seem like outsiders, but they too belong in our little circle. Here you'll see Marielle and Callum, Mae and Bryce, Chase and Heath, Bethany and Celia, Theo and Silas, and Hannah and Ryder all come together, bringing together every aspect of the story.

I hope you enjoy the end of this journey as much as I enjoyed writing it.

This is the first Crae Romance book that really expects a reader to already be familiar with the world. If you chose not to read the prior books, or simply want a refresher, these graphics should be useful:

WHO'S WHO

KNOWING THE
CREATURES OF THE
CRAE WORLD

GODS

Immensely powerful beings not seen on Earth anymore. Represent various aspects of the world (night, oceans, earth, winter, etc.)

DIVINE

Children of the gods. Created, not born. Significantly more powerful than anything on Earth, but not as powerful as their parents.

HALFLINGS

Children of the divine and creatures of Earth. Often have an unpredictable combination of traits from their two parents. Often have unexpected magical powers, but not as powerful as their divine parent.

SUPERNATURAL

The werewolves, demons, vampires, witches, and other magical creatures who walk the Earth.

HUMANS

Creatures of Earth completely unaware of the magical things happening around them.

FACTIONS OF OUR WORLD

Werewolves	• Creatures with a wolf spirit inside them with the senses and strength of a wolf • Live in a remote village • Notable wolves: Queen Celia, her mate Bethany, and the three princes, Bryce, Heath, and Callum
Demons	• Creatures with access to immense magic, but it has a cost • Typically live in Demonheim, a realm parallel to Earth that is meant to imprison the worst offenders who can't be trusted to be free • Notable demons: King Ryder, his halfling mate Hannah, and Chase
Vampires	• Creatures who drink blood, cannot go in the sun, and have above average strength and charm • Are loyal to one king, and spread over most of the globe • Their king has dozens of wives and dozens of children • Notable vampires: Silas, his mate Theo, crown princess Deidre, and Mina
Witches	• Creatures who have an inner magic that they can use to enchant things • Are typically very isolated creatures and don't share well • Notable witches: Mae, Clay, and Greta
Halflings	• Creatures born from the relationship of a divine and any creature of this Earth • Have an unpredictable collection of traits and a stronger than average amount of power • Notable halflings: Marielle and Hannah
Divine	• Children of the gods with incredible powers • Aren't supposed to visit Earth or form attachments here • Notable divine: Estrid, Rota, and Andreas

PROLOGUE

O nce upon a time, there was a god of night, and he had seven daughters.

There were many gods. As the world was born, creatures were born with it, each taking control of various domains, shepherding those domains and watching over them as they grew. Earth, sky, water, night, day, each season and type of weather—gods rose from nothing, the power of the cosmos filling them, and shaped the world.

The world bent to their will. They shaped the infant universe, made the world change by their whims, and had nearly unlimited power. And, despite this, they were lonely.

Very few of them considered the other gods good company. A god of night didn't talk to a god of the sea—what did they have in common? And so, to combat their loneliness, they invented a new concept: children.

They didn't have children in what would become the normal *way. The god of night wove children from the stars in the sky, taking qualities of his realm and infusing them into the stars until at last seven daughters emerged, born from supernovas. The god of earth hewed children out of the rocks and trees, birthing them from earthquakes and forest fires. The god of the ocean shaped* waves into companions, horrible tsunamis crashing over the land until children were born. And so on. Soon enough, the world was fuller.

Time went on, and all the gods birthed enough children to cure their loneliness. Whenever they felt the urge, there was someone for them to speak with, someone designed to understand them in a way no one else ever could.

But it didn't work both ways. We were their constant companions, their entertainment, and their source of joy. But soon enough, we weren't entertaining anymore. The gods, not ones to think about things like responsibility or parenting, couldn't abide by us when we no longer interested them.

We grew lonely too when the gods abandoned us like unwanted playthings, and too many of us turned to the new creatures populating the Earth as our distraction.

We didn't understand them. Even those with long lifespans were weak compared to us, and their experiences were so limited. We lived in realms they could never hope to understand, and they were so young by comparison. But they were company, and we took advantage until the natural result occurred.

The children born from these unions didn't belong with us. Closer to their other parents, they were too fragile, too short-lived. A measly few thousand years was a blink of an eye to us, and their power, whatever it may be, never could hold up to our own.

So the cycle continued. We sought companionship, and all the while, children were born that we'd never want. We, the unwanted children of the gods, made more unwanted children, over and over and over again.

CHAPTER ONE

ESTRID

No matter how hard I try, Earth keeps calling me back. I know I'm supposed to be happy at home. It's supposed to be the perfect little life in our idyllic gilded cage. Who could ever want anything more than their sisters and a palace in the stars?

I admit I was scared away from Earth for a long time. But over the last few hundred years, I've ventured down here more and more, checking in on the people I love, even if they don't know I'm here.

That's all tonight was supposed to be. I was supposed to come to this party, watch my family from a distance, reassure myself that they're okay, and go home before anyone is the wiser. It was supposed to be simple.

And then, I see the girl. Her power, her look—she's so obviously my niece that the truth is like getting struck by lightning.

Her name is Marielle. I came to the vampire's party to see my family, but I never expected her, because I never knew she existed. Yet she looks so much like Rota that she couldn't possibly be anything but her daughter. Her power is practically a beacon, declaring her strength and the lineage it must have come from. And of course she's in love with a werewolf; her mother's magic always did come from the moon.

I shouldn't be surprised to find previously unknown relatives kicking around. There are too many unwanted halfling children in the world; not powerful enough for us, yet always something *other* than everyone on Earth. It's become a fact of life really, to know that there are unwanted nieces and nephews down here.

But I didn't even know this one existed, and she thoroughly distracts me for days. Maybe it was the way she dismissed me. Maybe it was because her magic had been so strong, so familiar—almost enough for her to be considered one of us.

But *almost* doesn't make her one of us, I remind myself over and over. There are laws that say Marielle's of this earth, so she has to stay here. If she's one of them, she can't be one of us, and I have to leave her alone.

Besides, she flat-out rejected me. Marielle made it perfectly clear that she's found her family here, and I'm not part of it. The way she'd looked at that werewolf, and the way he'd adoringly looked back, told me enough. Marielle has a mate and a family and a home. So what if she's my niece? She doesn't want me.

That argument doesn't last very long. I have to know who she is, where she's come from. Call me a soft-heart; gods know all my sisters have over the years. But I can't abandon family, and I have to know who this girl is with so much pain in her eyes.

I wait for full night to find her. I'm no vampire, and I can roam about in daylight hours just fine, but I always prefer the comforting cloak of night. It feels almost like home, in its way. Fortunately, creatures like my niece always seem to prefer the darkness.

When I let the magic take me to her, I expect to wind up outside the home of the wolf she was with. I don't expect to land in a field of flowers nowhere near where I saw her last, only to have my ears immediately assaulted by the absolute racket of people fucking.

Good gods, what is he *doing* to her? I don't risk looking. A glance up tells me what I should have realized from the start; it's the full moon, and they're doing what werewolves do under the full moon, and I very much don't want to witness this.

There's a house over the hill that's presumably theirs, and it looks like a good enough place to escape to. It's probably not fair to ambush them inside their own house the morning after a full moon, but no one's ever accused me of playing fair.

The house doesn't look like a place a wolf would live. It's too stuffy and formal, but I make my way there, anyway. If they can't greet guests appropriately, then I'll see myself in, make myself comfortable, and wait for them.

Honestly. Would it have killed her to have a civil conversation with me at the ball? Vampires can always throw a good party, and it had been perfectly lovely, and I wouldn't be picking my way through a ruined garden.

I frown. That doesn't feel right. I don't know this girl, but a passing taste of her magic tells me she would never live in a place with a ruined garden. She's too attuned with the flowers and plant life around her.

The house reeks of death. The hair on my arm stands on end, and I think for a fleeting second about just disappearing from here. Something isn't right. But, like an idiot, I walk inside.

Call it morbid curiosity. Call it a lack of other things to keep me busy. Either way, I go in, and the smell of death only gets worse.

There are plants in strange places. They're ripping through the walls, cutting through furniture, all at odd, unnatural angles. I study them intently, knowing without having to ask that Marielle did this, and that no one would do this to their own home.

The bodies are in the basement, along with a cell and plenty of blood. Most of it presumably belongs to the corpses, and some probably belong to the wolf, but an uncomfortable amount smells like Marielle's magic. Something in me bristles at that.

She's *mine*. How dare they harm something that belongs to me? Who are they, and what did they possibly want with her?

Clearly, she took care of the problem herself. She's a lethal little thing, looking like the flowers she grows, but hiding something dark and cutting inside. The rose with its thorns.

Something in me warms knowing that.

I want answers, but I know I have no hope of interrupting what's going on outside, not during the full moon. It would take an army to separate a werewolf from their mate under the moon, and I don't particularly feel like bringing that level of force. So instead, I poke around the house, digging through the papers and files that scatter the basement and the large dining room upstairs.

I don't actually experience nausea, but I'm relatively sure that's what this feeling is. These spells aren't spells anyone should have. Enslavement, gruesome murder, even compelled love: magic that is theoretically possible, but practically unheard of. Spells that take an extreme level of magic, more than anyone should be willing to pay.

And what's worse is they're talking about chopping my niece up for ingredients to make those spells. Apparently, the magic in a halfling makes those *spell ingredients* extra powerful, and that means these horrid spells are possible.

No wonder Marielle wanted nothing to do with me. She probably thinks I and all the other divine knowingly abandoned her to this ugly, horrific fate. I wouldn't want to talk to me either, if that was the case.

I dig through the papers, setting the ones about Marielle and what they did to her to one side. I'll force myself to read them more later, but right now I might be sick for the first time in my entire existence if I keep reading.

"*Fuck me*," I whisper, rifling through the remaining stack of papers. There's a pile a mile high here, listing every disgusting crime against nature I can conceive of. They have spells for sale that make even my blood curdle, and I've seen a lot of terrible things over the years. I've done a fair amount of terrible things, too. When I'd still had a family, I'd been more than willing to put heads on pikes and torture to protect them. But these people target the defenseless. Children, unsuspecting people just going about their days who've never done anything to them—even humans.

I find a list of buyers for these spells buried deep in a stack of papers, and immediately pocket that one. That looks like a good place to work off some of this sick, angry energy coursing through me.

I can't stay here. I can't stay here and wait for Marielle to come back, if she'd even come back to this horrifying house. I can't face her when she thinks I abandoned her to this, when I did nothing, have done nothing—

But that doesn't have to be how it ends. I have more power in one hand than any thousand creatures on Earth. I can get answers. I can get to the bottom of this.

Frost creeps up the edge of the paper where I'm holding it, and I vanish from that damned house, papers in hand, without anyone being the wiser.

***

The corridor grows colder as I walk down it, ice crystallizing on the window-panes, blocking out the view of the starry sky outside. I'm sure if I looked back, there'd be icy patches in my footsteps. I usually have better control than this.

"I met your daughter the other day," I announce, sliding into the seat opposite Rota. I look over at my sister, studying the face I've known for ten thousand years. The girl I met could be Rota's twin with the freckles and red hair, except for the eyes. Rota's eyes are as ancient as the stars we were born from. The girl's eyes are ancient with pain.

I didn't know what it was when I first met her at the party, but now I have a good guess. What those people must have done to her... I shudder. She's supposed to be one of ours, and we left her to that.

Rota looks up from her book. "You'll need to be more specific."

"Red hair," I offer, although that's no help. "Druid? Powerful little thing."

"Hmm. I remember her. Two centuries or so ago, right?" She marks the page with a finger and gives me her attention. "What's so interesting about her?"

"Did you know what they did to her?" I ask, ice appearing under my drumming fingers.

"Who's they?" she asks, already returning to her book.

"The casters who cut her into pieces," I tell her. "Chopped her up over and over again for centuries. Carved her up like cattle." The paperwork I'd read had painted a grim but frustratingly clinical picture. My niece was used as *spell ingredients*. They'd carved pieces off of her for nearly two hundred years and kept notes like they were shearing a sheep or picking fruit from a tree. It was all so scientific, so precise, but I can imagine the very real pain in the very real person behind it all.

Rota goes still, and for a moment I think I've made her care. "And is she still there?"

"No. She's free now."

"Well, then," she says, flipping the page again, apparently no longer interested in me. "I suppose it's solved."

The cruel, callous response sets my blood to boiling. It shouldn't. I know what my sisters—and everyone like us—think of these halfling children. They're not like us. They can't understand us, and the gap is simply too big to bridge. We're never meant to bridge it. We belong with the gods and those children belong on Earth and that's that.

Marielle isn't like us, and therefore Rota doesn't give a shit. I shouldn't have expected any different, but somehow, I do, and I can't temper my rage. "Do you even care?"

"She's an adult," Rota says, still not looking up. "She's long past needing her mother. I weaned her, what, two centuries ago? She's not like us, Es. I can't help her. Her people need to look out for her."

I shouldn't have expected anything more. None of them have ever cared about the children before. They scratch an itch, then move on. If there are children as a consequence of scratching that itch, then they move on just as easily, giving them to the other parent like an unwanted present. Their lives are short compared to ours and their magic limited—why should we care about them?

And that's the question—why do I care about this one? I don't know. I rarely meet them, so maybe it's that. Or maybe it's thinking of my own child, and all I wish I could have done. Or maybe it's the pile of records dispassionately describing the pieces of her they cut off that does it.

I still have those records. I debate slamming them down on the table, making Rota read them, but what would be the point? She won't care. Thousands of years have taught me that. My own family taught me that.

Unable to deal with her for another minute, I walk away.

CHAPTER TWO

ESTRID

M en are so easy to kill. That's not new information to me, of course. The cold of the night kills as easily as anything else, and freezing men's hearts is particularly satisfying when they deserve it.

I know I'm not solving any actual problems by going after the men who bought those disgusting spells. I'm barely scratching the surface of what I found in that house, and what I'm doing won't stop them from finding some other victim to hurt all over again. That's the thing; I could spend the rest of my very long existence taking out people like this, but there are always more selfish, evil bastards to take their place.

If I want to really accomplish anything, then I need a more concrete answer to this problem. I need to figure out where they're getting magic like this, and I need a plan to stop them.

But first, I need more information. I need a way in, something beyond the men I've killed who are, at the end of the day, useless. They're absolutely evil people, but they have nothing I need.

It takes a month for me to get lucky. I'm waiting to break into a horrifically ugly McMansion—the elf living inside is several thousand years old, but apparently there's no accounting for taste—when a witch walks up to the door.

I let the shadows hide me completely. This might be interesting.

Using the shadows to cloak me, I creep closer, needing to hear what's happening.

"—The money, Gerret," the witch demands. He fidgets with something in his pocket as he demands it, and it's not a particularly intimidating move.

"Shove off." The elf tries to close the door, but the witch blocks it with his boot.

"You wouldn't say that if it was anyone else here." He says it with a lot of bluster, but his posture makes him look like a kid faking at being tough. He reminds me more of a snarling kitten than an actual threat.

The elf smiles nastily. "And they would send someone else if they were serious," he says, confirming my impression of this witch. "We all know they're scraping the bottom of the barrel with you. Shove off, little witch. Go back to what you're good at."

The witch growls, using the hand in his pocket and withdrawing a clunky pocket knife. I raise an eyebrow. If he wants to kill my target for me, then I won't complain, but what does he think a little knife like that will do?

The elf chortles. "What're you going to do, give me a paper-cut?"

He's too busy laughing to realize the blade has sunk into his gut. His laugh cuts off abruptly, looking down at the blade. "What a waste of a blade—"

"Poison is a nasty way to die," the witch cuts him off. "Slow and excruciating. Your body will fight it for a while, but eventually it'll give up." I mentally change my estimation of the witch. Poison that can actually kill an immortal is potent indeed, and not something everyone can make. He's probably more powerful than his fidgety, skinny little frame would indicate.

"You wouldn't have the brains—"

"I do," the witch interrupts again, tilting his chin up. "I know spells that would make your head spin. And, fortunately for you, I also know the counter-spell to this particular poison. But it has a cost."

"*Fucking witches*," he grouses, then hisses, doubling over, hands on the hilt of the knife but not pulling it out. "This burns," he says through gritted teeth.

"It does," the witch agrees, face giving nothing away, but I think I can see something in his eyes, some sort of uncertainty. I have to remind myself that he works for some evil people.

Well, unless the elf has been stupid enough to get himself involved with multiple organizations after him for money, and this witch represents some witch mafia or something. But I doubt that. I think this witch works for whoever makes these spells and who cut my niece up. I think I finally found the missing link I need.

The elf turns inside the house and returns, check in his shaky hand. "There. Happy? Now fucking cure me."

The witch grabs the check and shoves it in his pocket. "No," he says simply, turning to leave.

The elf howls after him, rage and frustration making him sound like a child. "They'll be pissed you killed me! I'm a paying customer."

The witch stops. "Barely," he mutters, and then keeps walking.

I send a shadow to follow the witch so I don't lose him, and then I stop and check on the elf before following my new target. I respect the witch's desire for him to die slowly—this elf buys girls, too young and human and brainwashed with spells to fight back—but I can make it painful and also ensure the job gets done. It's sloppy to leave a job half finished, and I'll tell him that whenever I catch up to him.

He looks terrible when I break in, the few short minutes making him a sweaty, stumbling mess. I have to suppress a smile. "Someone's having a bad day."

His eyes take me in. "Save me," he pleads, slumped over and looking more pathetic by the second. He removed the knife and discarded it on the floor, letting it drip blood onto his expensive marble. Judging by how much he's shaking, removing the knife didn't help him much with the poison.

"Now, why would I do that?" I murmur. "I think you and I both know you deserve to die some horrific death, don't we?" The question is rhetorical, and he doesn't respond. I click my tongue. "Do you have any girls here now?"

He whimpers. "I—"

I don't have time for nonsense. I let the shadows grab at his wrists, tugging them behind his back. I tighten the grip more than necessary, pulling his shoulders in their sockets in a way that surely tugs at his burning gut wound. Then I slowly walk closer, bringing my icy touch to his heart, letting my freezing fingers barely brush his skin. "It's a yes or no question."

"One."

"Thank you," I say, and then freeze his heart solid.

Immortals are hard to kill. Not as hard as we are, but still difficult. Removing the head completely from the body is the tried and true best method and the one most common during warfare. But I let the ice contract around his heart, freezing his blood and squeezing the organ until it physically bursts under his skin, and then smile grimly. There's no coming back from that.

I pick up the knife, studying the silvery blade while being careful not to let it touch my skin. It's an interesting and perhaps useful tool. Freezing hearts gets boring sometimes.

I flick it shut and store it in my pocket, then look for the girl he has here. And after I find her, I have a witch to catch.

CHAPTER THREE

CLAY

March's office always makes the hair on the back of my neck stand on end.

There's an acrid smell in here. It's magic, but only the rotten, vile leftovers of terrible spells. It's not fair that, when I can barely feel magic after what they've done to me, I can still smell this.

The smell is off-putting; the chairs are uncomfortable, and March watches me like he's planning how to cut me into pieces. On top of that, the leg I injured in a scuffle with a late-paying client almost a month ago *still* isn't healed, and it throbs painfully now. I don't know if that's in my head or if it's a real physical pain from trying to hide it so much. This isn't the type of place where I'd want people to know that I'm wounded.

They already think I'm incapable. I run errands for these people because they don't trust me to do more than that anymore, and the very last thing I need is for them to think that I can't even handle that much.

But when March calls, I go. I know better than to say *no* around here.

March loves his little power plays, loves ignoring me for a moment, making me wait even though he called me in here.

He looks through reports like they're the most urgent thing in the world, and I fight not to shift my weight again while I think about what it could be this time. I'm essentially Mr. Fetch-and-Carry now, bringing ingredients here or there or collecting payments. Needless to say, it's *not* the glamorous life I thought I would get when I signed up.

But I've already failed them twice. First, when I couldn't acquire Greta's magic shop, and the second time when I all but lost my magic. No one has *said* there's a three-strikes policy, but I think I can read between the lines. I don't think this organization comes with retirement benefits, and I'll do whatever it takes to stay out of the way and alive.

I fetch. I carry. Whenever I have enough magic for them to deem me useful, I give it to the cause without complaint. And sometimes, if a client particularly annoys me and I think I can get away with it, I stab them. It helps keep me sane.

Finally, March looks up. "We have a production slow-down we need you to fix," he says.

I blink. That's an unexpected way to say *we need you to pick up a delivery*. "Oh?"

"I'm sure you've heard the rumors."

No one gossips worse than centuries-old spell casters who do sketchy shit for a living. But this isn't exactly the type of workplace culture where you admit to having heard the rumor mill. We're not tolerant of people knowing more than they should.

"Our halfling has gone missing." *Gone missing* is a fascinating way to say *walked out and took down two* households' *worth of operatives*, if the rumors are to be believed. The rumor mill says that a whole host of werewolves killed everyone in their path to get to the girl. Then, once our side got her back, the girl and her werewolf mate killed everyone who took them. It was supposedly violent and devastating, and the carnage needed to be seen to be believed. Needless to say, it's not a story that makes us look particularly good. "Attempts to reclaim her weren't successful, and it's time to start over with a new subject."

I get a cold, sinking feeling in my gut about where this is going.

He pushes a folder across his desk. "We determined a couple targets. This one is yours. Bring her back by tomorrow."

Her. I clutch the folder without consciously grabbing for it and refuse to open it.

I knew about the halfling. I knew about the spell ingredients, the pure magical power contained in a halfling's body. It had been a part of some of those spells I'd used to cast for them, after all. The halfling's magic combined with my magic made some damn powerful spells. But I'd never seen her. Never had to face what they must have done to her.

But now there's a *her* in this folder, and it's my job to bring her back.

I nod shakily. What else can I do? I know the cost of disappointing March, and it's one I can't afford to pay.

"Don't disappoint us," March says conversationally, like this is all totally normal. "I know your capabilities are—*limited*—these days, but surely even you can handle retrieval." March raises an eyebrow. I don't know if he can see my hesitation or he just expects me to be useless, but the look is not a strong vote of confidence. "Any questions?"

"No," I manage to make myself say, and then stand.

"Clay?" I freeze. "Send Sarge in before you go. I have a file for him too."

***

It's not like I want to kidnap a kid.

I didn't get into this for kidnappings. I wasn't opposed, necessarily, but not random kids. Not like this.

But this is the job, and hindsight is twenty/twenty. Would I have made different decisions in the past? Probably, but I can't change my choices now. Once you're in this line of work, you can't go back. I burned all my bridges too long ago.

The target's name is Vesta. She's barely eighteen years old, and she's apparently living right here in New York City. She's trying to go to school. I guess the logic is that, as a student living alone, no one will notice she's gone for a day or two, giving us time to secure her somewhere.

I have to keep repeating the facts so I don't lose my mind. I can't think too hard about any of this, or I won't be able to do it. If I think about it like I'm just reading her file, then I can't think of her like a real person.

The kid isn't too hard to follow from her dorm. She's slight, a little wisp of a thing, wearing chunky heels and jewelry and a red scarf tied around her tight braids, presumably to hide her pointed ears. If I didn't know better, I'd think she was just another human teenager out for a night of drinking.

She's not *just some human kid*, I remind myself sternly. Whether she knows it or not, whether she likes it or not, there is a cost of being in our world, and it's always been survival of the fittest. It's not my fault if she can't look after herself.

The dance floor at this sketchy club that just let in a bunch of obviously underage college kids is packed. I dodge around writhing bodies, disgusted by the sweat and hormones.

I used to love a good party, although they looked a little different when I was younger. What's happened to me? When did I get old?

Thankfully, my body doesn't look that much older than theirs, so I blend in well enough with these kids. No one would mistake me for a college freshman having their first taste of freedom, but no one would think I'm too old for the club, either. I move through the throng, watching that red scarf through the dancers.

And then I'm eye-to-eye with the eighteen-year-old who grown men have already divided up for parts. I freeze, and she just looks at me for a moment like I'm any other person she stumbled across, and I don't know what to do. I should grab her or lure her outside. But I freeze up, unable to make the words come to start my lie. Unable to ruin this kid's life.

She just wants to dance. She wants to dance and go to school and have friends, and how can I *possibly* take all that away from her and turn her over to March to be tortured?

I turn away, hoping she doesn't recognize me for what I am, or at least doesn't put the pieces together. Then again, why should she assume someone wants to hurt her?

The cool air outside the club is a welcome relief, and I stumble away, needing more. I need to—I don't even know. All I know is that I feel like I'm burning up.

I stumble further away from the club, needing to put some distance between me and what I almost did. I need to re-group, to think of my options, but I can't even think through the screaming in my head, and—

I pause. Footsteps. Those are footsteps behind me, and not some casual tourist walking around where they shouldn't be. Those footsteps are determined, and the hairs at the back of my neck stand on end. Maybe it's a human thinking they found an easy target to mug, but my gut says that's not the case.

I walk faster, turning down another block. But the footsteps keep following me, and they're gaining.

I can't go any faster with my limp. I'm practically defenseless when it comes to spells right now. I have a knife in my pocket, and I grip it unsteadily, hoping it's enough.

A bolt of cold hits me in the back, icy spikes driving into my skin, knocking the air out of my lungs. I fall to my knees, gasping.

"What do you want?" I demand when I can get my breath. I try to stand, but something holds me in place.

Careful, light footsteps move around me. And unlike a moment ago, they seem in no hurry.

They stop in front of me, and my eyes trail up the bare legs, the dress-clad body, to find a face with pointed ears and icy eyes.

"There you are," she says, stepping closer, voice dripping with ice and contempt. "I have a job for you, witch."

"Who the fuck are you?" I demand, trying to pull free of whatever magic is holding me. Either I'm weaker than I thought or her magic is stronger than expected, because I don't move a muscle.

She rolls her eyes. "Did you hurt anyone tonight?"

"What the—" How much does she know? I shake my head, choosing to play dumb. "No."

"If you lie to me, I'll kill you and I'll make it slow," she promises, voice slow and even, and I believe every word she says.

"I'm not lying," I protest, and it's true. I didn't hurt anyone. I might have come close, but I didn't, and I'm sure I'll pay for that when I go back to March.

If. I look up at her, and I know it's an *if*. *If* I make it back to March.

She studies me. "Alright, then. You'll do."

"Do? What do you mean, do? I—"

And then the world goes black.

CHAPTER FOUR

ESTRID

I use the shadows to move him to a secure location.

I haven't been here in centuries, and I should perhaps have been more worried about the condition of the place before tonight, but in my defense I was preoccupied with hunting down the damn witch. In my mind, this is still the grand castle I lived in with those I loved the most, but the reality is a crumbling, molding mess of collapsing stones. My heart hurts just looking at it.

Even so, enough of it still stands for us to use it. Really, all I need is a room I can tie him up in, and there's plenty of space for that. I find a room on the second floor in an area without a surviving staircase. It's perfect for my needs, so I use shadows to pin him to an ancient bed frame and wait for him to wake up.

Honestly. These creatures are so damn delicate. A little bit of shadow travel and he's unconscious for almost a half an hour. Ridiculous.

I use the time to look him over, studying everything about him. First, I empty his pockets, robbing him of yet another pocketknife and his wallet. I set both aside, not bothering to examine them too closely. I don't want his money; I'm interested in the witch himself.

He's dressed for the club he went to tonight, a mesh top and pants so tight I'm sure he has trouble getting them on and off. I think he might be wearing a bit of makeup, but not enough to hide the horrendous bags underneath his eyes. This is a man who clearly doesn't sleep much.

He wakes up squirming and tugging against his shadow restraints, but they don't let go. They've held up against worse than him, but just to make the point, I tighten them around his wrists, squeezing.

"Careful there," I tell him, removing the shadows covering his eyes. "Wouldn't want to break those wrists. They'll heal, but magic might be kind of hard in the meantime."

"Who the fuck are you?" he demands, looking wildly around the room.

I give it a cursory glance. I know it's no longer pretty, but this castle was splendid once. I'm suddenly a little embarrassed for him to see it like this instead of its former glory.

Then I remember he's a man who works for people who do despicable things. He doesn't deserve a nice castle. He can have decrepit stones falling around him.

"My name is Estrid," I tell him.

"And who are you, Estrid?"

"Haven't you guessed yet?" I ask. My ears are usually the giveaway. That and the magic I use.

"What do you *want*?" he demands, tugging ineffectively at the restraints once again.

"A much better question." I study him as his tugs grow more and more feeble. Maybe he's just learning that he can't escape me, but the hatred in his eyes hasn't died away. He's not quitting. He's just weak.

Maybe I picked the wrong target. I don't need someone barely able to fight; I need someone who can infiltrate that organization and give me what

I need. I need someone I can re-shape to my will, and he can't be re-shaped if he's just broken.

"Did you cut apart that girl?"

He squirms again. "The one in the club? I didn't touch her, you insane—"

"Not her." I should probably care about her, whoever she is, and I make a mental note to add learning that to my to-do list. She's probably not *mine* in the way Marielle is, but at this point, it hardly matters. This is bigger than family. "The one who they kept for parts. My niece."

He freezes. "Your niece?" I can see the gears turning in his head as he frantically stares at me, realizing who he's talking to. I am a child of gods, and he should be terrified to be in my presence.

"You've put it together. Good. Now answer my question." I take one step closer to the bed. I rarely get to tower over people, but I use the fact that he's lying down to my full advantage, ensuring all he can look at is me.

"No," he croaks. "I never even saw her, I'm just..."

I study him closely. He's telling the truth. I can see it in his eyes, hear it in his voice, but I can't help but be even more disgusted at his desperate attempt to throw out an excuse. Like there's any justification that would make me forgive him.

"You're just a spineless, power-hungry piece of shit who isn't even good enough for them to show the *real* magic to," I conclude.

He jerks in his bonds again and sneers. "It's *my* power they use for those spells."

What a sad, pathetic response. "So you'll happily participate, but won't face what it costs. I understand." I've certainly seen men like him before in my lifetime.

"Let me out of here," he snarls. "Fight me. Don't hide behind your fucking shadows."

I shrug. "Alright." With a thought, the shadows drop, and before he can move, I pull out and open the pocketknife he left in the elf's stomach.

He freezes, eyeing the knife like a wild animal. "Where did you get that?"

"Where do you think?" I study the blade. "Nifty little spell you did."

"Don't play with that, I—" But I don't give him a chance to finish the thought, instead feinting to the left so he moves, then flicking the blade and landing it in the meat of his shoulder.

He screams, a blood-curdling sound that echoes off the stonework. "What did you do to me, you bitch!"

I *tsk*, stepping closer to him. "Is that any way to talk to the woman who's going to save you?"

"Save me?" he asks through gritted teeth.

"You told that elf you could create an antidote. I'm prepared to supply you with whatever you need for it as soon as you make me certain promises."

He falls back onto the bed, clutching at his arm. "There is no antidote, you complete psycho."

I study the way he's writhing and gasping. *Fuck, did I kill my source already?* "Well," I say pragmatically, "guess I need to start over. Anyone in particular you want me to return your body to?"

He takes several deep breaths, trying to center himself, which is entirely canceled out when his back bows off the bed. "Won't kill me," he says, although the way he whimpers tells me he's not so sure.

I freeze. "What do you mean?" But I don't need him to answer. I put the pieces together, seeing the clever lie he spun to that elf. It won't kill him, but he'll certainly feel like he's dying. That elf would have *lived* if I hadn't finished him off, because I'm now gathering that the witch is *soft*. He's vile and has no morals, but he doesn't have it in him to kill, and I can't decide if that's better or worse.

I click my tongue. "You were sloppy then, leaving the elf alive for me to deal with."

He doesn't answer. I suppose I can't expect him to.

I sigh. So now I have a sick, poisoned witch in my castle, and I don't have a cure to leverage his cooperation with. Fantastic.

"You'll thank me for this later," I murmur, then knock him unconscious again.

I restrain him to the bed. I have no desire to watch him for however long this takes, and while I doubt he can run away in his condition, and there are no stable staircases in this wing of the castle anyway, I don't need him rolling himself off the bed in pain. Once I'm sure he won't go anywhere, I begin to pace.

He'll be weak when he wakes. Assuming this hasn't broken him permanently, I can just start again. One icy touch to his heart will convince him how serious I am.

I just hate to *wait*. You think beings like me would be good at waiting, but very few of us are. When we want something, we're not used to being denied it.

This *fucking* witch. I know I need him, but I'm going to make him suffer for it.

He groans on the bed, being unconscious apparently not enough to entirely stop the pain. I frown and walk back over to him, standing over him like he's a bug on the floor. He squirms in his bonds, and some part of me reluctantly feels bad.

Yes, he's a terrible person, but I shouldn't pretend that I'm a *good* person. The idiot witch just had the bad luck to personally cross me. I can hate him and feel bad for him at the same time.

He's sweating, presumably from the pain of whatever poison he spelled that knife with. If I had an effective way to heal him, I might even consider using it. But that's never been a talent of mine, so I settle for pushing his sweaty hair off his face.

He's pretty. I don't want to think it, but I do. The witch is pretty even when he's in this much pain, and while I could do without the sweat matting his dark hair and dotting his brow, I can't help but see the sharp face and full lips and nearly perfect skin.

He takes four hours to open his eyes again. The sun rises in that time, and I might be going out of my mind. I should have brought a book, or one of those stupid cellphones everyone is so addicted to now. I drag a chair in, giving up on pacing, and put it near the bed, settling in to watch him.

I tap the bed with my foot. "Wakey, wakey. I have things to do here."

He glares at me, but it's as effective as a kitten glaring after his ordeal. "So you weren't a dream."

"Never been called a dream before," I tell him. A nightmare, maybe. I toy with the knife I plucked out of his shoulder. I have no intention of wasting my time and use it again, but he doesn't have to know that. "Are you able to talk right now?"

He groans. "And if I say no?" His eyes slip closed again.

"Then I kill you and move on." Will I? It would mean starting over, having to get lucky all over again. But I won't waste my time beating my head against a rock.

"I'm tired."

"So am I, but you don't see me complaining."

"I'm *drained*. Does a creature like you even understand what that means? You poisoned me, and I didn't have a lot left in me to fight the poison."

"You were limping when I caught up to you," I acknowledge. I'd thought that was strange at the time for a creature like him to be limping without obvious injury, but hadn't really cared enough to investigate. "Did they do that to you?"

He shrugs the best he can in his bonds, not looking at me. "Can you let me go?"

"No." I can see he'll try to run. He won't get anywhere, but that will just set us back further. And I need an answer to my question. "Tell me."

He still doesn't look at me. "Magic has a cost. And my healing relies on me having magic to use. So, something has been wrong with my ankle for a little bit. I don't have the energy to heal it. It's fine."

It's not fine, though. Because my magic differs from his, and I'm no witch, but I know that *shouldn't* be happening. There's no reason a normal use of magic would leave a functioning witch like this. "What kind of magic do they have you doing that's bleeding you dry like that?"

"You don't want to know," he says emptily, his face twisting as he tries to turn away from me.

"You're as much a spell ingredient as my niece was," I realize slowly. "They're draining you too. They might not chop pieces off you, but they're draining you just the same." I feel a begrudging rush of sympathy.

He chose this, I remind myself. They used him and hurt him, but he chose to be there. He was apparently supposed to kidnap a child last night. I shouldn't have sympathy for him.

He's silent for a long minute, and then he looks at me again. "And if I don't do it, then they'll probably chop literal pieces off of me. And I don't heal as efficiently as your niece does."

They probably would. They'd chop him up and then kill him, taking what they need before writing him off as a loss.

Well, that makes this easier. He should also have a vested interest in seeing the end of these people. Now I just need to convince him it's worth his while to help me end them.

"I need someone on the inside," I tell him. "Someone willing to get me certain information. Someone who will help me end this group."

"They'd kill me. Might as well just let you do it and save myself the hassle," he says dully.

26

"They're killing you either way," I point out. "And if you work for me, I'll protect you." I lean closer to the bed, trying to get him to look at me properly. He won't turn to me, instead choosing to stare at the wall.

"Nothing can protect me."

"You know what I am. You're saying I can't?" Knowing a divine is offering their magic should be all the reassurance he needs. He should be *trembling* in fear, *begging* to do what I ask of him.

He looks at me sidelong. "They also have some powerhouses on their side."

Bingo. An answer I've been waiting for, and I didn't even have to threaten him to get it.

I step closer to the bed. "Let's start there," I say. "Which divine exactly is backing your little venture?"

CHAPTER FIVE

CLAY

M y heart stops beating for a moment.

"Why do you even care?" I ask her, still staring at the wall, trying to keep her from seeing my face. "Your niece escaped, I heard."

"I'm still asking the questions here, actually," she says, and she touches the edge of the bed. All of a sudden, the entire bed is freezing cold, and I arch up to limit how much of it's touching me. I can't get away from it, icy fingers digging into me, stealing the breath from my lungs.

And just like that, it's over. Her point is made. She still has her magic, and I don't.

I could just let her kill me. What does it even matter at this point? Someone is going to kill me. At least if it's her, it'll be over fast.

Then again, she seems like a vengeful type of person. I bet she plays with her food. I can't count on her to actually make it quick.

"I won't wait all day," she warns me. She's still holding that damned knife.

Fuck, but do I regret taking the time to make that now. It had been a particularly good day, and I'd had energy for once. The spell isn't especially hard, and I'd found it in a book lying around one of the many houses we cycle through. The pain truly is as unimaginable as the spell book promised. It can't kill me, but I damn sure wished I was dead when she stabbed me.

"His name is Andreas," I tell her. "Mean anything to you?"

She doesn't say anything, but I see it in her eyes. She knows exactly who Andreas is.

And I don't. I'm the one being interrogated for information, and yet I'm the one who doesn't know much. I know Andreas has power that I couldn't imagine. I've spent decades scrounging up every bit of power I could, hoarding spells like the lifelines they are, but Andreas' power makes all that look like amateur hour. Andreas' magic blows me away.

I know he's like her. The few times I've seen him have made it obvious, and the level of magic he holds is inarguable. But what god's child he is, is anyone's guess. She would know better than me.

Do they have a club? Meet for yearly family reunions? Send Christmas cards?

"You know him," I conclude quietly.

"I'm asking the questions," she reminds me again. "Have you met him?"

"A few times. Not personally. From a distance, really."

"He gives you those spells?"

"Not directly, but yeah. Everyone looks to him." Andreas might not interact with us all on a regular basis, but self-important assholes like March are basically middle management. They report to Andreas, and then come back to us with his orders. We all know who keeps us fed.

"When would you see him again?"

I shrug, made difficult by the damn shadows still binding me. Insubstantial as smoke, they're nevertheless entirely solid and unbreakable. I'm beginning to understand why non-magic creatures hate magic.

"He shows up when he wants to show up."

She purses her lips, clearly not liking that answer. She's tapping the knife hilt against her hand, and I watch the blade, waiting for it to slip. Will the spell even hurt her? Would it give me a chance to get out of here?

"Only a few more questions," she says. "And then we're done." I don't like the sound of that. *Done* can mean so many things.

"Alright." Because what else can I say?

"Why'd you join them in the first place?"

I didn't expect that question, and something tells me a lot rides on the answer. There is definitely a wrong answer here, and I wish I knew what it was.

I opt for the truth. "Being a witch is about power," I tell her. "More power, more spells. We're protective of our magic, hoarding it. And they promised me more." My cousins Greta and Mae had always been good at making their own magic, but I'd needed to fight for every last piece. Creating just doesn't come naturally to me, so I'd need to rely on what already existed. It's dangerous work to steal and hoard magic, and I'd always hoped there'd be a better way. When I'd been offered access to so much magic, it had been impossible to turn down. "Guess some deals are too good to be true."

She purses her lips again, and I can't tell if that's a good sign or not. It probably isn't, and I wait for the killing blow.

I shouldn't care. What the fuck do I have to live for? There's nothing left for me. Andreas or someone else will kill me if they find out I ever had this conversation. Honestly, even if they don't, I'm not sure how many more times my body can handle this cycle of regenerating a little magic, then spending it all on one awful spell. I'd rather be taken out by a wrathful divine being than by my own body failing at magic.

"Alright then," she murmurs, and I hesitate to look over. She doesn't sound like she wants to kill me. "How'd you like to help me destroy one of the divine?"

CHAPTER SIX

ESTRID

His eyes go all wide like I spoke to him in some ancient tongue he can't understand, but I know I made myself perfectly clear. "Well? I'm waiting."

"That's a suicide mission," he stutters.

"I told you I'd protect you." Probably. I'm not too fussed about helping him right this minute, truth be told. But if he gets me what I need, then the least I can do is try to ensure he doesn't die. "And, be honest: what kind of future do you have if you don't take me up on this offer? You're intelligent enough to know that they're bleeding you dry."

He looks away, but not before I can see bitter understanding in his eyes. He knows they're killing him slowly, the same as I do.

"What exactly do you want from me?" He still refuses to look at me, but I can hear his defeat.

I study him for a second, then release his bonds. "I'm not having this conversation with a man restrained to a bed. Sit up and talk to me."

He shakes out his arms, slowly moving to sit up. At last, we're facing each other, and I study him again. This is a beaten-down man. This is a man who, despite being immortal, has been pushed to his limit. His body physically won't hold up much longer, and I need to temper my expectations of him before I send him back there.

"They took my niece," I tell him. "And then they cut her up for nearly two hundred years."

"I thought your kind didn't care about children who weren't as divine as you."

"We're not all the same," I snap, although alright, I hadn't even known she'd existed until a few weeks ago. I only know her name because I heard the wolf say it; she hadn't chosen to share it with me. She'd walked away from me because we'd abandoned her. I get his point.

He looks at me for a long minute, then chooses not to argue. "They're keeping a list of other halflings. They want a new one. That's what I was supposed to do last night. Was it just last night?"

"It was," I confirm, mind turning that over. So they're looking for more children to chop to pieces? "Any person with a conscience would want to do something about that."

"What the fuck do you expect me to do?" he demands. "In case you haven't noticed, you laid me out pretty easy. I'm fucked right now. I can't take out Andreas for you. I have nothing to give."

No, that's not quite true. He can go places I can't, learn things I can't, and give me information I can't get for myself.

Because yes, I want revenge for my niece. That's just common courtesy, to look out for family like that. But I've known since the moment I read those documents that the spells they're doing come from a higher power, and now that I know Andreas is involved, it makes sense.

I don't know Andreas personally, but I know who he is. He's as old as I am, one of the original divine children, except his power and godly parent lies in the realm of the Earth. His magic is no doubt incredibly old and strong.

I look over at the witch. *Strong* would not be the first word I'd use to describe him. Even if he were in better health, I don't think anyone would ever consider him a paradigm of strength. He looks more like a lean, lithe runway model than a bodybuilder, and while I know as well as anyone that magic is a deceptive sort of strength, I don't relish the idea of sending him up against Andreas in his current state.

"Rest up," I tell him. "You're going to need it."

He startles. "That's it?"

"For now." I don't know what he was expecting. He has an accurate enough assessment of his own strengths, so it's not like he's deluded into thinking he's capable of being what I want right now. Does he think I'd send him into danger anyway? That'd be a waste of a weapon.

"I'm going to restrain you again," I tell him. "But I'll give you a long leash. Don't try to force it—you won't win."

He grits his teeth but doesn't fight me, and that's good. That's progress. He knows this is inevitable now.

***

When I arrive home, it's like being made whole again.

The palace of starlight embraces me in the warmest hug, and I let the dark, cool night wash over me.

"You've been gone a lot," Avila notes, lounging on one of the benches outside, looking up at the stars.

"I have," I agree, wary of her response. Before, when I'd been leaving, it was like no one ever noticed. I'd go for a few hours and be back before anyone thought to worry. Now, I've been gone more than I've been here for over a month.

She pulls herself upright, studying me closely. "Are you in trouble again, Es?"

My throat feels like it closes at the casual way she says it. *Trouble again.* Like last time is just something we can brush over. Like what they did to me is so easy to simplify.

"I don't think so," I mutter, my voice choked.

"Oh, leave her alone," Amaris calls, walking through the garden of brilliant, bright blooms that only blossom under our night sky. "No one cares about that place anymore. She can do what she wants. Earth is unnecessary."

"We should still care about Earth," I point out. "The people—some of them are our relatives, Mar."

She shrugs, an ungainly move she somehow makes graceful. But that's Amaris, the beauty of all of us. Her eyes are filled with stars, and beings on Earth have been known to become spellbound when she looks at them for too long. She used to find that amusing, but I don't know the last time she even bothered to go to Earth.

"Come inside," Avila offers, standing. "Tell us about what has you so interested now."

We gather sisters as we walk. First it's Avila and Amaris, and then Nisha and Neve, and then Cosima, and finally Rota. We move to the grand library, a place where we've spent untold hours over the last ten thousand years.

We've read every book more than once, but if you let it take long enough, it's almost like the book is fresh when you get back to it.

"So, you're on Earth again," Neve says neutrally, her voice careful. Neve's shadows are always surrounding her, a perpetual darkness clinging to her skin. It makes everything she says and does seem a little darker, a little more threatening.

"I am." Let me not look afraid. Let me not show them I still think about the last time they deemed I spent too much time on Earth.

We've always been expected to police our own kind, and showing too much interest in Earth is against the rules. I paid for the last time I was *too interested*. It's only in the last few centuries I've felt even remotely safe returning, and I've been careful until now.

"Is this about my daughter?" Rota asks, and everyone turns to her.

"In a way," I tell her, my voice not as strong as I'd like. "What they did to her..."

"She's not our problem, Es," Nisha murmurs. "You know that. They're not like us. Let them solve their own problems."

"They are like us," I argue. "They might not be as powerful or live as long, but they're *our* children and they live lives too, Nish. Rota, she's yours. And she's been tortured."

Rota's eyes go hard. "That's why I don't understand why you like that place so much. They torture each other. They're awful to each other, full of so much evil. They have nothing to give us. Why would you ever want to spend more time there than you have to?"

"Why would you want your child there?" I challenge.

She scoffs. "What, you want her here? With us? She'd never belong." I open my mouth to retort, but I can't refute it. Marielle doesn't belong here. She isn't entirely like us, and she has a family on Earth now. Her wolf would never be allowed here, and I know Marielle would give up everything for him.

"I'm just saying, dismissing them entirely is wrong. And what's happening—"

"Estrid," Neve says carefully. "How far have you interfered?" The room is cold and for once, it's not my influence. Ice crystallizes inside me at my sister's threat. She'd say it's not a threat, but I hear it anyway.

"I haven't done anything," I deny. "I met her once, by accident. I haven't spoken to her again." Rota's and Cosima's shoulders relax when I say that. "But there is someone—do you remember Andreas? The son of the Earth?"

"Vaguely," Cosima says, waving her hand absently. "The others—they're not very interesting."

I wonder when the last time was when Cosima left this little gilded cage.

"He's the one who hurt your daughter," I tell Rota. "And he's hurting other halflings. And he's turning humans into his little cult, using magic he should never touch. Someone has to stop him."

If I expected everyone to jump up, I'd be disappointed. Their quickness in punishing me when I overstepped is only matched by their absolute lack of care about anyone else.

"Well?"

Nisha shrugs. "What do you expect us to say? He's not our problem."

"I think he's a problem for all of us."

"Not us. He can't touch us here. If he breaks the rules, his siblings can handle it. Or his father."

"And how has that worked out?" I ask, unable to help my bitterness. "Has our father given a lot of directions in the last thousand years?"

Neve sucks in a breath so sharp I can practically feel the icy wind whistling. "Blasphemy, Estrid."

"We're not his *worshippers*, Neve. We're his children."

"And he's a god. We serve him. It is what it is. If you're upset he doesn't speak to you, you have only yourself to blame."

"You talk to him then. Tell him what I found on Earth. Ask for help." Our father hasn't walked among us in a thousand years, but he and the other gods supposedly listen. No one ever responds to me, though.

It's absolutely silent for a long minute, and I hold my breath. "I'll try," Amaris offers me. "Maybe you should too. Maybe he'll listen to you now."

I doubt it. I haven't heard so much as a whisper in a long, long time. But I don't want to admit that, so I nod. "I can try."

Nisha sighs. "All this talk is exhausting. Come on. We're safe here, and we have everything we could ever need. Rest."

I look around our gilded cage. We have something, all right. I wouldn't call it everything, though.

But then I look at my sisters, all watching me with varying levels of worry, and that should be enough.

So I let them pull me in, hold me close, and we all fall asleep there, piled together, like we have so many times before.

***

I wake up still surrounded by my sisters, unsure how much time has passed. I'm the only one awake, and I carefully extract myself from the pile of limbs and make my way outside.

My father hasn't spoken to me in a thousand years. We were designed for the gods. We were their playthings and companions, with truly no purpose outside entertaining our godly parents. Now we sit around and wait and get ignored.

He doesn't speak to me, but I speak to him.

Usually at this ledge, looking into the void I love and hate so much. If I just reach a finger further out, I could touch the stars I was born from, that I know so intimately. I stay firmly on the ground.

I tell him about Andreas, about what kind of magic he's using. I talk about Marielle and the other halfling Clay was sent to capture. I talk about the human girl at that elf's home and how she suffered.

I get nothing. I squint over the edge, seeing if a star blinks a little brighter, try to feel if the breeze gets a little more insistent. Any sign, anything at all, that he's listening. I get nothing.

"If this is punishment, it's gone on too long," I tell him. "I was punished a thousand years ago. I paid my dues. And punishing me shouldn't hurt other people." Still nothing, not that I expected anything. It's not like I haven't raised this issue before.

"Why does Andreas get to interfere with humans when I couldn't?" I press. "Aren't the rules still the rules?"

He doesn't answer me, which isn't a surprise at all. The surprise is that, somehow, it still hurts.

Chapter Seven

Clay

Somehow, I manage to sleep, and when I wake, it's dark again, so presumably I slept the rest of the day away. It's the most sleep I've gotten in too long.

I feel slightly better. Not recovered by any means, but my mind is a little clearer. I can feel magic under my skin, too. Not much—it's a pittance compared to what I *should* have—but it's there.

Having been robbed of my magic burns. And it's worse knowing that just one day of rest—and rest while imprisoned, at that—is enough to help me start to recover. They've valued me so little that they wouldn't even give me that much.

Witches aren't supposed to run out of magic, but anyone can burn out if pushed too far. And here I am, barely a witch anymore, drained and empty and hurt and a fucking prisoner of some divine being with a touch so cold I want to die.

She didn't lie when she said she'd leave me a long leash. I can stand and move about the room and even to the door, but I can't go much further.

There's no bathroom in my radius, but then again, I doubt I'll find indoor plumbing in a castle so old it's literally crumbling around me. There's a chamber pot under the bed, which I'm going to ignore as long as possible.

I don't really have the energy to pace the room, though. I'd feel like a beast in a cage, and I don't like the comparison.

There's a chill in the air, and I know without turning that she's back.

"You look rested," she murmurs.

I sigh. I look nothing of the sort, and I've never missed my old apartment as much as I do right now. After Mae's boyfriend and his family threatened to murder me, it had felt prudent to skip town. Now I see it as just another chance for the organization to get their claws deeper into me when I was forced to depend on their generosity. But I miss that apartment, with my closet and my skincare products and, yes, running fucking water. What I wouldn't give for some face wash and hair gel. A change of clothes wouldn't be amiss either.

"You get what you need?" I ask dully.

"Not quite. But it's just a start," she says, refusing to elaborate. "Here—I remembered you need to eat."

She throws a bag of fast food at me, and I wrinkle my nose, but beggars can't be choosers. I open it, and at least it's still hot. "You don't need to eat?"

"I'm literally made of starlight. No, I don't need to eat."

"Must be nice," I say, thinking of the clawing hunger in my belly that's by no means the worst I've felt.

"Sometimes." The word sounds heavy, loaded with something she won't elaborate on.

I tear into the burger. It's not good, but it's somehow perfect, and I don't complain as I finish it and start the next one.

"How long can I keep you before they notice?" she asks when I'm halfway finished with the second burger.

"Not at all. They've already noticed."

She raises an eyebrow. "You're that valuable to them?"

"They'd sent me out to get them a halfling," I point out, side-stepping the question, because we are both fully aware that I'm not valuable at all.

She sucks her teeth. "And they want them. Right. So you've already failed at your task."

And that is something I haven't even let myself think through yet. When I'd failed to get Greta's shop, they'd allowed me to make it up to them by pouring my own magic into the spells, and that nearly killed me. I doubt they'll be so forgiving again. What's going to be the cost for not getting the halfling, something they probably consider more valuable by far?

While I'm fretting over what they're going to do to me, she's apparently thinking. "Tell them I took you then," she muses. "You can tell them I was angry about my niece. And tell them I roughed you up a bit."

"I don't look very roughed up."

"You're a witch. Glamor yourself."

"Even if I had the magic to do that, which I'm not convinced I do right now, they'll see right through it. This is literally an organization of some of the most powerful casters on the planet."

She raises an eyebrow. "And they let you in?"

Ouch. "I'll have you know that I used to be impressive." I used to be someone. People used to respect my magic. My name meant something.

"Used to be." She says it softly, and it doesn't sound like an insult. It almost sounds like pity.

Well, pity is worse than an insult. I don't need it and don't want it. "Are you going to actually rough me up so they believe it?" I challenge, desperate to change the topic.

She considers me for a long moment, but has the courtesy of taking the subject change and not try to go back. "No," she concludes. "Tell them I forgot about you and you escaped. Stay here for a week. A month, for all I care. Stay and get stronger so you don't get yourself killed when you go back.

And then tell them I forgot you and you ran when you could. They'll believe it. My kind isn't known for our dedicated focus."

"You want me to stay while they're cutting up whatever innocent halfling they *did* manage to drag back?" I ask.

"I want you useful," she says coolly. "And if it takes a month, then so be it."

I study her for a moment. Still standing, she cuts an imposing figure despite her small size. She's wearing a dress as black as night, and her ears and throat are dripping with jewels. Like stars, I think absently, glittering against all the black of her dress.

She's beautiful and deadly at the same time, and I feel like I've signed a deal with the devil. But it's too late to back out now.

And what other options do I have, anyway? The spark of magic beneath my skin is a stark reminder of the difference even a damned day makes. I might die in service of her, but at least I'll die with my magic back.

I consider it, then nod. "Give me a week," I say. "But I'll need food. A bathroom with *running water.* Clean clothes wouldn't go amiss, and a bed with linens from this century would be nice too."

"How demanding." She doesn't seem actually angry. Then, without her saying another word, the shadows rise and consume us both again.

When I can see, we're in what looks like the lobby of a fancy hotel. "Good gods," I mutter, trying to get my bearings.

"They're not listening," she says bitterly, and I turn to her, but with a completely different tone, she says, "I've released your wrists. Have the brains not to run."

I'm not embarrassed to admit to myself that I'd follow her just about anywhere for a hot shower right now. I nod and walk one step behind her as she makes her way to the desk.

I don't have any money, I realize abruptly. She must have patted my pockets down that first night and taken my wallet. Not that I'm loaded or anything, but I don't even have a credit card to put the room on.

I've never met a divine before this one, but my understanding is that they only come to Earth rarely, usually looking for a fuck, and as such, centuries can pass them by without them noticing. Will she try to pay with giant gold coins? Jewels?

She pulls out a flashy AmEx and slides it across the counter, explaining to the man there that she's looking for the penthouse for a week, and staring him down when he asks any questions.

I have questions, but at least I know better than to ask them in front of the mortal. Is that fake? Some sort of magic? I can't feel if it is, but then again, if it was a halfway decent glamor, I wouldn't expect myself to be able to see through it right now.

I don't listen to the rest of the conversation, but I follow her obediently to the elevator. I look ragged in day-old clubbing clothes, and I wonder what the mortals think of me. She looks like some sort of queen—or maybe a goddess—and I'm following her like a lost puppy. Do they think I'm her little boy toy? That this sophisticated, pretty model dripping jewels picked up the air-headed party boy?

I sigh, but keep walking. It's probably not the worst thing that's been thought of me recently.

The elevator ride is long, and when we disembark on the top floor, there's a floor-to-ceiling window that I eagerly peer out. "Where are we?"

"London."

She'd caught me in *New York*. "Why London?"

"Because I like it here. Come on." She says it like it's so obvious, and I don't know how to argue with that.

She opens the door and ushers me inside. "Make yourself at home."

Home looks like it belongs in an interior design magazine. It's a little sterile, but also practically smells like money. I salivate over it.

There's a living room with not one but three plush couches, an actual gas fireplace, and a view that is probably worth the price of admission alone. There's a dining table that could seat ten and a small kitchen through an archway. The kitchen, small as it is, looks high end. It's probably meant for staff to use, because some people apparently need a private chef even in a place with twenty-four/seven room service. There are a few closed doors around the perimeter of the room, presumably leading to different bedrooms.

There's a bottle of Cristal chilling on an elaborate dining table, and I suddenly get the itch to pop the cork and start the party. Maybe ten years ago, I would have. But right now, I'm just tired. I need a shower, and badly, so I *make myself at home* and start in one of the luxury bathrooms.

The hotel's complimentary products probably cost as much as my old rent. My hair feels softer than it has in memory, and I stay under the endless hot water until I can't take it anymore.

I refuse to put on my clubbing clothes, so I take one of the cloud-soft robes, tying it carefully around my waist and going back to the main room.

"Comfortable?" she asks sardonically. She's sitting on the couch, but still wearing her shoes and jewelry, still as put together as ever.

I decide that I have to just plow through it. I can't let her intimidate me forever. "Very," I agree, sitting opposite her. "Shower's free. And there's another robe, too."

"The shower was always free. There's three bathrooms in this suite."

Okay, I hadn't expected that. My eyebrow twitches up in surprise against my will. "Okay, moneybags. Where'd you get the cash for a place like this, anyways?"

"I'm old."

"I thought your kind didn't trouble yourselves with our world."

"I like nice things," she says flippantly. "And I made some wise investments over the years. Don't worry, witch. Your room service orders won't break my bank."

Some investments? That sounds like she spends a lot more time here than I'd suspected. Unless she really does just like nice things, and, hey, I can't exactly fault her for that. I'm in so far over my head now because I also like nice things.

But that's not the part of the statement I'm so stuck on. "Clay," I tell her.

"Hm?"

"You called me *witch* again. My name is Clay. You should probably know it if we're going to do this."

She looks me over, looking me up and down like she's trying to see how the name could possibly connect to me. No one bothers to call me by my name anymore—I'm *hey, you* or *witch* most of the time—but if she and I are really going to work together like this, then I want to hear her say it.

"Clay," she says graciously. "Call me Estrid, then."

"*Estrid.*" I try it out. It feels weird to call her by her name when she's technically my kidnapper, but what else am I going to call her? She nods briskly.

"Don't leave," she says, pushing herself to stand, apparently already done with me. "If you're supposedly my prisoner, then stay inside. Order whatever you want for food. I'll be back when I have a moment."

"Seriously?" I ask before I can stop myself. "This isn't your top priority?"

She raises an eyebrow. "*You're* not my top priority."

Ouch. I suppose at least she's honest.

And rich, I remind myself. Honest, rich, and willing to fund this place for me for a week. And if she's asking me to go on a suicide mission in a week—well, I have a bit of time before I have to face that, and at least I can enjoy the finer things before I die.

Chapter Eight

Clay

When I wake up the next day, still wrapped in that robe, I feel a little more magic pumping through my veins and hear a knock at the door.

The hair on my arms stands on end. Estrid didn't leave me any defensive magic, not even my knife that she seems to like so much. And while I have some magic back, I doubt I have time to properly enchant anything before whoever is after me bangs down the door.

I grab the champagne. I'm not proud of such a human weapon, but hopefully a blow to the head will give me a split second head start.

Except when I look through the little peephole, it's a human wearing a hotel uniform on the other side of the door. "Yes?" I ask, a touch more aggressively than perhaps necessary, but my blood is pumping and my heart is in my throat.

"Your purchases."

"I didn't purchase anything." He *looks* like a human, but who's to say a really strong glamor couldn't fool me right now?

"The woman with you did. Ms. Night?"

Ms. Night? Does he mean Estrid? Does she really walk around using the name *Night*? I know last names are a more modern invention, and that most immortals over a certain age don't bother, but that one sucks.

I suppose I shouldn't judge too hard. My mother, faced with the same dilemma about last names, decided to call us both *Sparks*.

I open the door, setting the champagne aside on a decorative end table before he can see it.

"Sorry," I say, trying to smile and hope he doesn't think anything is weird about this. Then I remember how expensive this hotel is, and how he's probably paid not to care.

"It's okay, sir. Your things?"

I didn't even order food last night, prioritizing getting more sleep. I hope it's a stack of pancakes as tall as my head, but I probably shouldn't be surprised that this man is only holding a box. Estrid doesn't even eat.

I open the box as soon as he leaves to find four changes of clothes and a set of skin care products I recognize the labels on. They're even more expensive than the complimentary ones in the bathroom.

These clothes don't come with anything as mundane as regular old tags. They don't have labels at all, but I get the gut feeling missing labels doesn't mean they're not designer.

I take another long, hot shower, using my new products that feel like money. *Fuck*, and I really have to pretend to escape this prison in a week?

Not a week. Five days now. I've slept more in the last two days than I have in weeks, and I think my limp is healed. If my aches and pains are gone, then I should feel my magic more and more.

When I'm dressed in the new clothes that somehow fit me perfectly, I call for room service, letting days of hunger order for me.

Does Estrid see the charges on her credit card, or is she the type of rich person who doesn't even look?

She did say I'm not her priority. She's probably not even checking. I could order whatever I want. I flip through the TV—the kind that you have to push a button for, and it rises from a discrete opening in a table—and find the pay-per-view.

Well. If she's going to be generous, I might as well.

***

I spend the next five days lounging around the place. I order more expensive food than I can eat, then feel bad about the waste and cut back to a more reasonable amount. I take long showers and even break in the giant soaking tub. I sleep ten hours a day, watch TV, nap some more, and wear the robe more than the expensive clothes.

Magic seeps back into my body, like a spring coming back to life, the fresh water of my magic washing away all the shit inside me. It's not everything I lost, but it's more than I've had in a long time now.

I hadn't even realized how much I'd given up, how low I'd been brought. Greta had a particularly bad boyfriend once when I was still a teenager, and when I'd—in all my teenage angst and confusion—demanded to know why she hadn't left sooner, she told me about the frog in the pot. If you shove a frog in boiling water, it'll jump out. But if you turn up the heat slowly, then the frog doesn't realize and stays until it boils and dies.

Fuck, I owe Greta so many apologies.

I don't think about it too deeply. Greta left everything behind years ago now, and I doubt I'll survive long enough to see her again. My magic is back, but Estrid is still asking me to go against Andreas, who could probably smite me with one finger.

As if just thinking her name summons her, Estrid appears by the dining room table. The shadows fade away and leave her standing there, as put together as always, in a pair of skin-tight pants and a black blouse.

"You look better."

I'm still wearing the damned robe. If she gave me any warning like a decent person, I'd have at least dressed to have company.

"Give me a minute," I grouse, stomping off to the bedroom to pull on one of the changes of clothes she purchased me. Is the proper thing to do to thank her for the clothes, or is this considered appropriate payment for the kidnapping?

When I walk back out of the bedroom, she's sitting on one of the couches, hands clasped and leaning forward slightly. "So. How are you feeling?"

I raise an eyebrow, sitting on the couch opposite her. "Do you care?"

"Did you recover or not?" she asks impatiently.

"I'm better." We're clearly getting right to business tonight.

"Good. Let's talk next steps." She drums her fingers together, and I watch the gesture nervously, although she doesn't seem conscious of doing it.

"Next step is you want me to kill a god."

"Andreas isn't a god. And you don't need to kill him."

"Then what *do* you want?" I ask carefully. It's a relief to hear she doesn't want me to kill a god—she hasn't outright lost all sense, then—but I doubt I'm going to get off easy.

"I need information. I need everything about their operation. Every spell Andreas ever gave over, every secret hidden stash. Any other halflings they have. All of it. And I need whatever you can tell me about Andreas. Why he's there. Who he interacts with. What he does, where he goes. If he's taking orders from anyone else or partnering with anyone. That's the important part."

I swallow. It still sounds like a suicide mission, but not as bad as it did before.

But fuck, dead is dead, isn't it?

"Why do you care?" I press. She opens her mouth, no doubt to tell me off, but I interrupt her. "I know you said you were asking the questions and told me to keep my mouth shut. But I'll be more useful to you if I know why this matters. It'll help me know what to look for."

That's partially true, but mostly I just need to know *why*. Estrid is too determined for there not to be a reason, and I'm going to make her give me something.

It's small, compared to what she's forced me to give up, but I'll take any win I can get.

"Is my niece not enough?"

"Not for you." I don't mean it as an insult, but we all know full well her kind don't care about those halfling kids.

She studies me like she's trying to decide what she can get away with. "Andreas is breaking some fundamental laws by doing this," she says after a long moment. "We're not supposed to interfere. It's the rule; there's a god for everything, but no god specifically owns any living thing. So no god—or their offspring—can interfere with them. It's seen as an attempt at a claim, and that's an insult to all the other gods. A fuck is fine because it doesn't mean anything, but no more. That's why if the child is even remotely like their non-divine parent, we have to give them up. They can't be one of us. And Andreas doing what he's doing—getting power like he is—that's breaking the rules."

"So why has no one stopped him?" I dare to ask.

She shrugs miserably, the first not perfectly put together sign I've seen from her. "That's what I want to know."

She's holding something back, but pressing might make her actually kill me, so I bite my tongue.

"Right," I say slowly, trying to find safer ground. "So, what's the plan? When I get the information you want, what do I do?"

"I'll find you," she promises, and I shiver when a shadow caresses my arm. "Don't worry, Clay—I'm never far." The way she says my name makes me shiver as much as the shadow touch did.

She leans forward. "Now—*escape.*"

Chapter Nine

Estrid

C lay runs out of the hotel like his ass is on fire, exactly as I planned.

He needs to get himself back to New York, but I'm not worried. I used the shadows to put my credit card and his wallet in his pocket before he left, and I'm sure he can get himself a flight from there. Judging by his spending habits, I'm sure he'll be drinking champagne in first class before the hour is up.

I should go downstairs, check out of this ridiculous room, and make my way back home. I've been busy these past few days, though, and taking a moment doesn't sound like the worst thing in the world.

I'd popped in on Marielle again. I hadn't left the shadows, but I wanted to check that Marielle was doing well. She's with her werewolf still, back at what seems to be their home. Thankfully, they'd been clothed and upright this time.

I've never been to the werewolf village, never felt a need to—my interests have long lied with the vampires—but from what I understand, her werewolf is some sort of prince there.

Well, Rota's child deserves royalty. And after what she's been through, he better treat her like a princess.

From what I can see, he does, so I don't interfere. She's recovering nicely, and while I doubt it's all sunshine and rainbows, her day-to-day looks peaceful enough. She doesn't need me.

Of course she doesn't. She wasn't wrong when she told me she didn't need anything from me or my kind at that ball. We'd never been there when she needed us, and it didn't matter that there are laws preventing it. She'd needed someone, and her mother had all but forgotten she existed.

After that, I'd gone and killed a few more names from the list I'd recovered. It was a good way to work through some anger and distract myself while waiting for my pawn to be ready.

I hadn't checked on Clay beyond monitoring the purchases as they hit my credit card. I hadn't lied when I told him I could afford whatever he wanted, and it seems like he wanted to put that to the test.

He looks better. He looks less like he'll keel over any second, and while I don't like his odds against Andreas, I at least can assure myself that I haven't instantly sent him to his death.

I check out of the hotel and spend half an afternoon in London, perusing the shops and just enjoying the streets. We're not allowed to interfere with the world, but nothing strictly says I can't be here. If I don't interact with them, if I don't make a real impression, then what harm does it do, anyway?

I admit that I'm a bit of an outlier. I've always liked the creatures of this world a little more than most of my kind. I'm not ready to give up my place and live among them or anything, and I'm certainly not forming a little cult of them like Andreas is doing. But I do enjoy diamonds, manicures, and designer dresses. I'll take the opportunity to peruse while I can.

When the bags become too annoying to carry, I pull out a specific necklace from the purchases, already having a neck in mind for it. Then I let the shadows take me away and deposit the bags back home before I find my way to my true destination.

This castle is much nicer than the crumbled one I took Clay to.

The king here is a paranoid bastard, and the crown princess even more so. She has eyes everywhere, but there are some shadows that eyes can't see through, no matter how hard they try.

Mina is bent over some sort of document, diligently making notes in the margin. I watch from the shadows for a long moment, taking her in. Her blonde hair is coiffed tightly at the back of her head, an immensely practical style that I hardly ever see her without. She keeps a knife on her belt, despite the fact that I rarely see her leave this castle anymore, and an extra pen is shoved behind her ear.

Mina is her mother's daughter. From what I hear, her son Silas is just like her, too.

She knows I'm here before I let my shadows drop. "Would it kill you to use the door?"

It wouldn't kill me, but it might kill someone. I doubt I'm welcome here, and I don't feel like starting a war to get to her. We've had this discussion before, though, and I'm not here to rehash it again.

I let the shadows slide away, stepping fully into her sitting room. "Busy?"

"I have a minute."

I sit opposite her, clearing a small space between her papers and books. "I come with gifts." I slide the necklace box across to her, leaving her to open it.

She opens it with greedy hands. Her position here as one of the king's favorite wives comes with fabulous wealth, but I love that Mina is still a little magpie, intrigued by everything shiny. It's endearing.

"What are you reading?" I ask her, watching as she clasps the necklace on. The shine is perfect, bright and beautiful against her skin, exactly as I expected.

She heaves a put-upon sigh. "War reports."

"War?" That's news to me.

"My *husband* apparently can only read so much, and so as always I pick up the slack." She picks up her pen again.

"Doesn't Deidre do that now?"

"She's the one writing the reports. Our crown princess apparently doesn't understand why the heir to the throne can't be a front-line spy."

Yes, that sounds like her. I've never met her, don't have any particular interest in doing so, but Mina talks about her sometimes. She's taken the girl under her wing since she came to the castle, and while Mina pretends it's about teaching her all the politics and how to navigate this world, I know she's genuinely fond of the girl.

Deidre isn't who anyone expected to be next in line for the throne, but Mina, raised to rule all her life and smarter than any two people here combined, is a good person to look after her. It doesn't hurt that Mina's son is so fond of her as well.

"She'll learn," I say diplomatically, although I'm honestly not sure she will. Deidre seems like she'll be the type of queen who does things her own way, rather like the woman in front of me now. "War?"

"Silas, who has never fought for anything except us all to leave him alone in his entire *life*, suddenly is passionately teaming up with werewolves and demons in a fight against some secret group of casters who have apparently been wreaking havoc for at least a few centuries."

My stomach falls out. "Oh?" I ask as neutrally as I can. I can't tell her I know everything about this fight. I'm breaking so many rules just by being here, and I can't make it worse by interfering with her actions in this war.

Having so many factions getting involved with this is an interesting development, and I can't decide if it's a good thing or a bad thing.

"What's Silas' stake in this?" I ask, looking for a question that won't tip off my interest.

"It's his mate," she tells me. "He has a sister, and this group kept her captive for centuries—chopped her up for spell ingredients, apparently. And the poor thing is out now, but they tried to take her back. Silas also suspects these are the people who enslaved Theo before they met, but of course he can't actually prove it."

No, but I might be able to. The papers I found confirm that those enslavement spells are a major product of Andreas' little cult, so it's a solid bet Theo did cross these people.

I don't bring it up. That's not how this relationship works, sadly, and I don't let myself feel too guilty about it today. They can plan their side of this war. I'll plan mine.

I don't like the idea of them going to war, though. Mina, Silas, and the girl they're talking about who can only be Marielle. I don't want any of them anywhere near these people, even if I don't have a good way to dissuade them.

"Should I leave you to your war plans, then?" I ask.

"You came all this way just to leave already?"

"I don't want to intrude."

"When will you be back, then?" she challenges, as she always does.

And like always, I don't have an answer. I see her far more often than she sees me, even if she is annoyingly good at spotting me through the shadows. "When I can be."

It has to be this way, I remind myself. There cannot be a world where someone like me interferes with the lives of people like Mina. That's just the way the rules work.

CHAPTER TEN

CLAY

Jaxon looks me up and down when I arrive back at the house. "You're days late. We thought you were dead."

"I almost was," I say, which isn't technically even a lie. Estrid certainly nearly killed me multiple times. The memory of her freezing touch and those terrifying shadows will never leave me, not to mention the poisoning. "Listen, something happened—"

"I'd say. You failed your charge, witch." The sneering tone when he says *witch* makes me bristle, but I can't exactly fight him over it.

My magic might be back, but I need time to build up an armory again. I need to spend some time enchanting the shit out of some weapons, really prepare myself for what I'm walking into. And anyway, revealing how much magic I have again isn't going to help me sell this story.

"Something happened," I repeat. "Listen, a divine got me, alright?"

He looks me up and down. "And what? She fucked you for a week?" He laughs like that's somehow a funny joke, and I want to throttle him.

Jaxon would knock me on my ass in a fight in three seconds flat, I remind myself. He's bigger than me, although that hardly matters. He's a demon, and while demon magic seems to come with a lot of rules, I know full well that this man could pulverize me with a thought.

"She imprisoned me and kept me tied to a bed," I snarl. Well, she did that for a day, at least. "I need to—I don't know. Who should I talk to about that?"

Please say Andreas, I beg mentally. Not that I want to confront Andreas, but the sooner I talk to him, the sooner I'll have something for Estrid, and the sooner she'll leave me alone. Hopefully, at least.

He pauses for a long moment. "You can meet with March, I guess?"

The doubt in his voice isn't reassuring, and I have no desire to meet with March. March is the guy I've been sucking up to for years now, hoping it'll get me somewhere. It never does.

But I can't exactly say that I don't want to see March. If I don't escalate this to March and really sell my story, then I'll never get any further.

"Where is he?" I ask, hoping my hesitation hasn't been too long.

"In his office."

Of course he is. Done with Jaxon now, I slip past him and make my way to the office, steeling myself while I walk.

I can do this. I can sell this story to March and set this plan in motion. I take a deep breath, knock on his door, and then push my way inside.

He's facing away from me, a giant *fuck you.* What kind of criminal underboss keeps his back to the door? The kind who wants us all to know he's not afraid of us, that's who.

I clear my throat, but he still doesn't turn around. "March?" I give in and ask.

He holds up a hand. "You made us wait a godsdamn week, witch. You can wait a minute."

"I was kidnapped," I say succinctly. "By a divine. Interested yet?" It comes out slightly more snarky than I intended, but I can't help it.

He turns toward me, albeit slowly, like he just can't let go of the little power play he's started. "Who?"

"Some ice bitch," I say, wincing internally even if I know it's how March expects me to talk. "Shadows, too."

"She was protecting the kid?" he asks.

"Must have been." And I suppose, in a way, she was. Still not a lie in sight.

"What did she do to you?"

"Tied me up in some old building. Monologued at me a bit."

"That's it?"

"Poisoned me at one point."

"You look like she took you to a fucking spa."

I probably do, because she basically did. But I can't confess to that. "I healed from it."

March seems barely interested, but I catch his left hand drumming against the arm of his chair. He's thinking, at least. I have to hope he's worried enough to bring this to Andreas. I hold my breath, hoping March is interested enough in my story to make that happen.

"You got caught," he says neutrally.

I don't say anything. The danger in the room is now palpable, the hairs on the back of my neck standing on end. I hold my breath, waiting for what he says.

"I'll pass along your concern," he says after a moment. "And people above you will work out how concerned we should be. Meanwhile, we have work for you."

"What do you need?" I try not to sound disappointed. I didn't expect this to be easy, but I confess I'd hoped *I got kidnapped by a divine who knows about us* would have been the type of statement to get escalated immediately.

"Unlike you, Sarge succeeded in his task," March says. "And we need someone to tend to the prisoner."

I swallow back my disgust. "And you want me?"

"You seem to only be good for cleaning up shit," March says cruelly. "So, go do that, witch."

The halfling is kept in the basement. I know the girl—Estrid's niece, I remind myself, because I've spent too long not thinking about her, and I should force myself to acknowledge that—was kept in a specially designed room, a working laboratory meant to be most efficient for cutting her to pieces. I never saw it, never even went to that house, but that doesn't mean I don't know about it.

In contrast, this halfling is literally shoved in what looks like a dog crate in the basement. She looks like a fucking kid, scared and filthy. My heart aches for her, and I wonder for a split second if I can just release her. But that seems like a fast way for both of us to get killed, so I restrain the urge.

I can't free her. Maybe Estrid can, but the best I can do for her is give her some modicum of care.

"Hey," I say quietly, hoping I can get her attention without terrifying her. I crouch down so I'm closer to her level.

It's definitely a damn dog crate, padlocked shut. I can feel the magic vibrating off the lock, and I know without investigating that messing with it would lead to unfortunate outcomes.

She turns away from me entirely, and I can't blame her. I study her closer, taking in her filthy sweatshirt. Has she been here for a week?

"Alright," I say quietly. "So, I'm thinking a meal. A fresh set of clothes. A shower?" I wince at offering that, because I don't want this kid to just think I want to get her naked.

I'm not a good person, but that's so far beneath me I can't even imagine it. But I know getting a scared, traumatized kid to believe that is a tall order. Fuck, did someone touch her in the last few days?

"Door's locked, dumbass," she spits.

I fight a smile. Alright, she's got a mouth. Good. I think Estrid would kill me if I told her there was a completely broken kid here.

"Shower might be a later thing," I agree, because it's not like March gave me a key. "But I can do the others. Thoughts?"

"Who the fuck are you?"

"My name is Clay. And you are?"

She's silent again for a long moment, then mutters, "Lorne."

"Hi, Lorne. I'm going to look after you."

She finally looks at me over her shoulder. "You work for them."

I can't exactly disagree. I *do* work for them, and I can't admit that I might be conspiring with Estrid. There could be ears anywhere. "Yeah."

"Then I don't fucking want anything from you."

What the fuck can I say to that?

I bring her dinner anyway, and a wet rag and a blanket I can shove through the bars in the dog crate. She doesn't touch any of it in front of me, so I just have to hope that she's not too proud to help herself once I'm gone.

"I need to be able to take her out of there," I tell March, barging back into his office after I'm done with Lorne.

"You need no such thing."

"You left a still-mortal kid in a dog crate. It's going to stink. It *already* stinks. Fuck, can't we get her a shower and a toilet?"

He raises an eyebrow. "Determined to get her in the shower, witch?"

I don't acknowledge it. I can't acknowledge it, because I can't shout at him. If he's accusing me, then it means he thought about it, and I have to swallow bile.

"Well?" I ask.

He sighs like I'm inconveniencing him. "Fine. You can see me for the key once every few days."

Well, I suppose I didn't expect him to just hand me the key. I nod, satisfied with what he offered. "I'll be by for it first thing in the morning," I tell him.

"Slacking off already?"

"She's pretty pissed right now. I don't want to deal with her fighting me tonight." I hate my own voice right then. "Give her the night to cool off."

"Good luck. That one's a hell-cat. I miss the old one—nice and broken in."

I have to leave before I actually vomit in front of him.

The worst part of it all is I can't retreat to somewhere private to freak out.

Not everyone stays in the various houses we operate out of, but when Mae and her fucking werewolves threatened me and I gave up my apartment, I retreated to this house, and leaving now would be the most suspicious thing I can do.

There are six beds in this room, and Sarge is already sitting on the edge of the one furthest from the door.

He looks at me and smirks. "Heard you were kidnapped." He says it with a twist on the word, like he somehow thinks it's funny.

I shrug. "I'm back now."

"And you lost us a halfling."

"You found one."

"And I heard you're her babysitter. Congratulations."

"Any advice?" I ask, just to have something to say.

"Yeah. Don't let her get her teeth on you."

"Her teeth?"

He mimes biting down. "Didn't you see?"

"She wouldn't look at me."

"Bitch is half vampire. Her teeth sting."

Good to know. While I'm working to convince Lorne to trust me, I need to stay clear of her teeth. It also means the meal I brought her was worthless, and the poor kid probably thinks I'm either an idiot or was taunting her. I'll have to go in with egg on my face tomorrow and apologize for that. And then I'll have to find her some blood.

I need to sleep; it's been a painfully long day. But all I want to do is let Estrid know I'm here and I'm trying to do what she asked. I don't know if I'll succeed, and I don't know what to do about the kid yet. I'm sure she'll know what to do, or at least have a place to start.

I lie in a bed and turn away from Sarge, hoping he takes the hint. Fully clothed, I tuck up my legs and close my eyes, but I don't fall asleep for hours.

CHAPTER ELEVEN

CLAY

S ourcing blood is a pain in the ass.

I end up cutting my own arm open and dripping it into a glass, but that can't be my long-term solution. For one thing, it took way too long.

"Hey," I say, stepping into the basement and approaching that stupid fucking dog cage. "I got something better for you. Sorry about last night. I didn't know."

She's still not looking at me, but she perks up slightly, presumably smelling the blood.

"Yeah, here, this is yours," I tell her, stepping closer with the glass in front of me. I have the key in my other hand, which is great, because I don't think I can fit the glass through the cage.

She still doesn't look at me when I unlock the cage, but as soon as it's open she moves faster than I could believe possible, turning and snatching the glass out of my hand and sucking it down.

I wince. "They hadn't fed you yet?"

She doesn't answer. I didn't really expect her to.

I debate offering a shower, but I think it's best to wait. "I don't know how often you need blood," I tell her quietly. "So if you have thoughts about it, now is the time."

She licks the rim of the cup. Fuck, the kid was *hungry*. "Every day."

"Every day?" I don't know a lot of vampires, but I'm pretty sure that's too often.

She shrugs. "I'm young. It's normal."

Alright then. I make a mental note to speed up my plan for getting her a regular supply of blood. Whatever I do, I can't let this kid starve.

"What are they going to do to me?" she whispers.

Fuck. Somehow, in all my thinking, I never planned on her asking me that.

The saddest part is the next few years will be the easiest it will ever be for her. They can't hurt her too badly while she's still too young; if they take her liver or something, she'll just die. But in ten years, all bets are off. Her liver will just regenerate, given enough time.

I'd known what things they used in those spells, what things they'd taken from the last halfling. But I'd tried not to think about it, tried not to focus on the real person getting cut up for it.

Well, now I can't think about anything else, and it makes my stomach curl.

This isn't my fault, I try to remind myself, but it rings pretty hollow now. I didn't bring her here, and I didn't personally cut up Estrid's niece. But I knew it was happening. I benefited from it. I didn't stop it.

"You have a lot of magic in you," I say, which isn't an answer, but I hope she doesn't push. What good will it do her to know what they want from her?

"I don't," she mutters petulantly, like we can have a debate about this and I'll say *oh, my mistake. Go on home.*

"Which of your parents is the divine?" I ask her instead of letting her indulge in the debate.

She frowns so hard I worry her face is going to stick that way. "My dad."

I guess that's not information that I technically need, but any information I get about this kid is a good start. "And your mom?"

Lorne's shoulders go up to her ears. "What about her?"

Got it. So her mom is probably not missing her, then.

I can't do anything for her here, but hopefully I can give all this information to Estrid so she can make *something* happen. She might know who Lorne's dad is, not that that will do much. We all know full well he's probably forgotten she exists.

"What else do you need?"

"A way out."

"Other than that."

She turns away from me again, her hand too tight on the glass. "Leave me alone."

"I can let you take a walk?" I offer. "Get you out of that cage for a few minutes."

"Yay, so I can walk in a circle down here? Going to put a leash on me too? Pass."

I huff. "Fine then. Have it your way. Give me the damn glass."

She hands it over willingly enough and doesn't even attempt to bite me, so I take it as a win.

***

I'm in the middle of trying to solve my issue about sourcing regular blood when March finds me. "Andreas wants to see you."

I nearly drop the phone in my hand. "He does? Why?" Did I say something too revealing to the kid?

March rolls his eyes. "Your little kidnapping, remember? Or did you decide it's not that important after all?"

Oh, right. *That.* "No, no. It's important. She targeted me *because* I work for Andreas. Andreas should know about her."

"Well, now's your chance to let him decide. He's in my office."

Of course he is, because March might imagine he's important, but we all know he's a little baby who bows and scrapes when Andreas demands something of him. Giving up his office is nothing; March would die for Andreas.

But then again, isn't that how we're all supposed to feel here? I should get better at faking it.

I knock on the office door and take a deep breath. This is game-time. This is what Estrid demanded of me.

Andreas is a mountain of a man. He makes March's desk look small, awkwardly crowding the place with his too-big limbs. "You're the witch who got captured," he says.

I'm not surprised he doesn't know my name, but I still feel like a mildly interesting bug he's studying. "I am," I agree.

"Alright. Sit down." Andreas has one of those voices that you can't help but listen to. He's firm in an immovable way, like you could never doubt him. I sit.

"Tell me what happened."

I tell him what I told March, about being tied to a bed and kept by a divine with control over shadows and cold. Selfishly, I want to hear what he thinks of that, if he knows who Estrid is.

"Interesting," he murmurs when I finish, leaning back in his chair. "I was wondering when someone would notice what I was doing here. Honestly, I made it far longer than I thought—but she's an interesting choice."

"Who is she?" I dare to ask. Surely curiosity isn't suspicious. If anything, it's natural and expected.

"Her name is Estrid. She's a daughter of the night, and she doesn't get to throw stones about interfering with this world." He shrugs. "Maybe she really did just care about the halfling. I can't imagine why, but it's possible. She's an odd one."

I fight the urge to push for more. "But she's not going to come after me again, right?" I ask, because I know that's what he expects me to worry about.

He raises an eyebrow. "You think you're significant enough for her to care about?"

"Probably not," I concede. I know he said it to insult me, to cut me down to size, and once it would have done that. The Clay of a few months ago would have hated hearing he's insignificant. But I know more than him right now, and I just remind myself of that.

"Don't worry about her," he tells me dismissively. "She's above your pay grade. March says you're watching the new halfling. Just take care of your job, and I'll take care of mine."

I will take care of my job. I'll give Estrid everything he just told me, as useless as some of it might be, and let her sort out what comes next.

Chapter Twelve

Estrid

I give him three days.

Three days seems like an appropriate amount of time to find out *something*. It also gives me more time to spy on Marielle and find out that, yes, she and her werewolf are indeed planning a war. I worry the shadows aren't enough to hide me from a werewolf's superior senses, so I don't stay long, but I'm there long enough to see the king and queen of Demonheim arrive to join their planning session.

They're taking this very seriously. Perhaps they can handle this on their own. After all, everything I've ever been taught tells me that interfering is the wrong thing to do. I'm supposed to let the creatures of this world deal with their own problems.

Maybe, but I won't. I already know I won't.

They can't take down Andreas. They might try, and they might even make a dent in his operation. But their combined power is still dwarfed by Andreas', and he will always win if I let them take him on by themselves. And I suppose my sisters would say that's not my problem, but I just can't let it lie. Marielle, Silas, Mina—they've all chosen this war. I can't let them walk themselves into a death trap.

So on the third day, I move through the shadows to find Clay. It's a risk to be this near to somewhere Andreas could possibly be, but it's a risk I'm willing to take. Thankfully Clay's alone, so I reach out of the shadows, wrap a hand around his bicep, and tug him into the shadows with me.

And then we step out in front of a restaurant in Los Angeles.

"What the fuck," he breathes, more an exhalation than a question. "Do you have any idea how *weird* that feels?"

I don't, because I've been able to do it since I sprung into existence. It's not worth discussing. "Well?"

"Give me a damn moment to catch my breath." He's an overdramatic fool. I didn't hurt him.

He takes big deep breaths, then finally looks around. "Why are we here?"

"Because you presumably have information for me." I let the threat of *you better* be implied. He knows what's at stake.

"I mean, at a restaurant. You don't eat."

"You do." And I like places like this, but have little excuse to visit. Mina doesn't eat either, and she's the only creature of this realm that I have regular contact with.

Plus, I doubt they've been feeding him well. He doesn't look as bad as when I found him, but the worn look is coming back to his eyes, and I have no desire to see him get that bad again. Why I care, I can't say, but I just know that if feeding him is what it takes to keep him going, then that's well within my abilities.

His eyes flick over the restaurant again. "A place like this needs a reservation."

"We have one." Money buys so many things.

"If you're not supposed to mess with creatures on Earth, then wouldn't investing in stocks or whatever the hell you did be violating that?"

Most definitely. But it's certainly not the worst violation I've ever committed, and it really doesn't require me to interact with too many creatures, so I just shrug. "You want the meal or not?"

"Alright, alright." He opens the door for me, smiling as I walk past. "I'm sorry—forgive my manners. You look very nice today, Estrid."

I *do* look very nice today, because I always look very nice. I'm wearing one of my purchases from London for the first time, and the dress fits me like skin. It's maybe a little too short for most fine dining, but I think I'll fit right in here.

"Thank you." I walk past him and go to the hostess stand. "Reservation for Night."

"That's a stupid name," Clay mutters as soon as she's out of earshot.

"I am literally made of stardust, Clay. I am the child of the night. What more appropriate name could there be?" He just rolls his eyes, and I don't push the issue, because I think this insistence on surnames is the real issue here.

As I requested, we get a table a little out of the way in an alcove. They clearly usually put a bigger table here, so our table for two looks a little small, but I take it without complaint. After the hostess promises us our server will be right over, we're left alone.

"So," I say, drumming my fingers on the table. Clay watches my hands with rapt attention. "What have you found out?"

He takes a deep breath. "I failed to get a halfling for them, but someone else succeeded," he says slowly. "She's a kid, Estrid."

It feels like a slap in the face. "Is she okay?"

"They haven't cut her open, but okay is stretching it. They're keeping her in a fucking dog cage, and I still don't know how to get blood for her consistently, and—"

72

"Blood?"

"Lorne's half vampire. Drinks blood. I've been giving her mine, but it's not a very efficient process."

No, and we just got him looking healthy again, too. He can't sustain that, although a part of me is warmed that he's been trying. "You've been feeding her?"

He shrugs. "They're mad at me for fucking up my job, so they think this is a punishment detail. To clean up after her and stuff. I mean literally clean up—they're keeping her in a cage. I'm washing up waste."

That poor child. "And you're protecting her, right? No one is touching her?"

"There's only so much I can do." He takes a deep breath as if to collect himself. "But so far, yeah. You need a plan to get her out."

I bite my lip. I should, but the reality is they'll just grab another halfling. It's better for all of them if we end this once and for all. It's better for this girl in the long run, because then no one can come after her again.

And if I say it to myself enough times, maybe I'll really believe it.

"And Andreas?" I ask instead of telling him what I'm thinking.

"He met with me briefly. He's sort of concerned by your presence, but not enough to make a scene. He told me to mind my business, basically."

"I need more than that, Clay." Just to drive my point home, I make the table ice-cold under my touch.

The waitress chooses that moment to appear. She's all smiles as she approaches our table, a carafe of water in one hand. "Afternoon, all. I'm Jen."

"Hey, Jen," Clay says absently, not even looking over at her. "We're going to need another few minutes."

He has his hands suspended over the table so he doesn't touch the icy surface. I've let the ice retreat, because it'd be awkward to explain to Jen why the water glasses are freezing on contact, but Clay won't look away from me, anyway.

"Don't threaten me, Estrid," he says, voice low and dark, as soon as the waitress walks away. "I'm doing what you want, and not just because you threatened me. I get it, alright? I'm the one looking at that kid every day. I get how fucked this is."

"And where was this hidden empathy when it was my niece, Clay?"

"And where was *yours*? You didn't rescue her. Don't tell me you couldn't have. Or did you not interfere when it was her, but now the rules don't matter?"

The blow hits home, but I fight not to let it show. I've had a long, long time to practice hiding my expressions, and I call on it all now. He's right, is the thing. Yes, I didn't check up on Marielle, or any of her half-siblings or cousins. I took care of my own child, and did a shoddy job at that. I'm well aware that my care has been lackluster at best.

"I asked you first," I tell him.

"I never saw your niece. I knew she existed, alright, but if I didn't let myself think about it too hard, if I just did as I was told..." He trails off for a moment, a look of disgust on his face. "I know what you think about me. And I'm starting to realize you're right, okay? I was selfish. Selfish is too mild a word."

It is, but I don't get to criticize him for it. I'm not that much better.

"And now?" I ask.

"I haven't wanted to be there for a while," he admits. "The work is awful and I know what it makes me. I only ever got a taste of what they promised me. The clients disgust me—you saw what I did to that elf. But you can't leave someone like Andreas, Estrid. It doesn't work that way."

Jen walks back over, a smile on her face. She's over-attentive, and she can't take her eyes off of Clay. I guess if you like the half-starved, dead-eyed immortal look, he'd be pretty attractive.

Fuck, who am I kidding? This is Los Angeles, and Clay looks like a runway model allowing himself to eat his first real meal in a week. If I were a human who dreams of proximity to the stars, I'd find him hot too.

"Any thoughts on meals?" Jen asks, looking blatantly at Clay.

"I'll have the pasta alla vodka," he says, not even glancing up.

She waits like she expects him to say more, but he's still looking at me, and I'm looking at him, trapped in this perpetual blame-game of a conversation.

"And for you?" she asks me.

"I'll take the same." I haven't read the menu and have no desire to. He can take the leftovers back with him.

Jen nods and walks off to put our order in, so I lean closer to Clay. "What did they promise you? Specifically?"

"What does anyone promise someone like me? Money. Power."

"What, your magic wasn't enough power?"

His lip quirks into a self-deprecating smirk. "Never such a thing as enough for a proper witch. We hoard spells, Estrid. Fight and die for them sometimes, too. Believe me, I've done my share."

I look him over. "I don't think you've ever killed anyone." It's a gut instinct, but Clay doesn't have the eyes of a killer. He's a schemer and he's not above playing dirty, but I highly doubt he's ever crossed that line.

"No," he admits after a moment. "I've stolen and manipulated my fair share, though. Witches either gather spells other people already made and hoard them jealously, or make them themselves. And I've never had much talent for that."

"So they promised you spells," I conclude.

"Like a library," he agrees. "Which isn't very traditional for a witch, perhaps, but the idea was with so much magic in one place, we'd pool knowledge and there would be *so much* for the taking, as long as I pulled my weight. But then it turned out that I had no idea what pulling my weight would entail. I thought we were researchers. Scholars. With a little business on the side, but I grew up in my cousin's magic shop, so what was the difference?"

I'm starting to see Clay for who he really is, and I can't decide if I like it. Not if I like *him*—that's a separate issue—but I don't know if I like knowing him. It's so much harder to endanger someone you know.

It's time to get back to business. I don't think I can handle anything else. "I need more about Andreas," I tell him again. I don't bother repeating my earlier threat. "I need actual information."

"I need something in return."

"You're not in a position for that."

"If I give you what you want, then you have to get that kid out. And I mean soon."

"And what about you?" I ask, tilting my head to study him. I expected the first thing he'd ask for is to get himself out. But I'm starting to wonder if I miscalculated there.

He shrugs. "I've made my bed, Estrid. And if that's the consequence, well—we both know I deserve it."

He says it so sure, like nothing can dispute it. And, to my utter shock, I find myself wanting to dispute it. Apparently, I've fallen for his soft-hearted act.

I'll get the girl out. But I'm getting Clay out, too.

Chapter Thirteen

Clay

She studies me like I'm a puzzle, and even when I can't bear to make eye contact with her, I can't look away.

If she wore that dress—that fucking skin-tight black dress, showing off most of her thighs and cupping her deliciously pert ass—to distract from the menacing air she always carries around her, then she failed. She can try to look harmless all she wants, but she'll never succeed.

Menace is somehow the *perfect* accessory to that outfit.

She clicks her tongue, and I don't have the balls to ask her if that means she agrees with me or not.

I told her the truth, or most of it. I've never told a single soul any of that before, and I spilled it to her like it's easy. I can't quite work my way up to explaining that my mom, along with Greta's and Mae's moms, had been poor. It's not an unusual state for witches, who hoard what they have and don't share, who don't usually do business well, and who sabotage themselves more often than not. And we'd all coped. Greta opened her shop because she is a massively unusual witch who can tolerate others. Mae acted more like a human and worked in menial jobs like she was their servant. And I—

Well, I wanted something no one could ever take away from me. I compiled spells, charmed people out of their money, and scraped by. I'd found my way into luxury in other people's beds, stolen more spells than I could count, and tried to make my name mean something. And then March found me on Andreas' behalf, and it sounded too good to be true, but I fell for it, anyway.

And here I am, being threatened by a divine being who just explained to me that she is literally made out of starlight. I've never felt quite so small and stupid.

Estrid nods. "Alright. But I need you to do something for me." I just wait, not even bothering to say something. There's always more.

"First, keep that girl as safe as you can. I'm not asking for a miracle here. But as much as you can do, do it. I will get her out soon, but it can't be right this moment." I nod; that has always been the plan. "And second, I need you to ingratiate yourself with Andreas. I need to know if he has any contact with the gods."

I choke. "And you think he'd just tell me that?"

She shrugs. "If you do it right, he might. That's the price, Clay. That's what I need to know."

Well, fuck. I'm fucked, if that's the case. Estrid can't just say she doesn't want to help me—she has to give me a suicide mission. "Why can't you ask around? Isn't one of them your parent?" I croak.

She looks at me for a long moment, then says, "The gods don't answer me when I call either, Clay."

My mind spins. Not even the divine? I know they don't answer *us*. I gave up on praying a long, long time ago. It's not like it accomplishes anything. But they don't even talk to their own children?

Or is it just Estrid? Estrid who flouts the rules, who seems to love it here on Earth and fights for her niece and for Lorne?

"I'm sorry," is all I can manage to say.

"Why should you be? That's the way of things. But it does make things like this more complicated. Andreas is breaking a lot of rules, and I need to know how aware the gods are of it before I act."

She keeps talking about these *rules*, but I have to wonder who's enforcing them if the gods don't talk to their kids any more than they do us. Is there some sort of council of the divine who enforces the rules? Are they policing each other?

"I can try," I say. "But Estrid, you have to know that might not be possible."

"Make it possible," she murmurs. "Use that charm I know is hidden under there somewhere, hm?"

***

When I've eaten my fill, the waitress comes back with the check. She slides it toward me with a big smile on her face, and I experience a momentary panic, because Estrid did *not* kidnap me with my wallet ready. Not that I could afford this place normally, regardless.

Estrid reaches smoothly across the table and takes the check. "I'll deal with that," she says shortly, manicured nails clipping along the folder.

I snort out a laugh; I can't help it. "Why is it," I ask, barely able to get the words out, "every time I'm out with you, people think you're my sugar momma?"

If I expected the ancient being to be unfamiliar with the term, then I'd be disappointed. "Because I'm the one with money, Clay," she says, smirking as she pulls out the same AmEx I saw at the hotel. "And I think you like it."

Fuck, she's not wrong. I shouldn't like anything about this. I shouldn't be enjoying the stupidly expensive stuff she buys, not when there's a kid in a dog crate I should be looking out for.

But I do like the way she looks at me, all mean and imposing, and I like the way her nails clack on the folder, screaming money in a way I never knew I needed. And I haven't laughed like this in I don't know how long.

***

Estrid drops me back at home with nothing but a spinning head and some nausea from the shadow travel. I decline the leftovers, although there are a lot and the food was damn good, because I can't afford to have anyone ask where I got it from.

I wish I had something now though, something to prove that this afternoon was real.

It's been a few hours. I doubt anyone noticed I was gone—they only notice me when they need something from me—but I should go check on Lorne.

I start by bleeding into a cup again. It'd probably be more efficient to just let her bite me, but if she tries to kill me, then I won't be able to protect her anymore. So I wait a long-ass time to bleed enough to fill the cup and then collect the key from March.

"You're mighty interested in that halfling," he says, holding the key like he's going to deny it to me.

"She stinks," I tell him flatly. "It takes a lot of work to clean it up. I'm not interested in a mess like that."

He grins and hands me the key. "As long as you know not to touch."

She's a godsdamn teenager, I want to shout but barely restrain myself.

I bring the blood to the basement, considering the key in my other hand. Could I sneak out and have it copied? Probably. Then again, the issue isn't really the key—with enough magic, I can work my way around the lock. The issue is where we'd even go, and how I'd get us out of here without being stopped.

"Lunch," I tell her.

"Is it lunch time?" She seems more interested in the answer than I'd expect.

I shrug. "Lunch time is what you make of it, I always say." She raises an eyebrow. "Alright, just eat. Drink? What do you call it?"

"Drink," she mumbles, reaching for the glass that I hand over. She frowns. "All the blood is coming from the same source."

"You can taste that?"

"Sort of. Blood doesn't taste vastly different, but there are little things. You know, blood type, health, all that stuff. I'm right though, aren't I?"

"You are."

"You have someone else in another room that you're bleeding dry for me?"

I show her the cut on my arm, still not fully healed, what with my short supply of magic. "Nope. I'm your source. Seemed convenient."

She purses her lips. "No one has that much blood."

"I'll be fine, kiddo. Can I interest you in a walk today?"

Surprisingly, she shuffles out of the cage. Her movements are awkward, and I brace myself to catch her in case she stumbles as she stands. "Could I get a shower?" she asks, almost bashful now.

"Still working on that," I tell her softly. "Sorry."

"Why are you pretending to be nice to me? It doesn't mean I'll suddenly be okay with this."

I swallow the lump in my throat. Don't I know it. "Good. Don't be okay with it." I glance around. No one else is down here, obviously, but that doesn't mean no one can overhear. There are plenty of magical ways to do that. I can't say too much. "But it's my job to care for you. I'm trying my best."

She's silent for a long moment, then whispers, "What are they going to do to me?"

Oh, this poor kid. My heart hurts for her. "I don't know," I say, a half-truth. I don't know all the details, but I know enough.

Livers and hearts and finger bones and eyes. So many eyes. Eyes are powerful, apparently. They carry a lot of intention, a lot of feeling. So many creatures take in the world through their eyes, and it's like a bit of a portal to the mind. Or so it was explained to me by March once. I hadn't wanted to know; witch magic doesn't require anything of the sort, and I wanted to remain in blissful ignorance, just contributing the raw power to make the spells work and be done with it.

"You fucking suck," she announces, and if it took her this long to come to that conclusion, then she has a lot to learn about the world.

"I know," I agree.

There's a creaking sound, and every cell in my body is immediately on alert. That's the basement door, and I turn to put my body between the door and Lorne. Not that it will do her any good.

Andreas and March both walk down together, sending tension shooting down my spine.

Andreas takes up so much room that he has to duck his head to fully enter the space. "Taking your new pet for a walk, witch?"

I shrug, hoping I can still fake nonchalance even when my brain is screaming that I'm about to die. "You told me to look after her."

"I meant make sure she doesn't keel over, not start making friendship bracelets. Don't worry—their kind is pretty indestructible. But don't fall for the sad eyes."

I don't say anything. What the fuck can I say to that? How can I argue for taking care of Lorne without dying?

"She settling in?" Andreas continues, as if we're not talking about a girl.

I shrug. "I guess so. Could use a shower though. She smells." Lorne gives me a betrayed look and I don't dare look back.

"That's what the hose over there is for, idiot," March says.

Andreas gives him a look, and he falls quiet. "Well, I'm here to check out our new subject. See if she'll be halfway as useful as the old one. Go on upstairs, witch; this doesn't concern you."

My feet are heavy as cinder blocks, but I move. What else can I do? Lorne's stare buries into me, but I can't look back. I can't help her. I have to leave her in Andreas' care, and I feel sick.

"Wait," March says, and I freeze. "The key."

I turn and hand it to him, hating myself every second, and then go up the stairs, leaving them to do what they will.

***

I wait outside the door. Part of it is punishment—if she screams, then I should be made to hear it, let the lesson really sink in—but part of it is strategy.

Estrid wants me to find out if Andreas is working with the gods? Fine. I still think it's a suicide mission, but I'm at least beginning to see a plan.

She doesn't scream. I don't know if it's stubborn pride, which I can already see that Lorne has in spades, or if they don't hurt her or if they gag or if they knock her unconscious or what, but regardless it's as silent as the grave through the door, and I don't know whether that's better or worse.

When they finally emerge, almost an hour has passed and I'm still standing there stubbornly. Andreas just raises an eyebrow at me, once more having to duck his head to get through the door. "We didn't damage the little pet bad enough you need to go clean her up, witch. Relax."

"I want to talk to you." I tilt my chin up and try to look as serious as I can. "Alone."

"What makes you think he has time for you?" March asks, snide as ever, but Andreas holds up a hand.

"I have a few minutes to spare. We'll take your office." Taking some sick satisfaction that he talks to March like that, I follow Andreas down the hall.

He closes the door behind us, taking the desk chair like it's his. "Well? Keep it snappy; I don't have all day for you."

"I want to do more," I bite out, running through the script I came up with while standing outside that basement door.

"You failed in your job just a few days ago. You've failed at procuring that shop for me, and your magic is so useless you can't even do the spells anymore. You're a barely satisfactory errand boy. Why would anyone trust you with more?"

I flush at the insults, but I don't let it deter me. It shouldn't matter if he thinks I'm a failure—I certainly don't want to be what he considers a success—but it hurts, nonetheless. "I was held hostage by a divine. That's not a fair fight and not one you could expect me to win. I took care of the prisoner—"

"—That's not an accomplishment—"

"I want *more*. I want to prove myself," I lie.

I hold my breath while he considers it. People don't speak this way to Andreas, and I'm playing a dangerous game, gambling that he'll be more intrigued than angry. At last, he says, "And what did you have in mind?"

"I want to find her. Take her out for you."

He actually laughs at that. "She handed you your ass last time. What makes you think this time will be any different?"

"I got away, didn't I?" I ask. "Look, with the right magic—"

84

"You don't have that kind of magic," he dismisses.

"But it could be taught, right? You could teach me so she couldn't do that to me again?"

"Look, witch, you're in over your head. There is no spell I could just teach you that would put you on the same playing field as a divine. Only a god can win against us. Another divine, and it's a battle of strength. But you? You're nothing. You're a speck of dirt beneath us."

I frown then, hoping it doesn't look too theatrical. That's about the answer I expected, and so far Andreas has played his part perfectly. The question is, will it continue? "So, do you have a way to stop her?"

"You let me worry about her."

It's not a yes. I need more, need to keep pushing, but I worry that I'm now on very thin ice. Andreas isn't known for his patience.

"She stopped me from taking the other halfling," I murmur. "She's cutting into business."

"Wasn't aware you kept our books."

"Surely there's some way we could take her out."

He sighs. "Estrid is her own worst enemy. I'm half wondering if I can convince her to my side; she likes this world and has already been punished once for messing with things she shouldn't have. I might be able to tempt her to join us, honestly. And if she can't be convinced, I'll make her disappear."

I hold perfectly still. Short of asking him *do you have a god on your side*, this is the best answer I'm going to get for now. He doesn't have anyone who can take out Estrid, or at least not that he's considering. Surely if he had a god on his side, he'd use them.

"Don't worry yourself, witch. Just do as you're told and you'll be fine. Speaking of, I have a delivery for you."

He hands me an envelope, and I take it with disgust, doing my best not to let it show. Let the dirty work begin once more, then.

Chapter Fourteen

Estrid

The girl changes things.

I should have expected them to find one. Taking out Clay temporarily didn't mean that I did any real damage to Andreas' little operation, and I should have known they wouldn't stop until they had what they want.

I do believe Clay when he says he'll do his best by her, but I know he can do very little. And that's not an insult to him, either; the situation he's in is a terrible one.

She's a vampire, too. I've always liked vampires. I wonder who her divine parent is. I wonder if I know them.

The girl herself probably doesn't know, or I'd have Clay get the information for me and then go kick their ass into shape. Let them rescue their child and call it their first act of child support.

What a wonderful, modern human invention. I wish my kind would take notice.

So now there's a girl, and I'm essentially condemning her to be tortured by not rescuing her right now. *For the greater good*, I'm leaving a child in the hands of monsters.

It's not forever. It won't be for long at all. Even if Clay can't get any information I need, then I'll throw away the plan and rescue the girl.

I'd like to know who is on Andreas' side, though. Surely he isn't doing this alone, with not a single god noticing. Surely he can't get away with the type of magic he's doing, the cult he's forming, the destruction he's causing, when I can't get away with a single child I'm a little overly fond of.

***

Neve glares at me when I appear outside our home. "You're gone too much, Estrid."

"I wasn't aware I had a curfew. Or was that a term of my parole I forgot about?" I try to sound light and airy, but I know I fail miserably.

"Don't joke." Her shadows grow so thick they practically choke all the light out from around her. "Like it or not, we *are* watching you."

"I haven't crossed any lines." *Yet.* "And I'm watching Andreas. Who is crossing lines, incidentally. Maybe we should be having this conversation with him."

Neve stands and steps forward, the movement the most terrifying combination of grace and lethality. "He is not my problem. *Earth* is not my problem. *You* are my problem, Estrid. Father expects us to maintain a certain standard."

All seven of us were born in the exact same second, but sometimes Neve acts so much like she's the oldest that I wonder if her star came into being a millisecond before mine. Her overbearing act is usually enough to get everyone to listen, but today, I lift my chin and square my jaw. "It's wrong, Neve."

"Rota was right," she says. "They torture each other down there. They hurt people, even people they love. Why would you want anything to do with it?"

Because there's so much *good*. There're manicures and diamonds and strangers who hold doors for each other. There're cute animals and random acts of kindness and art. There are the scents of freshly made street food and musicians on street corners and people who love so fiercely it knocks the breath out of me. People help each other during natural disasters and cry at both weddings and funerals. There's so much good on Earth, in that place that's ugly and painful and lovely. Whatever it is, at least it's not the stagnant cage of our home.

"Stop going there," Neve tells me. "Stop worrying yourself with them. You need a distraction, Estrid. You need to stay out of trouble."

A part of me aches to listen to my sister. All of me knows what kind of trouble I can bring down on myself if I don't. But that doesn't change what Andreas is doing. Lorne is counting on me. Clay is counting on me. Marielle, Mina, Silas—they're all counting on me.

"I won't," I tell her. "I'm not causing trouble, Neve. But I won't just let him hurt people. *Our* people."

"They're not *ours*, Estrid!" she shouts, but I ignore it, letting the shadows take me away again.

***

I spend a week killing Andreas' clients before I reach to pull Clay into the shadows once more. An entire week feels like an unconscionable time to wait, but I need to give him a moment to try to solve the problem.

He sighs. "I'm starting to get used to that," he mutters.

"Good."

"Debatable. Where are we this time?"

I gesture to the cliff in front of us. "Blue Mountains."

He turns and takes in the landscape. This is a popular place for hikers to stop, but the late hour means we have the spot to ourselves. The stars and moon provide the only light for miles, and a deep, soul-cradling peace settles into my bones.

"Beautiful," he murmurs. "This is beautiful."

"It is," I agree. I've always liked this particular view. I go to sit on the ledge, letting my legs dangle and taking in the night sky. "Come and sit."

"Going to push me?"

"There are much easier ways to kill you."

"Yeah, but I thought this might be a gift. A, you know, *thank you for trying* gift. *Enjoy the view as your last sight.*"

"You have morbid thoughts," I tell him.

He sits, surprisingly graceful. Or maybe not so surprising, considering. I keep thinking of Clay as awkward, but that's only because I met him at his weakest. He really does just radiate grace, and I can't help but watch him move. "Maybe. I've been thinking about death a lot."

That *is* concerning. "Are you okay?" I ask, surprising myself by asking. By *caring*.

He shrugs. "I spoke with Andreas. I don't know for sure, obviously, but it doesn't sound like he has a god backing him. It doesn't sound like he has any other divine either, if that helps."

It does, but I ask, "And how do you know?"

He shrugs. "Asked about magic to kill a divine."

"Ballsy." To Andreas' face?

"I pretended I was scared of you," he says, and he manages a half-smile at that.

Is he *not* scared of me anymore? Evidently, and I don't know what to do with that. "And what did he tell you?"

"That a god could do it, or another divine if they were stronger than you. And he said he'd get around to you when he felt like it. Or he'd convince you to join his side." He looks at me sidelong. "He hasn't come after you, has he?"

"No. Not yet." But I killed a lot of people this week. At some point, I'm sure I'll end up on his radar for real.

But Andreas doesn't have a god on his side. I don't know if I expected that answer or not. On the one hand, a god would explain how he's getting away with this, but on the other, it would be such a breach of every rule we've ever been taught. No one can interfere directly with the beings of the Earth.

"How does Andreas find clients?" I ask him, turning the pieces over in my brain.

"Word of mouth, I think. They recommend each other, and then they find him. A lot of repeat business, too."

Exactly like a cult, then. Andreas has essentially created his own brand of worshippers, both his loyal minions who look to him desperately for their next bit of power and knowledge and his loyal customers, who revel in the depravity he offers.

Fuck. I know exactly what Andreas wants. It's hard to believe, but it's staring me right in the face.

Forget having a god on his side: Andreas wants to *become* a god.

***

I'm thinking about it long after I send Clay back, long after I warn him to look after the girl on autopilot, long after I'm alone. It's almost unbelievable.

No one becomes a god. The gap between them and us is too great. It's just not *possible*.

But it is, is the thing. Yes, the powers of a god are unfathomable, but really what makes a god is worshippers. None of the gods own the creatures of the Earth, but every time one of them prays for help, says *oh gods*, or calls on any particular piece of the universe ascribed to a certain god—that's worship. And Andreas is setting himself up to become the god of living creatures.

Or maybe just the depraved creatures. But even if that's only his starting point, that's plenty.

The idea should have occurred to me sooner. I just hadn't seriously considered it possible, put it so far from my mind that it hadn't even been a thought until right this moment. A *god*.

I'd once been accused of the same, and I'd been punished for it by my sisters, even if that had been so far from my intention. I'd wanted my family, that's all, but that had been enough for divine retribution. And now, Andreas gets away with it all.

No, he won't, because I won't let him. It's ridiculous to think that I'm the only thing standing between Andreas and godhood, but if I have to do it, then so be it.

But first, I have people to warn.

***

Mina is thankfully alone when I find her, and I don't bother waiting to see if she'll sense me. I step right out of the shadows and sit opposite her.

"You're back sooner than I expected," she says, not even looking up.

I slide into the chair opposite her. "This isn't a social visit, I'm afraid."

"Is it about the war?" she asks shrewdly. Mina always knows too much.

"Stay away from it," I tell her urgently, leaning forward. "You don't know what you're getting yourself into."

"I've been to war before," she says mildly, now looking at me.

But she hasn't. Mina is a stateswoman, a clever strategist. She's not a fighter. She's planned battles, perhaps. Organized troops and information. But she's never been to war. When given the chance, she chose to marry her husband to end a war.

"You don't know what you're up against."

"A divine who is trying to sow war?" she asks, and when I balk, she shrugs. "Deidre is very skilled at getting her information."

You'd think people would learn by now not to tell Deidre things, but she always somehow worms the information right out of people. Perhaps it's a type of magic all its own. "She's not wrong. And it's so much worse than you can imagine."

"Silas has signed a treaty with the Craes," she tells me.

"Since when does Silas have authority to do that?" Since when has Silas *wanted* authority to do that?

"Deidre signed. Silas just insisted. But he didn't have to push her hard; you know she'd do anything for her favorite brother. And the girl, Marielle—Theo's sister—she's a Crae now. The treaty is signed. If the Craes are going to war for her, then we are too."

"None of you are prepared for this fight."

"Then help prepare us. You know more than you're telling," she says, staring into me like she can see the answers if she just looks hard enough.

I really don't know much more than she does, but I keep my mouth shut regardless, reminding myself of the lines. There are things we can't do. Things we *shouldn't* do.

"Convince your king to stay out of it," I tell her. I pause, hearing footsteps in the corridor. I can't be seen by anyone but Mina, and push to my feet. "For all our sake."

"I can't. I won't. I trust my son, Estrid. And he's not wrong about this one."

That loyalty will get her killed, but I'm in no position to judge her for it. I'm out of time, so I give her a serious look as I let the shadows take me, and just have to hope she takes my warning.

Chapter Fifteen

Estrid

I return to the palace of night with my chest tight and my heart pounding.

If Mina doesn't listen to me—if she and Silas get themselves in over their head—

If Andreas takes them away from me, then I don't know what I'll do.

I bypass the entire palace and go straight to the ledge. Surely my father has to listen to me now. "You've neglected the world for long enough," I tell him, then take a deep breath and start over. No need to piss him off to start. "Sorry, sorry, I—we need you here. Andreas is out of control." I look down at where the Earth should be, if I could even see it through the void of night. "Hear that?" I say to the Earth god. "This is your problem too."

No response. I keep trying anyway.

"Andreas is trying to become a god," I say. "He's trying to claim the living creatures, get their direct worship, and ascend into godhood."

Surely this will finally get their attention. Surely this will finally get a response. Any response. Just—something.

Silence.

"What do we have to do to make you listen?" I demand, voice broken. "Burn the world down? Is that what it will take? Because Andreas might be on his way there."

Nothing.

"Burn the world down it is, then," I say, a savage bite to my voice. If I'm not angry, then I'll be broken, and I can't afford to be broken. It's much, much better if I just let myself be angry.

Fire doesn't come naturally to me. I much prefer the cold, the biting chill of the night. But I'm all about using the appropriate weapon for the situation, and fire seems best suited for this occasion. I want to see this cage burn.

I go inside to grab a lighter and a candle, then leave again without seeing anyone else. I light the decorative grasses outside, but soon enough I trail the lit candle along the palace itself, needing to see it catch and burn deep in my soul.

And burn it does. Glorious, ugly bursts of flame catch on the side of the building, and I watch in satisfaction before moving on.

It feels like my last connections to my father are burning away. This prison he made for us, this gilded cage he could store us in until he wanted to be entertained again—if it burns, will we be free?

"Is this what you wanted?" I shout. I go to touch the candle to the next wall, but a hand catches my wrist.

I think for half a second it's my father, but the fingers are too slim. "What are you doing?" Rota screams at me.

"Getting their attention," I snarl, knowing I sound beyond reason and not caring. I am beyond reason. I'm beyond discussion, beyond rationality. This has gone on long enough.

"What the fuck does that mean?" she demands, eyes crazed. Maybe we're all crazy now. Maybe none of us were ever meant to live in a world without the gods, and now that they abandoned us, we can't handle it.

"Andreas is trying to become a god, and they won't fucking deign to set foot here to deal with him," I say. My words half trip over themselves, desperate to get out, for her to understand. I need someone to understand, someone besides Clay, someone who will get it. Andreas is hurting people in ways that should never be forgiven. He's broken all of our rules. How come they punished me but not him? Why won't they deal with him?

Rota drops my arm and steps away, a look of disgust crossing her face. She takes another step, like she needs physical distance from me, like whatever I have might be catching. "You've lost your damn mind."

"Is it so hard to believe Andreas would do that?" I challenge.

"Look around you!" she shouts, waving her arms. "This is our *home*. We are safe here, happy. This place is ours, not Earth. Not anyone else's realm. You're trying to destroy our happiness. You set fire to our *home*."

"I will burn it all down," I seethe. "I will crawl on hands and knees to wherever they are and *make them deal with this mess*." They took my family from me. They made the rules. They made us, dammit. This is all their problem.

"No, you won't. Because they don't want you, Estrid. Nobody wants you. You want that little world so bad? Then go. And don't come back."

And she uses two hands to shove me over the edge.

The fall back to Earth through the starlit heavens should be terrifying, but it's just horrifyingly numb. My sister. My own damn sister, born of the stars at the same moment I was, cast me out.

We were each other's companions for so long. Maybe not good companions, but companions nonetheless. Who else did we have?

I pull myself together before I crash. The crash wouldn't kill me, but I could do a lot of damage to wherever I land. I grab onto the shadows and let them take me to safety.

I end up in New York. Maybe I'm thinking too much about Clay and the job ahead. I never meant to be this close to Andreas, not yet. But I'm here, and I've liked this hotel in the past, so I go in and get a room.

After I book a suite for an indefinite stay, I clear my throat. "Find me a personal shopper," I manage to say. "I'm going to need to replace everything."

Chapter Sixteen

Clay

Estrid doesn't call me for two more days. Whatever set her off last time must be keeping her busy.

She probably thinks I didn't notice, but of course I did. The way she immediately got lost, the way her whole demeanor shifted—she knows something that I don't.

And that's fine. I know she won't tell me. It's not like I'm not well-adapted to understanding that I'm the lackey. The boss holds all the cards, and everyone else only gets exactly what they need to play. My only worry is if she's holding back information that will keep me from doing my job well.

She might think the information is *need-to-know*, but who's to say what I need to know right now? This isn't actually well-trodden territory.

Well, all I know is that I haven't seen Andreas again, March is an asshole, I'm still feeding Lorne my own blood, and the girl refuses to speak to me.

That last one has a lot to do with the *March is an asshole* bit. He's made me leave him alone with her four times. I know he can't do permanent damage to her, and whatever he is doing doesn't leave any blood or wounds for me to clean up, but she gets more and more withdrawn every time she sees March, so I fucking hate it.

I'm getting to the point where I'm ready to help her escape and damn the consequences. March isn't going to settle for bloodless action forever.

So when Estrid pulls me into the shadows, I plan to tell her immediately that we need to get Lorne out of there. Damn Andreas and whatever little pissing contests are brewing among the gods.

And I should say it. I should. But instead I'm standing in a hotel room with shopping bags scattered about, watching a woman dressed casually in a t-shirt and jeans, her bare toes sinking into the plush carpet.

They're painted a midnight blue. Somehow, I'm charmed by that little detail.

I'm less charmed by the mess. "Have you been shopping while I've been risking my life?" I demand.

"Yes." I just stare at her, trying to formulate a way to express my frustration that doesn't get me killed, when she sighs. "I have to start over. I have nothing."

"Nothing?" I can't quite process what she's saying. "What happened?" This woman always has something. This hotel room looks like it costs a pretty penny. A cursory glance tells me it's multiple rooms, and every fixture looks luxurious.

She shrugs. "We're alone in this. No one wants to help us. The opposite, really." She pauses a moment, looking me over. "Does that change how you feel about helping me? Knowing that none of the other divine will support me?"

"Are you saying they don't care what Andreas is doing? They're, what, going to allow it?"

"More or less."

"So they won't help us?"

"No one's coming to save us," she says, voice bitter. She takes a deep breath, and it's like watching her put a mask on, her face smoothing out and her posture straightening. I hate it; it feels like whatever small fragments of her and her honesty that I've seen are gone now.

"Can we even do this alone?" I ask.

Her spine stiffens. "Yes," she says shortly, not elaborating any further.

"Give me something, here. Talk me through this," I beg, stepping toward her.

She sits on the plush sofa, tucking her legs up under her. "What's there to say? I am no longer welcome back home. If we once had rules, apparently no one cares anymore. Andreas is going to be allowed to do whatever he wants, and I'm here. So if this is my realm now, then I'll take care of it the best I can. And you're still going to help me."

There's more going on here than she's telling me, and perhaps I shouldn't be surprised at that. Estrid isn't a very forthcoming person.

"I'm worried for Lorne," I tell her abruptly, deciding to let it drop for now. "They haven't hurt her too badly yet, but they're doing something..." I shake my head. "Estrid, there's only so long we can let this go on. The kid lives in a dog crate, for gods' sake."

She tenses. "I know," she murmurs, dragging a hand through her hair, turning it into a mess. "It's my first priority at this point. I don't think you're going to get more out of Andreas. And if no one is going to back me, I don't need proof in the traditional sense. You and I both know what he's doing, and that's enough."

I blink, because that's the most honest and open statement she's ever made. Estrid willingly gave me more information than I asked for.

"Why did you never ask your niece?" I ask her impulsively. I've been thinking about the girl for a few days now, every time I see Lorne's eyes grow more and more distant. "Surely she'd tell everyone what happened to her."

Her mouth twitches into a small smile. "She has," she acknowledges. "Her mate is going to war for her, and it seems like he and his family have recruited the vampires and demons as well."

I blow out an impressed breath. As a witch, I can't even imagine that. That kind of social connection is entirely foreign to me, but it makes me feel a little better that she has that after centuries of pain.

"So why aren't you talking to them?"

She looks at me for a long minute. "The last time I spoke to Marielle, I didn't know what happened to her. I offered to tell her about her family and she told me to get lost. That she had a new family now. So I did. She's not wrong; I'm well aware of what my kind are like as parents."

So she's doing all this for a niece she doesn't even talk to. I'm reluctantly impressed. "Don't you think that bringing this information to her would go a long way to mending bridges?" I don't know anything about mending bridges, granted. I have burned all of mine with prejudice. But this seems like the sort of thing that would help.

Besides, she wouldn't have to fight her battles alone if she went to her niece.

"They don't know where to start," she dismisses. "Their hearts are in the right place, but they have no idea what to do. They're mustering an army with nothing to direct it toward. How very werewolf of them."

My lungs squeeze. "Werewolf? Why do you say that?"

"Marielle's mate is a werewolf. One of those damned princes. I suppose it makes sense; her mother is literally the embodiment of the moon, so—"

Whatever else she's saying about Marielle's mother goes right over my head. The fucking werewolves. Those damned princes. "I've pissed off the wolves too," I tell her. "My cousin—" My throat closes for a second, thinking back. *Fuck.*

"Your cousin?" she prompts, leaning closer. It's hard to remember sometimes that Estrid doesn't really know me. It's like she sees through my soul every time she looks at me, but she has no idea who I am, what my past is.

That's what happens when you're forced to show someone the absolute worst parts of yourself first, I suppose. The only difference between me and someone else is I have so many other bad parts to share.

"My cousin Mae is mated to one of the other princes," I tell her. "And we didn't leave things on a good note." That's an understatement, to say the least. "I don't think she knows everything I've done. But she knows more than enough to hate me."

I expect her to get angry. I brace myself for her berating me, perhaps even threatening me again. I wouldn't blame her; I'd deserve it at this point, and it's clear she needs to blow off some steam. How I treated Mae is just one of my many sins, but it's one I won't forget.

Estrid sighs and lets her head fall back. "What a pair we make," she murmurs, like that's it. It doesn't feel like condemnation, either.

"I threatened her," I tell Estrid, because at this point I've opened my entire chest to this woman. I've flayed myself raw, cut myself open, and I might as well excise all the crimes of my past while we're in here. No one else has ever listened, and even if Estrid decides that my crimes are too deplorable to handle, then at least someone still heard them. "When our cousin Greta ran away, she left the magic shop to Mae. Mae didn't even want it."

"And you did?" she asks, head still tilted back and studying the ceiling tiles. "I can't picture you running a shop, Clay."

"Andreas wanted it," I admit softly. "Greta had a customer base he was convinced he could use. He told me to get the shop."

"So you took it," she says. Her tone is neutral, and I almost believe she's not judging me.

"I manipulated Mae. Greta left magic up to keep me out and I wheedled and manipulated and pressed. And when I finally found a hole in the spell, I took full advantage. I could have hurt her. I might have, if that werewolf didn't stop me. I fought hard, because I knew what the cost of disappointing Andreas would be." I can still feel the phantom aches and pains of that beating. Those werewolves pack one hell of a punch. "So, they don't like me either."

She rolls her neck so she's looking at me. "What a pair we make," she says again.

And somehow, that makes me feel warm inside again. Because we're a pair, because she's not abandoning me in this. Does she like me? No, probably not. I've probably burned that bridge before I even got to it, just like I burned all the others. But that doesn't matter, because I'm not alone.

"When do you want me to go back?" I ask hesitantly. She never lets me stay that long, not since I *escaped* captivity. And I know I have a job to do. Lorne is waiting for me, even if she doesn't want to see me. There's always the possibility that I could overhear something useful for Estrid, but to do that, I have to be there.

I know what my job is. And I can do it, too. I'm willing to do it. I just wish I could have a moment first.

She looks at me for a moment, then sighs. "Just don't ruin it, alright, Clay?"

With no damned idea what I could be ruining, I nod hesitantly and keep my mouth shut, and we stay like that for the better part of an hour, just the two of us, together in a long silence.

Chapter Seventeen

Estrid

Clay is in my home, and I have no desire to throw him out.

Maybe it's because this doesn't feel like a home yet, just a hotel room I've filled with whatever random objects I thought might help me feel better. It's not my home of thousands upon thousands of years. Maybe it's just I've never lived without my sisters before and I'm lonely.

But no. This isn't like having my sisters here.

This is like having all my worst impulses, the worst moments of my history, laid bare and inviting him back, regardless. Clay has made terrible choices in his life, but I can't pretend I made better. We both hurt our families. We both failed the halflings.

And now we're here, and somehow neither of us has left. He could get up and walk out, and I even think I'd let him. I don't need him anymore, and I can't pretend that there's so much evil inside of him I'd need to kill him.

I doubt I could. How do you look at someone in your darkest moments and then turn around and kill them? I just don't think it's possible.

But he hasn't left. Whether it's because of me or because he wants to save the halfling, I don't know. Maybe it's both, or neither. Maybe his own crimes are weighing heavily on his soul.

He looks tired again. I don't ask him if he's sleeping because I already know the answer. I don't think they're asking him to lend his magic to any of their deplorable spells, or at least he hasn't mentioned it. Maybe they think he's still entirely drained. Or maybe he has been doing them and is just too ashamed to bring it up without me asking directly.

I don't ask. It wouldn't change anything either way, and I can't help him. Not yet. But I will soon, and not just for the girl. Leaving Clay there would be just as bad as all the years I left Marielle there.

"Are you hungry?" I ask him after a few more minutes of silence. It's not a bad silence, either. Just two people existing, living in the same place, probably thinking the same thoughts. It's been a long time since I've had that.

"You think about food a lot for someone who doesn't eat," he says.

"Are you hungry or not? Because I hear the room service here is top-notch, but if you would rather I send you back and you eat there..."

"Alright, alright. You have a menu?"

"On the desk."

He stands to go retrieve it, and I watch him move. Clay deftly navigates the admittedly impressive pile of things I accumulated in the last two days. He was wrong when he accused me of caring more about shopping than Andreas' cult, but I admit I let the personal shopper get a little carried away. I thought it'd make this place feel like home, but somehow filling it with stuff makes it feel even more empty.

"I'll call for it," he murmurs. "You want anything?"

"Don't eat," I remind him, although I know full well that he knows.

He shrugs and calls down, ordering some sort of sandwich with French fries. Then he throws himself back down on the couch while he waits.

"So, do I Cash App you for the food, or..."

I look at him blankly. "I have more money stored away than any immortal could spend in their lifetime."

"I know," he says, and he gives me a small grin. I have to stop myself from doing a double-take. His face lights up, his eyes get a mischievous tilt, and I want to see it again.

And that's foolish, so I squish the thought. "Then why did you ask?"

"Because it's polite. And I'm working on being polite."

"And that's new for you?"

"You don't get to talk."

"I'm perfectly polite."

He raises an eyebrow. "I don't think so."

"Little shit. I haven't murdered you yet. Is that polite enough?" There's no heat behind my words, though, and judging by his smirk, he knows it.

"Forgive me for being polite, Estrid. Won't happen again."

"See that it doesn't," I sniff. I sound foolish, but I don't care. I don't stop.

I might never have my sisters to be foolish with again. If this is all I have—well, it's not the same. Clay certainly doesn't replace them. We're all born of stardust, all the embodiments of different pieces of the night, and Clay will never be that. He's too much flesh and blood, too squishy and soft. But this might be close enough. This might make something in me feel a little better.

He'll eat his dinner, and then I'll send him back. I have to; he needs to be there for the girl. But it won't be for much longer. I need to get them both out, set them both free, and make a plan to be done with this myself.

CHAPTER EIGHTEEN

CLAY

Estrid makes me eat every bite of my meal before she lets me go. I tell her I'm full, that I'm not used to eating this much, but it doesn't matter. She insists, looking at me the whole time with something that I might describe as worry on anyone else. I'm probably projecting. I know I'm a tool and I shouldn't forget it, but I can't help feeling a little warm and fuzzy under her scrutiny.

It's stupid, but I can't control it.

Once I've eaten enough to satisfy her, she extends a hand, and I take it. Before I know it, I'm back where I started, in an alcove in the damned house. I'm getting used to that shadow travel. It doesn't even upset my stomach anymore.

I want to tell Estrid that, but she's already gone. I don't know when she'll be back, don't know what the plan will be. I trust her to have a plan. I think I even trust her to have my best interest at heart. At any rate, I don't truly believe she'll just leave me here anymore.

I just have to hope it's soon. Lorne and I can't take much more of this.

It's late now, and I've already fed Lorne today. I want to go and keep her company, but I know she wants nothing to do with me. She sees me as an enemy, and the poor girl is allowed to feel that way. I certainly haven't helped her.

Sarge is already in the bedroom, but thankfully he's asleep and doesn't have any questions about where I've been. Not that I think he'd ask them anyway; no one around here seems to give a fuck what I do, as long as I'm where they need me when they need me. I should have realized a lot sooner that these people didn't give a fuck about me and my life.

The sheets on this bed suck. I used to have silk sheets I shelled out a lot of money for in my old bed back in my apartment. I'd saved for those, too. I bet Estrid has soft sheets. I bet hers have a thread count higher than I could ever even imagine.

I drift off to sleep thinking about Estrid's bed.

***

A piercing scream sends me flying upright, my heart pounding and breaths barely coming.

That's *Lorne*. I don't know how I know, except I do, because who else could it be? That's Lorne.

In a fog, I grab my shirt and pull it on, shoving my feet in shoes and running down the stairs, taking them three at a time.

What the fuck could be wrong at this hour? I didn't exactly check my phone, but a quick glance at the windows I'm passing tells me it's still the middle of the night. Something must have happened, and I feel my throat tightening at just the thought. Someone is down there with that child.

I scramble for the one measly pocket knife I've managed to enchant since Estrid took my old one. It's pathetic that this is the sum total of my magic now, but I clutch it like it's a lifeline. For Lorne, it might be. I can't let anything happen to that kid. I turned a blind eye for too long, letting my own selfish ass come first. And I just can't anymore.

If I die today—well, I really don't want to die. My life has just started to get interesting again, and if I die, then I'll never get to see Estrid again. But if I do, then that's the cost of what I've done, I suppose. You don't walk away clean from that.

I throw the basement door open wide, not bothering with any sort of subtlety. Lorne's screaming was loud enough to wake the house; subtlety left us in the dust long ago.

Lorne is strapped to a steel table a few feet from her dog cage, and her side is ripped open. I can see her chest rising and falling, so she's still alive, although how she's surviving this wound is anyone's guess. "What the fuck are you doing?" I snap, stepping closer and trying not to look at the gaping hole in the kid.

Andreas shrugs nonchalantly, turning toward me with bloody hands. "She doesn't need both kidneys, witch. Now go away. You're not needed here."

"Let her go."

He has a scalpel in hand that he points at me now. "Watch yourself."

I hold up my pathetic knife. "Let. Her. Go."

He looks me over slowly, raising an eyebrow to convey just how little he sees me as a threat. "Listen. You're already on your second chance, witch. There won't be a third. Make a smart decision now."

"No," I tell him. I look up at this man—no, not a man. This divine being, born of some power too big for me to understand. And it's just me and a stupid fucking pocket knife.

But I'm the only one here for this child. My eyes dart around, taking in the scene, trying to come up with a strategy. If I can hit him with my knife, maybe the poison will be as hard on him as it was on me. And that'll distract him enough for me to get Lorne, and maybe if we're both stupidly lucky, I can get us both out of here. Maybe.

It's a long shot, but what other choice do I have? I throw the knife, hoping for the best.

It bounces off of him like it's some sort of prop knife made of rubber. He looks down at it slowly, as if he can't believe what just happened.

"Dumb fucker," Andreas curses. "I'd kill you slowly, but I need this to be quick so I can get back to the girl." He glances at her. "They bleed out so easily when they're still mortal."

I want to run. I want to run and hide or beg and plead. I don't, holding my ground.

Last stands always sound so much more romantic in fiction, and, I'll be honest, I wasn't even sold on them then.

I fall a few inches, a sudden jerk knocking the breath out of my lungs. I take my eyes off of Andreas long enough to see that the ground has *swallowed my feet*. I'm trapped up to the ankle. A rock rips through the basement floor and shoots at me, pummeling me in the sternum before I can even hope to move. A scream rips out of me as my ribs splinter under the force. Another rock hits me, this time in the spine.

Fuck, I'm pretty sure I can recover from a broken spine, but I've never tested it before, and I don't want to.

Another rock, this one from above, and I barely have time to raise my arms to act as a shield. I need something, need a weapon, need a plan—*anything*.

Another rock. He's going to bury me alive, and I don't know if it'll kill me—probably not. But it'll be damn unpleasant, and I'm sure he'll just come back to finish the job later.

Then it's a barrage, like me realizing his intent gives him permission to finish it. I try to shield my head, but it's like holding an umbrella against a tsunami. I pass out for a second, the pain of a rock hitting me in the head knocking me senseless, and when I come to, it's entirely dark.

I'm entombed. Andreas brought the earth down on me, and no matter how hard I shove, I can't move it. I'm trapped here, just waiting for him to finish me off.

Or not. What's to stop him from leaving me here in my misery, alive and regretting it? My breaths come faster, panicky and thin, and I bang against the rocks.

No. Andreas doesn't leave loose ends like that. It's not much of a comfort, but it's something.

I need a plan. I need something to enchant, something to be ready. I need to be able to defend myself, because even if it's going to be useless against Andreas, I won't forgive myself if I just lay down and die.

I could enchant the rocks. I could make them shrink; I know an easy enough enchantment for that, and that would give me a gap to escape from. But from there, I'll be defenseless again, so I need a better plan before I can do that.

I look around furiously, but it's too dark in here to see anything that might be in here with me. I have no idea what's useful nearby, not through this thick shadow, and—

I stop. Shadow.

Estrid uses the shadows. I don't know if it works both ways, but it's the only thing I have left to try. "*Estrid*," I hiss into the shadows. "Estrid!"

Chapter Nineteen

Estrid

I hear him calling for me.

I usually don't. The shadows aren't my secret spy network—that's a lot of work for not a lot of reward. But there was something about tonight, the way he looked at me, the morose set to his eyes. The story he told me, maybe. I couldn't leave him, not entirely, so I left a shadow on him, just a touch.

And I hear him calling my name.

I leave my stupid, lonely hotel room behind and appear beside him, only to find myself in a dank, blood-soaked basement with a nearly dead girl, a pile of rocks, and a divine being striving hard for godhood.

Andreas turns to me. "Estrid. What a surprise. Did you come to join me finally? I always suspected you would."

"What about me made you think I'd rip apart innocent people?" I demand, staring at the girl on the table.

"You tried to take over the world once. Your mistake was just not knowing how to bide your time. And now, it's time. We're alone here. The gods stopped watching. Everyone else is too lazy and content to care. Earth is for the taking. I'd be happy to give you a corner of it."

A *corner*. He thinks I'd sell out this girl's life for some corner of the world. "I think I'll just kill you, actually," I say, and watch in something that feels almost like delight as his face twitches with disgust.

He flicks his hand at me and more rocks rise, but I bat them away with the shadows.

His lips purse. "What do you get out of being such a nuisance? If you don't want your share, what could you *possibly* want here on Earth?"

"Give me both of them," I tell him quietly, "and I'll leave."

Will I ever leave him alone? No. Gods or no gods, what Andreas is doing is wrong. No one is supposed to be the god of living creatures, and he's just cruel. I won't tolerate it, even if I have to fight it alone. But I'll get Lorne and Clay out first.

"*Them*? You want *them*?" he demands, laughing incredulously. "Her, I get. I heard you like the sad little halflings. But what's so special about that witch? You know he's defective, right?"

"He's mine. They're both mine." I try to reach for the girl with shadows, but Andreas throws a rock at me to break my concentration.

"Yours? You taking in strays now, Estrid?"

"You don't know me."

"I know your sisters punished you for over a century because you liked those sad halflings too much. They were worried you were making yourself a goddess of vampires, weren't they? And I thought you were too, but now seeing you—you're just that pathetic, aren't you? You were just playing house."

"They were my family," I say coldly. "I wasn't *playing* at anything."

He laughs cruelly. "I should have known better than to think you might be a worthy partner. If you were good, you'd have won your war. You'd never have allowed your sisters to punish you. But you're nothing but a nuisance,

Estrid. And I don't have patience for anything that stands in my path. I already took care of that witch you're pining after."

The room gets colder without me consciously trying, and I have to desperately try to pull it back, worried about hurting the girl. Where is Clay? Is he *in* that pile of rocks?

I send the shadows probing around, and yes, he's in there. And he's not conscious.

Fuck.

I'm not in any position to fight someone like Andreas. I'm not equipped to fight like that, not someone who is so violent and cruel. Andreas has spent his life preparing for that type of war. I haven't.

I just need to get my hands on Lorne and Clay. For now, that's all I can do.

Clay will be easy, already embraced by the shadows inside those rocks. There's a light glaring down on Lorne, banishing my shadows, but one step at a time. I can send him away right now, and I concentrate for a moment and do it, sending him to my hotel room. Hopefully, he's okay. Hopefully, he wakes up there now that he's free, realizes what's happened, and takes care of himself.

The rocks crumble now that his body isn't holding them up. Andreas raises an eyebrow. "Well, you got your worthless little toy. Maybe did me a favor; disposing of him would have been messy."

My entire existence has been as cold as ice, so I don't expect the white-hot rage that consumes me when he says that. But I'm practically shaking with it, so furious that he would ever say that about Clay.

Clay is not worthless. Clay is foolish, misled, and greedy. Clay also was willing to die tonight for the girl there on the table. Clay is someone, and someone important. The gods themselves won't listen. My siblings won't listen. Everyone who is supposed to be powerful, who is supposed to rule this realm, won't listen. But Clay listened.

The temperature of the room drops dramatically, down to well below freezing. Ice crystallizes on every surface, even Andreas' clothes. "Give me the girl," I tell him. I need to get her. Need to get her and get to Clay, need to make sure they're both alright. I promised, and while everyone else might have forgotten their promises to this world, I never will again.

"Over my dead body."

"That's the plan."

He studies me for a second. "You're bluffing. You don't have what it takes. You could have ruled the world, Estrid—and you *let them* punish you."

I don't know how much *letting* was involved, and I fight to not remember those awful years. "I listened to the will of the gods."

"The gods are *gone*, Estrid. They don't answer us anymore. I've waited and waited, but I won't leave this power vacuum any longer. It's just us now, and if I'm the first person brave enough to fill that void—well, I'll gladly do it. You could have been at my side, the second of the new gods."

"And when you're the god of living creatures, what will I be?" I ask, pretending to entertain this nonsense, hoping that if I keep talking, it'll disguise how fast my heart is going. *Gone.* He says the gods are *gone.* Is it not just me they're ignoring?

He shrugs. "You want the night? It's yours. Just throw your support behind me, and it's done."

"I rather die like a mortal than serve under you," I sneer, bracing myself for whatever comes next. I trace my shadows a little closer to the girl, inch by inch, waiting for the perfect moment to strike.

"You're a pathetic waste," he says. "But if that's how you want it." He raises a rock to throw at me. I freeze it in mid-air, then try to secure him in place with my shadows. All I need is to stall him long enough to bring my shadows to the girl—

He dodges away, faster than any creature who isn't divine can move. But it's enough, and I wrap my shadows around the girl's leg and suck her into the darkness with me.

***

I land on the floor of my hotel room, disoriented and panting. Shadow travel has never hurt me before, never took so much out of me, but I can barely breathe right now.

I grab the girl, knowing what kind of condition she was in. She's too young, and her divine blood will have made her hardier than most, but she's young and fragile. Mortal, really, and my heart jumps in my throat.

I rip my wrist open and drip the blood in her mouth. She's a vampire; surely the blood will help her. Surely once she has blood in her system again, she'll start to recover.

While I'm waiting for her to take the blood—and she's just lying there, unresponsive, but I'm hoping the scent of blood will wake her—I turn toward Clay.

He's still unconscious. "Wake up," I snarl, mean and unfair and I know it. He's unconscious because of me. *I* put him in that position. But fear is taking over every inch of me and making me mean, and I can't stop it. I need him here. I can't do this without him. "Wake up, Clay," I demand. "You have to help me with her, she's—"

She's still not taking any of the blood. It's dripping into her mouth, but she's not actually swallowing any, and the wound in her side is bleeding more than I can give her back. What the fuck do I do here?

Staunch the bleeding. I know that much, but I've never done it. My own little one had a remarkably safe childhood, what with me following him around practically everywhere. Scraped knees and elbows were the worst of it, and they never bled like this.

I shove my hand into the wound, trying to put pressure on it. With my other hand, I fumble around for a pristine white pillow, tugging it off the couch and pressing it against the wound.

It turns red, and she doesn't stop bleeding.

There are organs in there. I have no idea which one Andreas was trying to dig out of her, and I have no idea how to check that he didn't do damage to anything else. She needs medical attention. Real, proper medical attention from someone who can actually help her.

And I seem to know someone who can do that.

Well, *know* is putting it strongly. But I've been spying on someone who might be able to help.

She knows more than I do, at any rate. And if she can't help Lorne—or if she rejects me entirely, which I wouldn't be surprised about—then I'll have to try a human doctor, which will lead to too many questions.

I grab Lorne with one hand and Clay with the other, and then let the shadows take us away.

***

Marielle and her mate are cuddling on the couch when I appear out of the shadows in their living room, two unconscious, bloody bodies still tight in my grip. The werewolf jumps up, stepping between Marielle and us, but I don't move. "Help us," I croak. "Please. I—please."

Chapter Twenty

Estrid

M arielle moves toward us, but the werewolf throws out his arm to block her path. "Who the fuck are you?" he growls.

Marielle touches his arm. "She's my aunt. Remember her from the party?"

He grumbles for a second. "And how the fuck did you get in here? The village is supposed to be warded against outsiders."

"Shadows," I gasp, not giving a fuck about what he's asking, just needing Marielle's help. I look at her and only her. "Please, I—she's like you."

She stares for a moment, as if she's trying to piece together what I'm saying, but then she nods. "What happened to her?" she demands softly, stepping out from around her mate.

"The same people who took you, they took her—he's the one who stopped them tonight, but they tried—I don't know what they were after, but she won't stop bleeding, she won't take blood, and she's too young to heal right, and I just need *help*."

Marielle crouches down next to me, the werewolf hovering behind her. "I'm not a doctor."

"You're good enough." She bites her lip but nods, determination in her eyes.

"Marielle, I—"

She holds up a hand to stop her mate. "I have to try, Callum. Go get me my bag?"

He hesitates a second. "Are you sure—"

She turns to give him a quick, almost painful smile. "I'm sure I can handle myself, and we both know it. And I'm sure that this girl will die without help. Go. Please."

He does, moving so quickly that I have no doubt he'll be back within moments. "Her name is Lorne. She's half-vampire, but I can't get her to take blood like this."

Marielle nods and strokes Lorne's hair off her face. "I'd guess we need to close the wound first. There are some things I want to use, to ensure it heals cleanly—when they're so young, that's important. But get me the plant over there?"

I look where she's gesturing to see a flowering plant near the TV. I jump up to grab the pot, checking over Clay as I do. He looks awful, still unconscious, but I doubt he's dying, at least.

Marielle takes the plant from my hand. "Alright," she murmurs, keeping one hand on the stem and another on Lorne. "Let's try."

The werewolf practically runs back in with a bag in hand, skidding to a stop right behind Marielle. "Mari—"

"Shh," she interrupts. "Not yet."

With a furrowed look of concentration, she turns her full attention to Lorne. Before my very eyes, the wound in her side starts to close up, the bleeding slowing as the gaping wound gets smaller. The plant withers slightly under Marielle's grip, but the wound keeps healing.

There's an awful ripping sound, and it takes me a long moment to realize that it's a sob and it's coming from me. I never cry in front of people, never lose my composure, but it feels like that's all I've done for days. My father, my sisters, Clay, and now these people, who despite being family, might as well be strangers. But I can't stop the sound and I can't stop the tears.

I fall to the floor, halfway between Clay and Lorne. With Marielle having Lorne well in hand, I crawl back over to Clay, touching along his head. He was bleeding here earlier, but the wounds stopped gushing blood even if they're not fully closed yet.

"You're a fool," I whisper to him between sobs. I doubt I'm as quiet as I think, but Marielle is consumed by Lorne and her werewolf is consumed by her. "Why didn't you call me? No one told you this was your job."

But I had, is the thing. Or at least I'd let him believe it, and he really could have died tonight. I'm so godsdamn lucky that he didn't.

I couldn't stand it if this man died for me.

No. I couldn't stand it if this man *died*. I like his stupid little smirks, rare as they are. I bet they weren't always that rare, and I've wondered if I can draw them out more. If I lost that chance...

Marielle is mixing together some ingredients completely unidentifiable to me. "She needs blood," she tells me, and I don't need further instruction. I take the knife she's using, slice open my wrist, and hold it to Lorne's mouth.

This time, she takes from me, and I feel my whole body sag with relief.

The werewolf watches with interest, still hovering protectively behind my niece. "Is your blood going to hurt her?"

"Callum," Marielle scolds quietly.

"I'm asking. She's different from us, and it's a valid question."

"Vampires can take my blood just fine," I promise him. Plenty of vampires have in the past. I watch the blood drip and Lorne reflexively swallow. Good. That's good.

"Should I call Theo?" Marielle whispers, and I know she's talking to her wolf and not me.

"Maybe?"

"Theo?" I croak.

"My brother," Marielle says. "He was at the party the night we met. The host, actually."

Ah, that Theo. Silas' Theo. I still haven't quite worked out how he and Marielle are siblings, but now isn't the time to ask. "I know enough about vampires to help. But if you'd be more comfortable, sure. Is she going to live?"

"She'll live," Marielle confirms. I turn my attention to her as she pushes her sweaty red hair off her face. I know the magic she just did took a lot out of her, but I also know she can do it. It's how I knew who she was the moment I saw her; in addition to looking like her mother, Marielle has serious magic. Maybe not as much as a divine—so not enough for her mother to keep her—but more than the average halfling. She's somewhere in-between.

Her werewolf kneels down on the rug with us and braids her hair, just silently taking over and sectioning it, moving with neat, efficient, but still gentle strokes. My heart softens toward him a bit.

"And him?" I ask, turning to Clay while still keeping my wrist in Lorne's mouth. "He's not a child, he's not dying, but he got clobbered and I'm not sure—"

"I recognize him," the werewolf interrupts, tying off her braid with a hair tie on his wrist while he stares at Clay.

"Who is he?" Marielle asks.

"He's Mae's asshole cousin."

Fuck, I forgot Clay told me he has history with the werewolves too. "He's changed."

"Can't have changed that much." Callum frowns. "What the fuck is he doing here?"

"He's the one who almost died trying to save Lorne here. He's been protecting her for weeks now, waiting for a chance to free her."

"Weeks?" Marielle asks, her already pale face growing paler. "They had her for weeks?"

Marielle reaches for Callum's hand, and he's already reaching to take her in his arms. "It's alright, beautiful," he murmurs to her. "She's free; you healed her. She'll be okay."

"Weeks," she murmurs, almost a painful moan.

"They had you for two centuries?" I ask, needing to confirm that the records I read were true.

Callum turns hard eyes to me, his entire demeanor changing. "And you didn't protect her."

"I didn't know," I point out, but I can see it in his eyes that he knows as well as I do that it's not a valid excuse. "I protected this one."

"Are there others?" Marielle asks softly. "We've been trying to find out, but we can't really get any sort of foothold in that organization—we didn't do a good job at taking prisoners when we had them—"

"They made you carve out your *eyes*," Callum snarls. "I wasn't going to let them continue to breathe."

"I helped," Marielle reminds him. "They took you and I wouldn't—I couldn't—let them live. But we weren't thinking long-term."

"Damn right," Callum agrees. "And no one can fucking blame us for that."

Marielle takes a deep breath. This is clearly a well-rehearsed conversation, and I watch it like the spectator I am, but I want to get back to the matter at hand. "Are there others?" she repeats.

"Not that Clay knows about. That doesn't mean there aren't, though. They didn't tell him much. And speaking of Clay..."

But he's already stirring. "I didn't do that," Marielle whispers, but I tune her out.

"Clay? Clay?"

"Fuck, Es—" he groans, and my heart jumps. He's never called me Es before. "Where are we?"

"Crae Village."

That gets his attention. "Crae Village? What the fuck are we doing here?" He still hasn't opened his eyes, and when he moves as if he's going to sit up, I pin him with my shadows. "No fair."

"You looked dead to me five minutes ago, Clay. Wait a damned minute."

"What are we doing here?"

"Nearest place I knew to save Lorne."

"So she's okay?" he asks, and he finally opens his eyes.

I feel Marielle and Callum watching us like a tennis match, eyes going back and forth between us. I wish we were alone, but this is the cost of coming here. "She'll recover," I say, because *okay* is stretching it right now.

"Her organs are knitting back together," Marielle tells him. "Right now, blood helps."

Clay clumsily raises his arm. "Take mine."

I pin that arm too with my shadows until I have restraints around his waist and both arms. It's like all the way back to the first days where I imprisoned him, and I can't say that I like the comparison. "Settle down. You lost enough blood tonight."

"But she's used to mine," he murmurs, like that makes any damn difference.

Apparently, it does to the werewolf, who tenses. "What do you mean, she's used to yours?"

"Clay's been feeding her," I interject. "Because they were starving her."

"She's a child," Callum snarls, and it doesn't take a genius to see the way he looks at Lorne and his mate. This is a man who probably has thought endlessly about Marielle's captivity, who probably thinks about where he was when she was being hurt.

"I know," Clay says. "I tried—Well, Andreas is fucking divine. I tried."

"Andreas is more than divine," I interrupt. I've kept this to myself, but it's too late for that now. These people were already planning war, and as much as I wanted to keep them out of it, I know coming here means I've thrown my lot in with them. I don't have anyone else I can trust, and while it's a stretch to say that I trust these people, they're as close as I'm going to get. It's time for them to have all the information. "He's bordering on godhood."

An uneasy silence descends on the room. "We should call everyone," Marielle tells her mate.

There's a scuffle at the door. "I texted them," Callum says, staring at Clay and I with hard eyes while the door swings open and the whole Crae clan descends on us.

Chapter Twenty-One

Clay

I honestly thought it might be best if I never saw Mae again. It's because I'm a coward, yes, but mostly it's because she deserves to not have to deal with me. I know what I did. I know what I tried to steal from her, and I know I made her afraid. She shouldn't ever have to deal with me again, and she certainly shouldn't have to deal with my problems.

And now, she's the first one to come pushing in the door while I'm still groggy, fuzzy-headed, and shadow-restrained to the floor. Wonderful.

She looks good, is my first thought. The Mae I knew always had an edge to her, her fake confidence only hiding so much. There'd been a fear there, an old hurt that never seemed properly satisfied. But this Mae, while still physically looking the same, looks so different.

She's fulfilled, I think. Greta would be thrilled if she knew.

She's also pissed. "You," she hisses, stepping toward me before stopping, looking around bewildered and maybe a little hurt. "What's he doing here?" she asks the couple whose house this is.

I'm presuming she's Marielle, which means I'm in the home of a were-wolf prince and his mate who has been horrifically harmed by an organization that, until recently, I was very much a part of. This night just keeps getting better and better.

"I want to know that too," another werewolf growls. This one is Mae's, and I'd recognize him anywhere after the beating he gave me. Bryce, I think his name is.

A tall woman crosses her arms. "Same here. Callum, what is this?"

Estrid steps in front of me. She's physically shaking, and I wonder what happened after I passed out. The details are blurry, but I know I called for her and she must have come. I have no idea why she brought us *here*, other than Lorne looks better than she did when I first saw her on that table. What happened between when I passed out and now? Did Estrid have to fight Andreas? Is that why she looks like she's about to fall over?

"We came here to ask for sanctuary," she says, her voice as shaky as the rest of her. "And to offer our help."

"What help could you offer us?" Bryce growls.

"We know more about the organization you're looking to take down than you do."

"Because he's part of it!" Mae interjects, voice forceful.

My heart plummets. I was hoping she hadn't put that together yet, although I don't know why. It's not like I was going to get away with not admitting it.

"I had a change of heart," I say, my voice raspy.

"Don't talk," Estrid scolds.

"Too little, too late," Bryce says at the same time.

"And who the fuck are you?" another one asks Estrid.

"My aunt," Marielle says quietly. "On my mother's side."

That much is obvious. Even as shaken as she is, Estrid radiates a type of deep magic that no normal being could possibly approach. She's divine through and through, and people eye her with respectful caution.

"And what the fuck do you want?"

Estrid holds her chin up like she's the one with something to prove. "I didn't know what happened to Marielle. Not until after. But I won't let it happen to another one. Clay has been my spy, gathering me information."

The woman who spoke earlier looks interested. "And do you have any?"

"I know more about Andreas than any of you do," she says.

"She said he's a god," Callum interjects, and all eyes turn to him. He's holding his mate, his big hands deceptively gentle on her, and I think he might be holding her upright. I don't blame her; just seeing Estrid and Lorne is probably too much for her. She survived two centuries of the shit they put Lorne through. I'm surprised she's functioning at all.

"Not a god," Estrid corrects. "Just bordering on godhood."

"Oh, *bordering* on it, never mind then," one of them snarks. I lift my head to look at him. Demon, and I think I remember seeing him around Mae's shop once upon a time.

There's a stand-off happening, and I can see Estrid warring with how much to tell them. She hasn't even told me this about Andreas, and I know how much she likes to play things close to the chest. But I already know we're not getting out of here without full honesty.

The werewolf queen has a reputation for being a straight-shooter and ruthless when she needs to be. We can't lie to them.

"Estrid," I mutter. "Let me up."

She glances back at me. "You're still recovering."

"I'm better now."

"Keep him tied up," Mae says. "No telling what he'll get up to."

It cuts. We're cousins; Greta practically raised us both. I'm not saying that I don't deserve it; I definitely do. But it still hurts regardless.

"Estrid," I say again, ignoring Mae for now. I can already tell that we're going to have it out, but right now isn't the time.

She heaves a sigh. "Fine, see if I care when you fall on your ass." The shadows fall away, and I push myself to my feet.

"We mean no harm," I mumble. "And I'll leave. But please—listen to Estrid. She knows what she's talking about." I try to catch Mae's eye, but she won't look directly at me. "And Lorne. Please, she's done nothing wrong."

"We don't hurt children," the third brother says. The emphasis on *we* is so obvious he might as well come out and say *unlike you*.

"Clay stays," Estrid says calmly, like she has any sort of bargaining power here.

"Careful," Callum rumbles. "I'm not sure *you* get to stay at the moment."

"No," Marielle says softly. Callum immediately turns his full attention to her, and I relax now that it's off Estrid. I know she can handle herself. I know that even someone as strong as these werewolves doesn't truly stand a chance against her. But that doesn't change that I don't like the way he was looking at her.

Good gods, what is *wrong* with me? Estrid can take care of herself, and, outside of the deal we struck—a deal I'd say I've fulfilled my end of, at this point—we owe each other nothing. I certainly don't owe her jumping between her and angry werewolves. I have my own issues with angry werewolves to contend with.

"We need them," Marielle says softly, unaware of my rushing thoughts.

Mae scoffs. "We don't need people who abandon their families, Marielle."

It hurts, but it's true, and I don't argue. I don't look at Mae, either. I'm not going to win this with her. I just watch Marielle, and everyone else seems to do the same.

"Are you sure?" Callum asks her. "You don't have to let them stay here. No one would blame you if you wanted them gone."

"I can remove them right now," the demon promises her, cracking his knuckles like he's actually going to fight a divine.

Marielle turns to the queen. "I want to hear what they have to say. But it's your decision."

The queen looks Marielle over for a long moment, frowning, then says, "I'll leave this one to you. If you want them here, then they'll be here. If you want them gone when you hear what they have to say, then just say the word and they're gone. But we should contact the Emricks about that one," she says, nodding to the still-unconscious Lorne.

Estrid shifts. "I told you, *I* can look after her—"

"I don't trust you to look after a rock," Callum interrupts. "We need to find her family."

"She told me she doesn't have one," I say, grateful to finally have something to contribute, even if it's bad news. "She doesn't know who her father is, and it doesn't seem like she wants to see her mom, if she's even alive. She wasn't clear."

"And she told you all this while you were torturing her?" Mae asks.

"I never tortured her. I never tortured anyone." Mostly true. I might have threatened some people, might have even hurt some people, but those were all clients of Andreas' who refused to pay. At least they were undoubtedly terrible people who deserved whatever I did to them. "I did my best to keep her alive."

"He almost died for her tonight," Estrid points out. "Andreas would have killed him. He *tried* to kill him."

I can feel Mae's eyes on me, her hostility temporarily broken by curiosity. "You're not talented enough to fight off a divine. You're talented, and an unscrupulous fucker, so I'm sure you have some surprises up your sleeve, but you're not that talented. He'd decimate you."

"Thanks for the vote of confidence," I say dryly. "But no, you're right. Estrid saved me. Saved us both."

"I'm calling Silas," the queen announces. "Or rather, Marielle can. I want him here for this. And Chase, get Ryder. We might as well all hear what they have to say."

"Right now?" her mate asks quietly. "It's four in the morning."

Is it really that late? I can't decide if I'm tired or not. There's a bone-deep exhaustion in me, but my blood also hasn't stopped racing since I first heard Lorne scream.

"Right now," the queen agrees. "Let's hear if they're worth keeping around before we bother to find them a place to sleep."

***

It takes over an hour for everyone to show up, and in that time, Lorne wakes.

"Oh, thank the gods," I murmur, and Estrid gives me a dirty look for saying it, but it doesn't change how I feel. Fuck, it's like I can properly breathe again. It wasn't all a waste. Lorne is going to be okay.

Marielle crouches down beside her as she wakes. "Hi Lorne," she says. She has the type of voice that always seems gentle, and I hope Lorne can sense that she's not in danger. "You're free now. My name is Marielle. Can I check your wound?"

"Where am I?" Lorne asks groggily, trying to sit up.

"Careful, girl," Estrid says from her seat on the couch. Callum is hovering right behind Estrid, like it's his job to keep her in check and prevent her from getting near the rest of us. He tenses when Estrid speaks. "Or I'll restrain you."

"Don't," Callum says, his voice a raspy threat. "Don't you dare threaten that girl."

130

"She'll hurt herself."

"You won't be restrained ever again," Marielle tells her. "But you should stay lying down. You're in my home, in Crae village. Can I check your wound?"

"How bad is it?" Lorne asks.

"It's better now," Marielle says. "Can I check?"

Lorne nods, so Marielle lifts the bandages she applied earlier. There's a thick layer of paste over it, but apparently that's a good thing, because Marielle doesn't touch it, just studying the skin. "I think you're in good shape. I've never treated a vampire before; do you need more blood?" She looks ready to cut herself open to provide the blood.

"Mari—" Callum begins, but she quiets him with a look.

"I'm alright," Lorne murmurs. "I just—did he take anything?"

"Not that I can tell," Marielle says, voice still incredibly gentle. "I'm not a doctor, though; later today we can take you to find one, maybe? They have tests for that now, right?" She looks at Callum again when she asks it, and he nods, although I doubt he knows any more than she does about modern medical technology.

Lorne looks at her. She doesn't answer the question about the doctor, and instead she says, "You're like me."

"In more ways than you think," Marielle agrees. "How old are you?"

"Seventeen."

"I was sixteen when they took me. Two centuries ago."

Lorne sucks a deep breath. "When did you escape?"

"Not too long ago. About five months."

"Oh, gods," Lorne whispers. "I'm going..."

Marielle seems to know what to do better than any of us, because she helps the kid sit up and rubs her back. "You're okay. It's okay. You're safe now, and you're not going back."

"They just... they just..." She takes deep, gasping breaths. "They kept me in a fucking dog cage."

Marielle keeps rubbing her back. I don't know how she's staying so calm when all I want to do is scream. What they did to this girl—what I allowed to happen—is deplorable.

It's worse watching Marielle keep her shit together when I want to lose mine. She went through it too.

"It gets better," Marielle says soothingly. "You can get your life back, Lorne."

Lorne gives a bitter, broken laugh. "What life?"

Marielle's hand stutters for a minute, and I think Lorne stumped her, but then she says, "I get it. I never could have imagined what I have now—but I do. I have a mate and a family and I'm happy, and you can be too. We called Silas and Theo. Silas is a prince, and he's the crown princess' favorite sibling. And Theo is my brother. They can come and help you get somewhere safe. You can start figuring out how to be happy."

"I want to kill him," she says, startling nearly everyone in the room. I don't get why *that's* what they all react to. Of course she does. If someone locked me in a dog crate and tried to remove my kidney, I'd damn sure want to kill them, too. Fuck, he hit me with rocks and I'm all in on killing him, and I didn't suffer half of what Lorne did.

"Kill a god? Foolish," Estrid says, and Marielle glares at her.

"Es," I mumble, trying to get her to back off. She's not wrong, but we can let the child have her dreams. Revenge is probably a powerful motivator for recovering.

"You couldn't kill him even if you tried," Estrid continues, pretending not to have heard me. Or maybe she just wants me to know that I don't get a say. Either way, the whole room grows more and more tense as she continues. "You rest and get better. I'll be taking care of it."

Callum looks over at me, and with a low, menacing voice, says, "Control your friend."

"You vastly misunderstood the situation if you think I can control her," I tell him. Estrid does what she wants.

Lorne looks around, taking in everyone, and then says, "I'm not leaving. I'm going to stay."

Marielle and Callum share a look, a little confused and frazzled. I don't blame them; a stubborn seventeen-year-old is unpleasant for everyone involved. I remember when Mae was that age.

It's definitely not the time to bring that up, though. Mae stormed out of here earlier, and I doubt reminding anyone that she has a legitimate grievance with me is the right move.

"We'll see," Marielle says at last. "We can talk with Silas, and see."

Lorne frowns, but she doesn't argue. But I can see it in her eyes; she doesn't give a single fuck what the adults say. She's going to do what she wants.

I respect the kid for it.

There's a loud cracking upstairs, then a "Make sure the damned blinds are closed!"

"They are!" Callum calls back, having closed them as soon as the sun even threatened to peek over the horizon, and then there's a whole series of footsteps down the stairs.

The first is the brother with a scar through his eye, then his demon mate. After that are two vampires, one blond and painfully angular, the other darker and stockier.

Estrid tenses up like they stabbed her, her eyes wide. Her mouth falls open just slightly, and I wait for her to say something, but the sound never comes.

No one else is watching her. No one else sees it. But I do. I tilt my head, wondering. Estrid never seems afraid of anything, but this is most definitely fear.

Marielle abandons Lorne to run over to the shorter of the two vampires, hugging him fiercely and being hugged back. "Thank you for coming," she whispers to him.

I side-eye her mate, wondering if everything I've heard about were-wolves and their mates—the fierce jealousy and possessiveness—is true, but he just watches them with a small smile.

"Always come when you call," the vampire says. He picks up his head from Marielle's hair to take in the rest of the room, and his eyes land on Estrid, Lorne, and I. "I'm Theo. This is Silas."

Silas *Emrick*. A vampire prince. Maybe an insignificant one, but all Emricks are dangerous. I shrink back slightly, hoping they don't notice me, but that's already a lost cause.

Estrid still doesn't say anything, so the man turns to Lorne. "You must be Lorne."

"I am." She's still sitting on the floor, but the way she looks up at them tells me our conversation about fighting a god isn't over.

"We're glad you're safe," Silas says. His voice is silky, like he's always trying to convince you to do something. This man could sell water to fish.

Lorne wrinkles her nose. "No thanks to you."

"Lorne—" Marielle begins, hesitant, but Lorne isn't having it.

"*They* saved me," she says, throwing an arm wide to gesture to Estrid and me. I wince, thinking that movement probably pulled at the wound, but she doesn't react at all. She turns to me. "That's what you were doing there. Right?"

It would be *so easy* to let her think that. To, just for once, be the good guy. But I doubt anyone in here would let me get away with it, so I shrug. "I wanted to. But don't pretend I'm perfect; I did bad things for Andreas too."

"But you protected me."

"Badly."

"But you did."

"I—"

"Accept the damn compliment, Clay," Estrid says, the first words she's said since the vampires arrived. I look around, and the demon has the gall to look amused while watching this. I want to flip him off, but thankfully I have enough self control. I like living.

"If that's all," he drawls, "Heath and I are off. We have more guests to pick up."

"Thank you, Chase," Marielle says fervently.

He walks over and kisses her gently on the top of her head. "Anything, and you know it," he murmurs, and then he grabs his mate's hand and disappears.

Theo and Silas sit on the couch, facing Lorne. Marielle navigates back to Lorne's side, and Callum moves slowly closer, clearly torn between wanting to be at his mate's side and worrying about how the girl will react. He's not wrong to worry; he's a huge guy, and he definitely looks scary.

"Let's start with saying, no matter what you choose, you're safe here," Callum says to her. He sounds like a prince now. "The Crae family always takes care of people who need it. Another halfling is more than welcome here."

"But," Silas cuts in smoothly, "you are also more than welcome with us. You're a vampire, Lorne, no matter what. You're part of our kingdom." He looks her over. "Heath said you weren't in contact with your mother. Who was she?"

"Elizabeth Orlette," she mutters, not looking at him.

He chokes. "No shit. Well, we're family then, of a sort. Your mother is now married to one of my brothers."

"Your brother is Brutus?"

He huffs. "Unfortunately. I take it you don't care for him?"

"He didn't want me."

The pieces are falling into place. No wonder the poor girl was on her own, ripe for the picking, when Sarge went looking for her. Her father left before she was born. Her mother abandoned her in favor of her new husband, most likely her mate. And suddenly, there's no more room left for Lorne. The kid who should have been protected was left alone, easy pickings when Sarge came calling.

Damn Andreas for taking advantage of a young girl in that position. I know he's not above it in the least, but it's a particular kind of despicable.

"And your father?" Silas asks, but he looks at Estrid when he says it.

Lorne shrugs, but Estrid says, "One of the sons of the spring, I'd guess."

"How do you know?" Lorne demands, spinning to face Estrid, brow furrowed.

"It's a feeling. A type of magic beyond you all. But it's as accurate as I can be without knowing more."

Silas considers this, then nods. "Details don't really matter there, I suppose. Lorne, I want you to know that, cousin or not, you have a place with us. You don't have to go back to your mother and Brutus if you don't want to, either."

"I haven't been with them in two years. I'm not going back."

"Alright, then. You can stay with us for now, and we can decide what a good place for you is, and—"

"No. I'm not leaving."

Theo raises an eyebrow. "Made an impression already, Marielle?"

She looks as helplessly confused as everyone else, but no one says anything. "Lorne is looking for revenge," I cut in, because it seems like no one else is going to say it. "And I personally think she's entitled to it."

"Good gods, shut the fuck up," Callum mutters. "She's a child."

"I'm the one who was in a dog crate," Lorne says resolutely. "I'm the one who got cut open." She turns to Marielle. "Aren't you here for revenge?"

"I'm immortal now," she points out. "And my magic is stronger. So I'm a little harder to kill."

"I'm strong," Lorne says.

The front door pushes open. "Thought we'd pick everyone up," Chase says, and he opens the door wide enough to let in Heath, two demons, and the rest of his family. Mae doesn't look at me again, but Bryce stares me down like his eyes can light me on fire.

"Let's table this for later," Callum says lowly, and then he gently pulls Marielle to sit with him, tugging her onto his lap to make room for all their guests. Once everyone is seated, he turns to Estrid. "You're only here because you said you had information. Talk."

The atmosphere of the room shifts. This is a war camp now, and we are most definitely at war.

CHAPTER TWENTY-TWO

ESTRID

All eyes are on me, and I can't take my eyes off Silas.

I haven't seen him this close in years. I'd take opportunities to catch a glimpse, finagling party invitations just so I could check on him, but I never approached him like I did his mother. Mina has known me since she was a little girl, but I couldn't risk letting Silas be so close to the secret as well.

But here he is. He watches me calmly, not a single hint of recognition in his eyes. They're the eyes of someone who would be a good ruler, although I understand he turned down that role. His mate sits by his side, and from what I've heard, they're very happy together. They seem it from here.

I watch him a moment too long, and one of the werewolves clears their throat, clearly waiting for me to say something. Right. I have a job here.

"Once I found out about Marielle, I did some digging." I neglect to mention seeing them in that meadow, or the specific details I found out. Marielle doesn't need to relive that. "And I found out—well, everything. So I set to digging into the group, looking for their leader. I found Clay and persuaded him to help me. He gave me a fair amount of information, most crucially that Andreas was the one leading that little cult. I was suspicious of the spells. That type of magic is too big. We'd be forbidden from performing it in this world, because anything that interferes with free will and how creatures of Earth act is forbidden. It unbalances the power toward one god or another, and gods are never supposed to interfere with the living creatures of Earth. Clay investigated, but he and I are confident now that Andreas doesn't have any gods working on his side. And now, since I spoke with him, I know my theory is correct; he's trying to become a god."

I think about the way Andreas spoke, the things he said in our brief confrontation. *The gods are gone. I'm the first person brave enough to fill that void.* I suppress a shiver. What Andreas is talking about is beyond imagination. The gods can't be gone. They formed the universe. They are the night and earth and spring and summer and daylight. They are the water and the plants, the icy winter wind, the feeling of war on a battlefield. They're everywhere.

But I've felt alone for a long time now.

The room is silent for a minute. "And that's possible?" the big demon asks. Ryder, the king of the demons, looks the part in every way. I've been interested in him for a few weeks now, once I realized his mate and queen is a halfling, but I haven't managed to work my way into Demonheim to check him out. I watch him as he watches me.

"Gods are based on worship," I say. "The more worship, the more power. And worship doesn't have to mean prayer. Any acknowledgement of the god will do—even negative, or neutral. Andreas is essentially forming a cult of loyal followers. That counts, and it's damn dangerous."

"Why?" Hannah asks me. "Why is it so dangerous?"

"Gods and their children aren't supposed to mess with the affairs of all of you," I tell them. "It's the one hard and fast rule. Because that might lead to creatures of Earth worshipping them directly, and that would shift the balance of power—Andreas doesn't just want to become a god. He wants to become the king of all gods."

"How do we stop him?" Celia asks, ever practical. The calm, easy way she sits would lead anyone to believe that she deals with threats like this every day, but I can see it in her eyes; this is so much bigger than she ever thought she'd have to tackle in her lifetime.

"*We* do nothing," I say firmly. "You all go back to your lives. This is a problem for my kind."

"Then where have they been?" Lorne asks, speaking up for the first time since everyone arrived. A few people startle, not expecting the child still sitting on the floor to speak. "Where the fuck have your kind been? My whole life, I knew they didn't want me, but if this is *their problem*—why didn't they stop this?"

There's a general murmur of agreement around the room, and I shift uneasily. This is a delicate dance. So much of this is about trying to find exactly how much is appropriate to tell them. I need them to back off.

"Your sisters threw you out," Clay murmurs, and I throw him a dirty look at the betrayal.

"What?" Bryce demands.

"Her sisters. They threw her out. Refused to help," Clay clarifies. "Estrid has been trying, but—"

"But nothing," I interrupt, before we have to listen to whatever excuses Clay has imagined for me. "I'll deal with it. I just need a little time."

"Is Andreas going to go after another halfling?" Marielle asks.

I bite my lip. "It's possible," I admit. "I don't know how the spells work entirely, but I know it takes a lot of magic. And halflings are *made* of a lot of magic. Combine that with someone's power," my eyes flick to Clay, "and boom, you have some horrific spells. So if he wants to stay in business—and he does, because that's how he's gathering his followers—then he'll need another halfling. But that's presuming he doesn't already have one."

Lorne flinches. "I wasn't the only one?"

"We don't know for sure," Clay tells her. She gives him a look that I can't quite read. Deep and complicated, this child has complex feelings about Clay and his role in her recent life. I can't say I blame her.

"Why protect me and not them?" she whispers.

Mae scoffs. "Yeah, Clay. Why protect this one, when you let so many others be hurt?"

He winces. "Mae—"

"Marielle was there for two centuries. She's been there longer than you've been alive. But you didn't feel bad about that when you joined up, huh?"

Marielle tilts her head. "I can't say for sure, but I don't think he and I ever met."

"You couldn't see the people who hurt you, Mari," Callum reminds her. His voice is soft, almost delicate, but Marielle tenses up nonetheless.

"I never met you," Clay says quickly. "I never was even in that house. I won't pretend I didn't know, at least a little—I was a part of some ugly things. My magic was used for the spells. But—"

"Greta would be so ashamed," Mae interrupts, digging the knife in deeper. "She taught you everything and you use your magic for *that*."

Clay opens his mouth, but Ryder is apparently over the family drama, because he cuts right across him. "Back to what we're all here for," he says, his booming voice insistent, "what can we do to help?" He wraps an arm around his mate almost subconsciously.

"If you can somehow find all the halflings out there and protect them, be my guest," I say. "But no one's ever kept a record of them. So the hunt might be difficult."

"Andreas had a list," Clay pipes up. "That's how March assigned people to pick up halflings." He looks apologetically at Lorne when he says it, but she doesn't flinch. Either she's getting a thicker skin, or she's in shock. "I don't know how many are on it, or if it's complete. But it's probably the most complete list there is."

Heath and Chase look at each other before Chase clears his throat. "We could procure that if you had an idea where he'd keep it."

"March's office," Clay says almost immediately. "That's where he had the files, at least. But that's dangerous."

"Kind of you to worry, but this is kind of what we do," Chase says.

"And if you're engaged?" Celia asks.

"We could kill—"

"March, yes," I say, even though I've never met March. But at least I know March isn't divine, so they stand a chance against him. "But if you see Andreas—run. You're not equipped to take him on."

Hannah raises a lazy eyebrow. "These two took down the former king of Demonheim, survived the cages, and a thousand other things besides. They can handle themselves."

What are these people not understanding? "Andreas could bury you beneath the earth for a century or so without blinking," I say bluntly. "He cuts open teenagers without remorse; he buried Clay in a rock slide. And that was *easy* for him. He plans to take over the world and has the magic to pull it off. You are *ants* to him."

"Way to check a guy's ego," Chase mutters, but then nods. "Message received. Hands-off. We can handle what you're asking for. But," he says, turning to Clay, "we need you to come."

"Me?" he asks, voice barely above a squeak.

"I need someone who's seen the place," Chase continues. "I have a vivid imagination, but it's not that good. Your mind will be my channel."

Clay gulps, but looks resolved by the time he nods. "Alright, then. When are we doing this?"

"As soon as we get all the information we can," Celia says. "We're allowing you to stay, but only if your information is worth something. You two have done too much harm to my people. I won't forget that."

"What else do you want?" I ask, because I'm genuinely running out of information to give. Not just information I'm *willing* to give: all information, in general. I've told them most everything I know that's relevant to this situation. "You will protect the halflings. I'll recruit my sisters and the other divine. We'll punish Andreas."

"Not punish," Callum says definitively. "Kill."

"You can't kill something like us," I dismiss. Many have tried, many have failed. "Only a god could do that."

Callum sits up a little straighter, and the energy in the room immediately shifts. The beast who's led the wolves' army for almost a millennium is clearly present now, and everyone can feel it. Even his family looks slightly unsettled, although they're not afraid. Only Marielle, still snuggled into his side, doesn't react.

"Andreas *bought* my mate," he growls. "He bought her, had her father drug her food, and dragged her out of that godsdamn house when she was a *child*. They chained her for *two centuries*. They cut her up, blinded her, starved her, raped her—" Marielle flinches slightly, but she doesn't make a sound. Callum rubs one of his enormous hands up and down her back, so gentle and at odds with the rest of his body. "I found her like that. Chained and blinded in the darkness, terrified and alone and hurt and I will never, not for a single second, forget her face that day. And you want me to accept that we have to just *punish* him? A slap on the wrist?"

I swallow. Callum says it so starkly that it hurts me too. I feel his pain, and Marielle's, and I don't know what to say.

"The point of the gods is that no one is more powerful than another," I say, my voice barely a croak. "So their children aren't more powerful, either.

We can't kill each other. We can fight, and *maybe* a group will get lucky, but it's not likely. And Andreas has made himself *more* powerful."

"I will fight the gods myself for the right to kill him," Callum growls. "So, start figuring it out. You owe Marielle that much."

It's true. It's more than true, but it doesn't mean that I have an answer for him.

Marielle lays her hand on Callum's thigh, and the tension in his eyes fades away in an instant. "I'm okay," she whispers to him. "I'm here now, with you, and we're both going to be okay."

Everything about him softens. I see the conflict in his eyes—Marielle being *here* doesn't negate anything he just said—but he can't help it. She soothes him.

"You're talking about killing a god," I say bluntly. I don't particularly like delivering bad news, but I'm not here to sugarcoat anything. "And that's just not possible. But as for punishment—" I think back on my own punishment, those years I spent as *nothing*, with nothing. It would be a fitting end for Andreas. "I'll see what I can do."

And, done with the conversation, I let the shadows take me back home, ready to see my sisters for the first time since they cast me out.

Chapter Twenty-Three

Clay

Everyone is left gaping as Estrid disappears, and unfortunately, it's me they all turn to, like I have more answers.

I shrug. "If she says she'll do something, she'll do it."

Emrick sighs. "That was rather underwhelming."

"Not enough information for you?" the demon king asks. It's almost a taunt, and I feel the temperature in the room rise.

"Enough," one of the werewolves says. The blonde one, sitting next to the queen. I'm going to need to learn their names before this is over. I hate being in a room of enemies and not knowing their names.

No, not enemies. I don't know what we are, but I don't think we're enemies anymore. *An enemy of my enemy* and all that.

"We still need to find the halflings," the demon queen points out. "Not one more child will go through that."

Lorne tenses, and I ignore everyone else to turn to her. "What do you need?" I ask her quietly. I don't delude myself into thinking that not everyone is listening, but they're not invited to participate in the conversation and I hope they know it. "More blood? A place to sleep? Are you in pain?"

"No, maybe later, yes," she says.

Marielle jumps up. "I can give you something for the pain." She reaches for that mysterious bag again, pulling out little vials and mixing things together.

Theo watches her fondly. "You got even better at that," he murmurs.

Marielle shrugs. "Time. And maturity."

"And not having Rowan over your shoulder?"

She smiles briefly. "That too." She hands Lorne whatever she mixed. "Spread this right on the wound. Or if it's hard to reach, I can do it."

"I got it," Lorne says, a stubborn set to her eyes. I want to tell her she has nothing to prove, that it doesn't matter if she's entirely self-sufficient or not. But I keep my mouth shut, half-watching as she contorts to reach through her ruined shirt to spread the salve over her wounds.

"She needs somewhere to sleep," I say firmly, looking at the werewolf queen. "I don't care if you let me stay or not. But Lorne needs somewhere to sleep."

"This is where we revisit you coming back with us," Silas says. "We have a large home, Lorne. You wouldn't be in the way."

"I'm not going anywhere until this is over," Lorne says stubbornly. "And I'm not changing my mind."

The queen huffs. "Stubborn teenagers." She looks over at Callum. "Remind you of anyone?"

He ignores her. "Lorne, we—"

"No," she interrupts. "I need to be here. If you take me from here, then you'll be tying me up just like they did."

That puts a damper on the room. I'm almost proud of how manipulative she's being, although fuck, she's making it hard to do the right thing.

"Give her a place to sleep, at least," I suggest. "She needs rest."

"You don't get to talk," Mae snaps at me.

Not unexpected, but it is exhausting. "Can we not do this right now?"

"Sure. You can leave, and then we never have to do it."

"Mae—" Chase begins.

She turns and glares at him. "You saw him. You heard him. You know what he did."

"And I know we need him now."

Mae's mate wraps his arms around her. "Absolutely no one is going to make you talk to him," he assures her, glaring at me as he says it. "But we are going to use him."

She looks at me for a long minute, then looks away and ducks her head. "Keep him away from me."

I bite my lip. I have a lot I want to say to her, and I know all of it is unwanted. It'll just make things worse. Maybe there's no such thing as making things better. Once you burn certain bridges, maybe they can't be rebuilt.

"When do you want to leave?" I ask Chase, ignoring Mae like she wants.

"Now, if you're up for it. I understand you got conked on the head tonight."

And I still feel the pain of it, but I'm not going to let them know that. "I'm fine. Let's get this over with. Maybe we'll be lucky and the chaos of what we did will keep them distracted."

I don't mention the obvious; they could all be sitting in March's office, planning their next steps. I'm sure Chase and Heath are smart enough to know it.

"Here's how this works," Chase begins, but I cut him off.

"I know demon magic."

"Right. You have demons in your little cult."

The demon king's face twists. "Traitors. Do you want backup, Chase?"

"If you go, I do too," his mate says firmly.

Ryder turns to her, mouth opening and closing but not saying anything. She gives him a firm look.

"You should stay," he says finally. "They're after halflings."

"If you go into danger, then I go with you," she says again. "That's how it's always worked, Ryder. Nothing changes that."

The room is silent, and I realize belatedly they're looking at me. Because I'm apparently the expert here, I'm the one who has to make the call.

That's a lot of trust to put in me, and I don't take that lightly.

"The more the merrier," I decide. "We don't know exactly what we're walking into. I was unconscious, but it sounds like Estrid broke some things there."

Ryder continues to look at his wife. "You should stay," he says again.

"Are you staying?" she goads. "After what they did to people just like me?"

I can practically hear his teeth grinding together, but he doesn't say anything back. The demon king stands. "Alright then. We do this quickly. And safely," he adds, looking at Hannah. He extends a hand to his mate, helping her up. She keeps a hold on his hand, and then he reaches for the rest of us.

"You need to be touching me," he warns me, although I've already said I understand demon magic. I nod and hesitantly put a finger on his other arm.

"Think of the office," Ryder tells me. "Focus on it and nothing else." I nod, centering my thoughts, and tune out everything else.

Once we're all touching, the world spins around us, and we disappear.

We land in March's office, the world spinning for a second. Maybe I've just gotten used to Estrid's shadows, but this is somehow worse. I take a moment to get my balance, then a moment to look around and breathe a sigh of relief that we're alone.

"Dig through the desk," I whisper. "I don't know exactly where it would be."

Everyone starts digging, going through drawers and files. Ryder goes through a file cabinet with a single-minded ferocity. Heath and Chase crack the wall safe, and Hannah searches for what I presume are secret compartments, pressing along the wall like she can somehow sense something I can't.

I tackle the drawers in the desk itself, not looking at the chair on the other side. How many times had I sat there like a naughty kid in school, waiting for my next terrible assignment? And how many times had I taken the assignment, no questions asked? White hot shame bursts through me, and I have to fight it down so I can concentrate on my task.

Chase and Heath pop open the safe, which reveals a pile of cash but no papers. "I'm taking it anyway," Heath decides. "We can donate to a victim's fund or something. The last thing these assholes deserve is their money."

"Less talking, more searching," Ryder murmurs, setting yet another file on the desk after flipping through it.

"Those are *all* duds?" I ask.

"Financials mostly. A client list that I might have to go murder later. No halfling list."

"Got something," Hannah mutters, and all eyes turn to her. She's prying at a spot on the wall, and, sure enough, there's a seam there. "Just need to..." She grits her teeth, trying to dig a knife she produced from who-knows-where into the seam.

"Here, love," Ryder murmurs, walking over to her and touching her knife. All of a sudden, the secret compartment pops open, and at the same time, an alarm blares.

"Fuck!" Chase curses. "Out?"

"No," Heath says. "We need what we came for."

"Take it all and run?" I suggest desperately.

But Hannah shakes her head. "We won't be getting back in as easily. Make sure it's what we need, Clay. We can hold whoever it is off."

Ryder growls at her. "You'll be fucking careful," but she just ignores him, flipping the grip on her knife, and moves in front of him.

So I'm left to flip through the pile of files while the four of them stand uneasily around the door, waiting for it to open.

They don't have long to wait. Jaxon comes running in, March right on his tail, and Sarge somewhere behind him. I do my best to ignore them, trusting the three demons and the werewolf to keep me safe. It's a novel experience to trust someone like this, but we're not getting through this if I don't.

"Traitor," Ryder says, presumably to Jaxon.

"You're not *my* king," he snarls.

"Did you follow my father?"

"I follow Andreas. He's the one who's going to lead us to greatness. He'll succeed where your father failed."

I can't listen, I remind myself. I just have to trust. So far, I've found a slew of unsavory spells. I've seen some of these before, in bits and pieces. I shove them in my pocket even if they're not explicitly what we came here for. More information is always better than less, and I'll be happier knowing these spells aren't in March's office anymore.

And then, at the bottom of the pile, I find it. A list of names, and near the top, circled... Lorne. Bingo.

"Fuck!" I narrowly dodge Jaxon swinging a sword at me. Hannah intercepts him, stepping between the two of us, blade raised.

Jaxon sneers at her. "What's the bitch-queen going to do, huh? Heard you can't do any magic at all."

Her sword moves so fast that I don't even see it. A cut on Jaxon's cheek starts bleeding, and Hannah moves again, aiming for his neck.

"Never needed magic for the likes of you," she says darkly. Jaxon raises a hand, but Hannah's faster, chopping it off. Then she's at his neck again, and the sword cuts clean through in a stroke she makes seem effortless.

That's a shit ton of blood. I look away, shoving the paper in my pocket before it gets stained from any more splatter. "I found it," I say weakly.

Ryder unceremoniously drops March's corpse and storms over to Hannah, grabbing her with his huge hands and pulling her closer. "Are you hurt?"

Heath rolls his eyes. "Anyone would think you two didn't meet in the middle of a war. Where she protected your ass, I remind you."

"Like you're any better when your mate is in danger," Hannah says tiredly, submitting to Ryder checking her over. I don't think Jaxon's sword came anywhere near her, and I got the feeling that she controls every fight she's in. But she lets him check anyway.

I glance around, confirming all three men are dead. "Lorne will be happy to hear they're gone," I say faintly. "Only Andreas left to haunt her nightmares."

"Let's go," Ryder says, reaching out his arms so everyone can grab hold, and then we're gone.

CHAPTER TWENTY-FOUR

ESTRID

*H*ome feels wrong.

The air smells different. The dark night sky doesn't feel as comforting. And, most of all, the cold is glacial, not inviting.

There is no warmth here, no love. It's a blank wall, and I have to take a moment to brace myself.

"Please!" I call, not wanting to walk further, not wanting to upset them before I even start. "Hear me out."

"Why?" Nisha's voice is a whisper on the wind, a caress from the shadow. I close my eyes, trying to lean into it, but she pulls it away. "Why would we want to hear from you?"

"Does ten thousand years mean nothing?" I ask.

"You burned our home."

I look; I can see the damage, but it's still standing. Their gilded cage is scorched but still perfectly functional, and I admit I'm a little bitter that I didn't manage to do more damage.

"Please," I beg. I've done more begging tonight than I have in a thousand years.

And the last time I begged, I was right here, facing my sisters. I'd begged to save my son, I'd begged for my family, for the life I'd built. They'd done me the courtesy of physically looking at me that day, though. But it hadn't been a relief; their faces had been cold and merciless, and I'd known even before I started begging that I'd lost.

"Please," I say again, hearing the echo of the past in my voice. "They're my family."

"*We're* your family," Neve's voice is a rasp, whip-thin and just as painful. "And you have betrayed us again."

"I have *never* betrayed you," I tell them, forcing myself to stand tall, because *I am not in the wrong here*. "I can still love you *and* want to protect our family on Earth."

"Earth isn't our problem," Amaris murmurs. "We don't interfere. You know this. You know the rules father left us with."

"Andreas is—"

"Andreas isn't our problem either," Rota says, and somehow her voice hurts worse. I know she doesn't care about Marielle, but that's her daughter. "Your problem is you care far too much about Earth and what happens there."

"They're our children!" I protest, trying one last desperate grab to get them to see reason.

"They are *other*."

We're other, I want to reply. We are what's other, this strange, in-between power. Neglected by our parents, too strange for all the creatures on Earth.

"He doesn't even talk to you anymore, does he?" I ask. "You made me think it was just me, it was my fault—but he left you too, didn't he?"

When they nearly destroyed me, I thought it permanently severed something. I've felt so alone, so miserable. But I wasn't alone. I was never alone, but they made me feel like it anyway.

They're silent for a moment, but I won't have it anymore. "You won't even stand up for yourself now that he's gone?" I push. "You'll let the children get hurt because you're *scared* to cross a god who made you and abandoned you?"

When they punished me for my son, for my *home*, it'd been carried out in the name of the gods. They dragged me off the battlefield, brought me here, and condemned me in the name of the gods, just for loving my family. And then they'd all worked together, channeling enough magic to equal a nuclear bomb, and turned me back into the stardust I was born out of for more than a hundred years.

I still remember the feeling, being nothing and everything simultaneously, being pure power and yet not having a way to channel it. It'd been torture, and I'd been so *grateful* when they released me, even if it meant the war was over and my family wasn't protected.

"You're cowards," I tell them, sniffing back tears I refuse to let them see. "If you won't defend the people down there, if you prefer this cage and waiting for a man who is *never coming back* over helping—then you're not worth the magic you have."

It's silent for a minute, not even the slightest breeze making a sound. Then Neve's voice cuts through the darkness. "Then you leave us no choice."

I tense, my whole body thrumming. I won't allow them to take away my choice again. I can't let them take me out of this fight—I won't lose another family.

Their power whispers in the air, hands made of shadow and air reaching for me. I draw the shadows around me like a protective cloak and jump over the edge.

The empty blackness, pin-pricked with distant stars, crashes around me as I fall, my whole body numb.

I failed.

I almost want to quit and just let this happen, let myself fall among the stars. But I need to go back. If I give in, then they win. Andreas wins. And I won't fail.

I stop myself from falling, using the shadows to bring me back to that spot in the mountains that I took Clay. I need privacy, and I certainly won't get that back in that house.

Just like that. They didn't even listen, deciding to write off all of Earth just like that, at the whim of people who don't even speak to them anymore.

I thought the gods talked to them still. I thought it was just me they abandoned. But no, we've all been waiting here like discarded toys, and this is how they've chosen to react.

Anything would be better than nothing. I would take any support, any offer to help. Anything to know that I'm not alone.

Because the truth is, I can't do it alone. I'm just one daughter of night, and there's nothing particularly powerful about me. Andreas, by contrast, has been consciously and sadistically building strength for at least a few hundred years now. I have no idea how to stop him.

The sun has set here, and I bask in the darkness on the mountainside. But even the night—always my biggest comfort—feels different now. The stars shine differently, the wind whispers with a discordant, ripping noise. I debate for a moment retreating to my hotel room, but dismiss it quickly. There's nothing for me there.

What I need is to not be alone, but my sisters won't take me back. For ten thousand years, they have been my comfort. They have been my family and my source of solace. When we were abandoned, at least we had each other. When we were lonely, caught between worlds, we had our little family. But now that's done.

I should go to Mina. But Mina doesn't comfort me; I comfort her, ever since she was a little girl with scraped knees. That's how our relationship works, and I can't allow that to change. Not now, not when she could start asking questions I'm not prepared to answer.

No, I don't want Mina. I want Clay, I realize, and before I even know what I'm doing, I reach through the shadows to find him.

It's getting easier and easier to do that. I find him without trouble, sending the nearby shadows to him in a caress that's meant to be gentle, although I don't know if I succeed. I don't bother to go to him myself, don't bother to check his surroundings. I just bring him to me, allowing the shadows to cradle him as he lands on his knees at my side.

He blinks at me, looking around. "Es?"

I tremble. I can't help it, as much as I want to, as much as I don't want to show Clay my stupid, trembling limbs. No one should see this. This is mine, my shame, my family disgrace.

"What happened?" he asks, voice coaxing as he leans forward. Hesitantly, slowly, like he thinks I might bite him or something, Clay wraps his arms around me. I let him, leaning into his touch.

It registers in some part of my brain that, a few months ago, Clay would not be selflessly trying to comfort someone. I've broken him, but I can't say if it's for better or worse.

Who am I kidding? It has to be for worse. I broke him, but I have no idea how to put him back together correctly. Being good is as unfamiliar to me as it is to him.

At my best I've just *been*. Neither good nor bad, a neutral, self-serving force traveling through life. Exactly as my sisters are now, I realize dimly, and I hate the thought.

"We're on our own," I tell him dully, refusing to elaborate. "They won't help us."

He sucks in a hissing breath. "Fuck," he mutters. "Any chance they'll change their mind?" He rocks me slightly, a subconscious swaying that I can't help but lean into.

"Do you know a god?" I ask rhetorically. "One who answers when you call?"

"Can't say I do."

"Then no."

"How do we take out Andreas, then?"

"I don't want to talk about this," I say, because I don't have an answer and that won't hurt to admit.

"Alright, then. We found the list. Pretty much all of them left to warn halflings. They're offering them sanctuary too, if they want it, in a whole host of places. And we stole a bunch of other information too, like—"

"I don't want to talk about that, either," I interrupt. I should want to talk about it, should want to know exactly what they stole. Should want to know why there's blood splatter on Clay's face, should want to know that everyone is unharmed so far. Should ask after Lorne, or any of a million other things. I don't want to. No, not that. I *can't* right now. I physically can't take any more news.

"Alright," Clay says. "What do you want?"

"Make me forget." It's out of my mouth before I consciously think it, but as soon as I say it, I know I mean it. I need to forget what's happening. Forget that everything has changed forever, that we're screwed, that I somehow have all these halflings—and the entire world, even if they don't know it—relying on me.

Clay freezes. "And what'll make you forget?" he asks carefully.

I know what he's thinking. His blood is boiling, his pulse picking up. And it's not a bad thought, either.

"Just a distraction?" I ask him, checking. I know the reputation my kind has, so I'm sure he already knows, but I can't have any ambiguity between us. This can't be permanent. At this point, I'm not even sure I'm permanent.

He smiles, slow and a little wicked. "Just a distraction," he agrees, pulling back a bit to look me over. We both don't look our best right now, and neither of us has rested since who-knows-when. But when I look at him, I see promise and warmth in a way I can't quite describe.

Just a distraction, I remind myself. That's all we are. All we can be. I cannot get involved with creatures of the Earth.

"How do you want me?" he asks. "I'll warn you; it's been a while, and—"

"Me too," I say, because it's true, and, for some reason, I don't want him to think that I'm like the worst stories about my kind, using and discarding people at every opportunity. "So, we'll just do what feels good?"

"Get naked for me, then," he says, leaning into my space. "Let me see you."

Oh, so he thinks *he's* in charge of this show? I smirk, mind already lighter, already focused on something else, and peel my clothes off, only to hide pertinent pieces of my body behind walls of shadow.

"No fair," Clay complains.

"I never said I played fair. Your turn."

He undresses without further complaint, spending the entire time staring at me like he'll suddenly develop the ability to see through shadows. I wait, spreading my legs a bit, letting the shadows spread with them.

"You are a menace," he accuses.

I ignore him—he's just complaining to complain, and won't have another word to say once I tease him with a little peek—and look him over. It's my turn to stare, and I take him in.

What once might have been lean muscle is more skin and bones now. The magic Andreas wrung out of him took its toll. Still, the lean lines and proud cock catch my attention.

Thoroughly distracted, I drop the shadow, letting Clay look his fill, and I smirk when he goes completely speechless. "You act like you've never seen a naked woman before," I tease.

"Not like you," he says, voice barely a whisper.

I roll my eyes. "*You're not like other girls* doesn't actually impress women, you know."

He finally looks me in the eye, shaking his head. "You don't get it. There's something about you—"

"This is a distraction," I remind him, half-panicking as I blurt out the words. Fuck, this can't be any more than a distraction. We can't be anything real. I'm not supposed to want anything real with guys like him.

Something complicated and dark crosses Clay's face. I want to soothe it away, but what can I say? I can't take it back.

He pulls together a smile. "Right," he says. "So, let's distract ourselves, hm? What do you want?"

I want to ride this man until he can't see straight, until he loses his mind and can only babble out my name. I want to know that, when he closes his eyes, all he'll be able to think about for a little while is me.

"Lay back," I tell him. Then, just to drive my point across, I use the shadows to hold his wrists in a gentle grip, tugging him back into the dirt.

"Kinky," he says, looking at his wrists and grinning. "Be honest: were you thinking about this the first time you restrained me?"

No, because I'd been thinking about killing him then. But I've thought about it a few times since, not that I'll be telling him that.

"You talk too much," I tell him, straddling his hips.

"Come up here and keep my mouth busy then," he returns. When I just raise a brow, he smirks. "I've been told I'm very good at that."

Somehow, I have no doubt. And the idea is tempting, but... "Not this time," I say, before I can catch the slip of the tongue. I can't take it back now though; that'll just draw more attention to it. "This is going to be hard and fast."

He shrugs, raising his restrained arms as far as he can. "You're the boss, then."

"Damn right I am." I stroke over his cock, touching the hard flesh. He feels good in my hand, heavy and hot, and I know he'll feel even better inside me.

I feed him into me, rocking my hips experimentally as I take more and more. My eyes close almost against my will. I want to watch him, want to see him react, but it's all too much.

He fills me so fucking good, and I can't help but rock on him right away, wanting to feel that perfect spot—

"Fuck," he bites out, and I open my eyes to watch him. His eyes are hungry, almost frenzied. "I want to touch those pretty tits."

"Not this time," I say again, almost like a compulsion now. A stupid, stupid compulsion. "This is my show."

"Damned right," he says, watching my tits instead of my face. I can't blame him; I do have nice tits, and I know it.

I leverage myself all the way up, almost pulling off of him, before I fall back down. Clay hisses my name, and I feel a swell of pride. That's it. That's what I was after.

"Let me touch you," he begs as I do it again.

I lean real close, watch him strain his neck like he's reaching for a kiss, then pull back, circling my hips. "No. Not yet."

Not *ever*, because I have a sinking suspicion if I let go of any amount of control, if I let him touch me, this will all feel too real. And I can't have that.

I bring my hands to his chest, digging my nails in as I rock myself on his cock. He bites his lip, staring at me before his eyes dart down to where my nails are no doubt leaving marks.

"Please, Es," he begs. "Fuck, I just need to make you come."

"You are making me come." I squeeze my cunt around his cock, hoping to emphasize the point. Clay's cock is certainly going to make me come, and soon by the feel of it.

"Fuck, I'm so damn close," Clay admits, bucking his hips up into me. He stops asking to touch me, stops asking for anything. "Estrid, Estrid, I—"

Music to my ears, and I finally give into my instincts and lean forward and kiss him. "I know, Clay. Come for me."

With a gasp that sounds like my name, he does, bucking wildly against me, filling me with hot come as his eyes roll back in his head. He looks like a desperate man, one driven completely mad, and I revel in it, letting him fill me deeper and deeper.

"Let me make you come," he rasps, voice wrecked as he comes down. "Estrid, gods, let me *make you come.*"

Even I'm not so heartless that I'd deny him such a desperate request, so I let his wrists go free, and Clay wastes no time, reaching up to palm my left breast with one hand and rub the fingers of his other across my clit. My movements against him stutter, caught in the feel of his thumb on my clit and two fingers teasing my left nipple.

"Harder," I grit out.

"Let me play."

I work up the energy to grind on his already-spent cock, feeling smug satisfaction when he hisses. "Harder," I repeat. "Get me there, Clay."

"Oh, I'll get you there, Estrid, don't you worry—"

I'm about to argue with him, but he finally puts more pressure on my clit, and I see stars and tumble over that edge.

Clay takes me into his arms, holding me gently and kissing my hair. "You're fucking beautiful when you come," he murmurs.

I bask in that for a second, but then the world comes crashing back. We can't be doing this. We can't be here with sweet words, because we're not people who have sweet words. Clay might have rehabilitated himself, and maybe someday he'll find a partner who can keep him in check, but that partner won't be me. I'm not meant to be here. I can't have him.

And we have work to do. It's like a cold bucket of water. "You made me forget," I murmur.

He grins lazily. "That's good, right?"

"Maybe," I allow, because fuck, we did agree on it, and it's not his fault that it's left me empty now. "But we have to get back to the real world, Clay."

The relaxed, languid energy he's had since I came disappears in a second. "You're right," he says shortly. "Time to go."

Chapter Twenty-Five

Clay

The mixed signals are killing me.

It's not her fault. It's not like she lied. No, if anything, Estrid was perfectly up front. She said this was just a distraction. It was my own stupidity that got in my way.

But she kept talking about *next time*. I can tell she didn't mean it, that it's a slip of the tongue, but a guy can't be expected to be rational when Estrid is riding him and promising him, accidentally or not, a future.

When I told her it's been a while, I hadn't been exaggerating. When I told her she's special to me, it hadn't been a line.

Estrid imprisoned me, poisoned me, and threatened me. Estrid had no qualms about hurting me or sending me into danger, and if the mission turned into a suicide one, I doubt she'd have blinked an eye.

But somewhere along the way, that changed. For me and for her; whether or not we're just a distraction, I know she's attached to me now. She saved me. She called me here. She didn't have to; she could have curled up alone to lick her wounds, gone anywhere in the world, been with anyone. But she chose me.

And I chose her too. I didn't realize I had, not until I'd been in Callum and Marielle's house, facing down all those people and realizing it felt like Estrid and I against the world. She's the person who changed me, who gave me a chance. She's my salvation.

And now she's going to want to forget it. I can already see it in her eyes, the shuttering, the putting all this behind barriers. And I doubt I'm strong enough to climb those walls and drag her out again.

Well, maybe she'll need another *distraction*. I'll be happy to provide.

I should feel bad about that. I do, because I know full well her sisters throwing her out again hurt her, and I don't wish losing your entire family on anyone. But I didn't orchestrate that to happen, and I won't be sorry about comforting her if she needs it.

"Finish getting dressed," she tells me, her voice quiet now. "We have to go check in."

"Most of them will be gone. They're off finding the halflings," I remind her, tugging my pants back on. There's dirt everywhere now, but I don't think asking Estrid to take us somewhere we can get a shower before we go back sends the right message.

Although I'd *love* a shower with her. But those are the thoughts I'm not supposed to be having. I'm supposed to keep my mind off that, and switch back to thinking about this damned war. I'm supposed to be done with my distraction now.

Estrid is fully dressed, and if I thought that'd help me re-focus, I was mistaken. She's been fully dressed every other time I've seen her too, and I can't get this woman out of my mind.

Dark hair and pretty pointed ears, still covered in jewels despite us just rolling around in the dirt, a wicked, sharp smile, and eyes that seem to see right through me. What's not to like?

164

She's also as unyielding as stone, has a tongue that could cut me, loves fiercely but quietly, and has a core of goodness that I see no matter how much she tries to hide it.

But I'm not supposed to be thinking about any of that.

I pull my shirt over my head. "Let's go."

Back in the Crae household, Marielle and Callum are the only ones there. "Good timing," Callum says, quickly glancing over at us. "But also, if you ever appear into my house without warning again, I'll cut your head off."

"Callum!" Marielle says, aghast.

He doesn't back down. "I don't play when it comes to the safety of our home," he says to her, but he's still watching the two of us.

"I'd like to see you try, wolf," Estrid jeers, but then softens. "But I appreciate you protecting my niece. So: noted."

They stare each other down for a moment, but at last Callum nods. "Alright then. I'm about to head out, just had to get Lorne settled."

"Where is she?" I ask, because she's not in the living room anymore, where she stubbornly stayed even when we were discussing retrieving the other halflings.

He turns his glare to me. "She didn't like you disappearing on her."

"That is my fault," Estrid says, and I blink. I doubt Estrid has ever admitted fault in her life, and while yes, this was undoubtedly her fault—I can't exactly teleport myself halfway around the globe using nothing but shadows—I'm surprised she's bothering to defend me to Callum.

"Fine, then. You can tell her that."

"Where is she?" I repeat.

"She's asleep, finally," Marielle says. "Upstairs. I want to check on her one more time before we go."

"Go?" Estrid asks her.

Marielle squares her shoulders. "Go. We have our own portion of the list."

I worry for a moment Estrid is going to say something, try to stop her. I get that Marielle is her niece, and I know this woman has been horrifically hurt too recently. But we don't need to piss off our hosts any more than we already have.

But all Estrid says is, "Do you want a ride?"

"That weird shadow thing you do?" Callum asks, then turns to his mate. "Can you do that?"

"Not that I know of. We'll take it. Give me five minutes," she says, heading toward the stairs.

Callum purses his lips and looks at us. "Can I trust you in our house while we're gone?"

"Think we're going to steal your silverware?" I ask.

He raises an eyebrow. "From what Mae said about you? Distinct possibility."

"I won't touch your damn silverware. Or anything else. I won't snoop. I need sleep; I plan to crash on your couch," I tell him.

He looks for a half a second like he's about to say that I can't have that either, but he closes his mouth. "Alright, get a nap. People will be in and out." He turns to Estrid. "Do you need to come with us?"

"I do if you want a ride back."

"You haven't slept either," I interrupt, because how much more can Estrid be expected to do? I'm sure she somehow needs less sleep than me. Maybe she doesn't sleep. I've never seen her sleep. Does she not sleep, like she doesn't eat? "Do you need to rest?"

Estrid opens her mouth, no doubt to tell me off, but Callum doesn't let her. "I'll just call for Chase," he says. "Sleep. When everyone gets back, I'm sure they're going to have plenty of questions for you."

Marielle comes back downstairs, dressed in comfortable clothes, her hair tied back, and two knives visible on her belt. "Ready?"

Callum takes her hand and presses a kiss to the back of it before turning to Estrid. "So, how's it work?" he asks, but I can already see the shadows rising around him.

"You tell me where, and I send you," she tells him. "Simple as that."

He gives her an address, and before he even finishes the words, they disappear.

"You could have warned them that it makes you nauseous as hell," I say.

She raises an eyebrow. "It doesn't make *me* nauseous as hell. The rest of you, that's your own concern."

I smile, unable to help it.

"I'll take this end of the couch," I say before I say anything stupid. Thank the gods that Callum and Marielle have a giant sectional. "You should sleep too."

"For a little while," she agrees, but I can see it. She's absolutely exhausted. We both settle down to sleep on opposite pieces of the sectional. If I thought it'd be hard to sleep here—I'm not much for sleeping on couches, especially in places where people might want me dead—then I'm immediately proven wrong. I'm so exhausted that I couldn't keep my eyes open if my life depended on it.

***

Rocks. Everywhere, and now darkness. Stifling, suffocating darkness, the kind you just know you can't get out of, crushing in from all sides, and—

I wake up with a firm shake, a hand I somehow already know is Estrid's on my shoulder. "Wake up, Clay. Wake up for me."

I peel open my eyes. It almost hurts to do so, but I force myself, following her voice. And there she is, sitting next to me, hand still on my shoulder. "You're alright," she murmurs.

Am I? I have the compulsive need to check my body for damage, despite knowing full well the damage from what Andreas did healed already.

"It's fine," I mutter. "I'm fine."

My heart hasn't slowed down, and my pulse is pounding. My mind can't stop turning over what it felt like to be trapped there, buried alive in those rocks. But I'm fine. I am literally, physically fine, and we're here because Andreas tried to cut Lorne's kidney out. I'm well aware I don't have any room to complain.

There are footsteps on the stairs, and I curse. Either someone is home, or I woke Lorne. Neither is a good option.

Lorne comes down the stairs, wearing sweats a thousand times too big for her. Callum's, I suppose. She's about six inches taller than Marielle, so I guess Callum's clothes were the best option she had until someone more her size returns.

"What happened?" she demands.

"Nothing. Go back to sleep," Estrid tells her, not sparing her so much as a glance.

But I'm looking, and I see her nostrils flaring. "I'm sick and tired of being told to butt out," she nearly growls. "I understand, alright? I got the lecture from Callum. I can't fight, and even if I could I'm not strong enough to kill him. Message received. But I'm not an invalid who needs to be excluded from everything."

Estrid looks over at her. "Clay is entitled to his privacy. Or is your need to feel included more important than that?"

Lorne freezes. "That was harsh, Es. She can sit down here if she wants," I say tiredly. I'm not going to stop the kid from doing anything she wants. If anyone is entitled to have nightmares, it's her.

Lorne moves hesitantly, like she's sure she's going to be scolded again at any moment. "How're you feeling, kid?" I ask.

"Like someone tried to remove my kidney," she says bluntly. "Marielle's done her best to dull the pain."

"Do you need any blood?"

"I had some earlier."

"You lost a lot," I remind her.

"And Estrid gave me some, right?"

"I did," she acknowledges. "But you'll tell someone if you need more."

Lorne has the gall to roll her eyes. "Everyone here is a worry-wart. I've gotten that lecture a hundred times today."

"Good. See that it sticks."

Lorne settles deeper into the couch, unknowingly taking up the spot where Estrid was sleeping before my little nightmare. "Why did you save me?" she asks Estrid quietly.

Estrid jerks her chin to me. "He did most of the work."

"But you told him to, right?"

I turn to watch Estrid fully, seeing an interesting battle play out across her face. She doesn't want to lie to Lorne, but she also doesn't want to let her know that she's secretly such a softie. I don't step in to help her.

"I didn't know what Marielle went through until it was already over," she says. "And I wouldn't see it happen again."

"But I'm not your niece. You and I aren't related, right?"

"Not if your father is who I think he is, no."

"So, you'd have done it for anyone?" Lorne checks.

Estrid raises a brow. "Does that make it worth less, do you think?" She holds her breath, and I get the feeling that she's really waiting for Lorne's judgement.

"No." Seemingly satisfied with Estrid, Lorne turns to me. "What did you dream about?"

Is it too late to back Estrid and tell the kid to go back to bed?

But no, because that's selfish, and the kid is entitled to know. "I dreamed of that night," I tell her. Was it last night? Two nights ago? I honestly can't keep track anymore. All I know is I'm both exhausted like it was a million years ago, and scarred like it was moments ago. "And the rocks."

Estrid squeezes my shoulder again. She doesn't say anything. Maybe she has nothing to say, or maybe she doesn't want to say it in front of Lorne. But just the squeeze is enough.

We're not a damned *distraction*. Maybe she doesn't feel like we can be more, but she feels something. Estrid isn't the type to comfort people she doesn't care about.

"I'm sorry," Lorne says, like she has any business being sorry for me, like I in any way deserve her apology.

"Don't be sorry. It's certainly not your fault I made bad choices," I tell her.

She glares at me. "You came down there to rescue me. And I was a dick to you."

"You," I say, speaking slowly and clearly, hoping she gets it, "were a scared kid in a terrible situation who had every right to be scared. And every right to be a dick. And to be much more of a dick than you actually were." I try to force a smile. "If you want lessons about how to actually be a dick, then you've come to the right place."

She looks me over. "You don't have to be a dick to yourself, you know."

I just blink at her, and before I can formulate a reply, there's a crack upstairs, and then Heath, Chase, Callum, and Marielle walk down the stairs.

Estrid releases my shoulder like it's on fire. "Did you find them?"

"Yup," Chase says. "But they're six hundred years old and powerful enough they almost killed all of us before we could explain. Understandably, they're not super convinced they need protection."

Heath nods. "Most of the halflings we found were older. One or two younger ones—including the one you told us about in New York, Clay. She's with Silas and Theo now, getting settled."

Estrid nods. "It's amazing what the invention of reliable birth control can do."

I raise an eyebrow, somehow unable to picture Estrid popping the pill every day, but I realize I fucked her raw last night and didn't even ask. Now seems like a bad time to bring it up, though, and if Estrid didn't want something to happen last night, then she wouldn't have done it. That was her show.

We *will* be having the conversation before next time, though. Because there will be a next time if I have anything to say about it.

"What news did you get from the divine?" Heath asks Estrid, and even with her not touching me anymore, I can feel how she instantly tenses up.

"Nothing good," she says shortly, and I can see how hard she's fighting to keep her tone even. She might have been willing to break down in front of me at her sisters' betrayal, but she'd rather die than show these people a sign of weakness.

"What happened?" Marielle asks, a soft compassion that I didn't expect evident in her voice.

Estrid shrugs. "They don't dare mess with this world. They're too scared of the gods, or too comfortable in their power, or both. They won't help."

"So, what do we do?" Callum asks after a moment.

"I figure it out," she mutters mulishly. "And you all keep doing what you're doing."

There's silence in the room for a moment, and then Marielle says, "Come on, Lorne. Let me check that wound. I didn't expect you to be up and about yet."

Lorne doesn't even try to argue, which is progress. She and Marielle head upstairs. Heath and Chase head for the door while Callum just looks at us.

"I want you out of my house in the morning," he says. "You're upsetting my family."

"No arguments from me," I say, even though I have plenty of arguments. Namely, I have nowhere else to go. But the sooner I can stop being stared at here, the better.

"But before you go, everyone is meeting in the morning. And I highly encourage you to have a better answer than *I'll figure it out* by then."

And with that, he goes upstairs.

Chapter Twenty-Six

Estrid

M orning comes too soon, and I haven't slept a wink.

Clay has two more nightmares, and I want to be awake to lend him what little comfort I can. This goes far beyond just being a *distraction* to each other, but I won't deny him this. What, am I supposed to sit on the other side of the couch and just *watch* him suffer? Not even the gods are that cruel.

I wince. It's a poor comparison, because current circumstances tell me they absolutely are. They'll watch people suffer and do nothing.

Well, I won't. I can't.

I'm wide awake, turning over the problem Callum threw at my feet, when Marielle wanders downstairs. She stops when she sees me, then nods her head towards the kitchen.

I bite my lip, checking on Clay, but he seems to be sleeping well for the moment, so I get up and follow Marielle.

The floor plan is more open-concept, with just a half-wall and kitchen island dividing the living room from the kitchen, so the gesture is more symbolic than practical. Marielle begins making coffee without saying anything, and I lean against the counter as she goes through careful, precise moves.

"Do you drink?" I ask her, curious. I've known very few halflings to compare, but I know they're all different. My own had drank blood like his father, but he could go longer than any vampire I knew between feedings. What each halfling inherits from us is an interesting mix.

"Sometimes. I don't need to, if that's what you're asking."

"But you like it," I surmise.

"Coffee? Not especially. But Callum does, and when I'm up first, I'll make it for us."

Marielle has only been free a few months, such a brief span in her lifetime, nevermind mine. But I can see it, the comfortable domesticity she's settled into, and I hope for her sake that it lasts forever. I hope there're thousands of years of this, of coffee and the family she clearly found for herself. I hope that werewolf loves her enough to make up for all she's suffered.

She finishes setting up the machine and, without turning away from it, says, "When we first met, you said you could tell me about my mother."

"She's my sister," I tell her. "Her name is Rota."

"Rota." She says it like she's tasting it, then shrugs. "Did she ever want me?"

No. Rota never wanted her. Rota wanted to not be lonely for one night, and Marielle was the undesired consequence before reliable birth control existed. I doubt she's spared a thought for her since she gave the infant to her father. But I can't tell Marielle that.

"We're trained to reject anyone not like us," I say carefully. "If the baby isn't like us, then we're supposed to let them live their lives here, on Earth, and not get in the way."

"Why?" she asks. "What would be so bad about knowing me?"

My heart aches for her, but I remember the brave girl who stared me down and told me she didn't need me or my family a few months ago. "You didn't need your mother," I try to say soothingly.

Marielle finally turns around, and there's fury in her eyes. "I spent the first sixteen years of my life tip-toeing around a man who didn't want me, who casually threatened to sell me to the highest bidder. I watched him abuse Theo and waited in fear for the day he'd kill him and sell me. And then he did. Only it wasn't a marriage, but instead it was..." She can't finish her sentence, and she starts to tear up. It takes her a second to master herself, but then her fury is back. "Two hundred years, Estrid. I could have used my mother. I could have used *anybody*. And I've talked to my *new* family, and I know no parents are perfect by any stretch of the imagination, but at least they all fucking tried."

She's right. She's right and I can't even dispute it, and there's not an excuse in the world that would make what happened to her or all the others okay. Lorne, Hannah, so many others. We spent so much time saying that they're better with their own kind that we never asked ourselves if that was even true.

Callum calls down the stairs, voice frantic. "Marielle?"

"I'm fine," she calls back.

"That fern thing you put in our bedroom just grew three feet."

"Whoops." She closes her eyes again, taking deep breaths, and I can feel the magic coming from her. It feels different from my own, but still familiar in its own way. "Better?"

"I'm coming down."

"No," Marielle says. "I'll be up in five minutes."

He hesitates a moment, but then says, "Whatever you want, Mari." Marielle turns to the fridge, pulling out the creamer.

"You're right," I tell her. "About all of it. We owed you better."

She sighs. "It's done with now."

"We still owed you better."

"I'm furious with my mother. But you—you didn't owe me anything. But you went after Andreas anyway. And that means a lot." She turns to look at me. "Am I going to get to meet my mother?"

"Probably not."

"Because they all turned you down. They won't help."

"Yes."

Marielle squeezes her eyes shut again, then nods. "Did you tell her about me? That I'm in the middle of this?"

"She knows," I tell her. "The gods' rules about mixing, they're strict. Your mother is just following the rules." That's the most charitable way to think about my sisters' decision, at any rate.

Marielle swallows. "And the rules matter more than me." She unexpectedly reaches over and squeezes my hand. "Thank you for being here, anyway. I know you had to choose us over them. And I appreciate it."

I don't deserve her thanks or her appreciation. We owe her so much better. But before I can formulate a response, she squeezes my hand again and then lets go, grabbing the finished coffee and walking back toward the stairs. "The others will be here in an hour," she says. "We need a plan then."

"Others?" I ask, like an idiot. Like I don't know who's coming. My only excuse is my brain is scrambled, still trying to parse through the conversation that we just had, Marielle's condemnation, so rightly deserved, and her forgiveness, much less rightly so.

"All the Craes. The demons and the vampires too. We're all in this together. We don't plan without each other."

Great. Silas will be here again, and I'll have to face him and the memories he brings once more, and I doubt I'll be able to disappear so easily today.

It's strange, looking at someone you feel like you know who has no idea who you are. It's much safer for him that he doesn't, of course, but it still feels like a slap in the face.

Marielle doesn't look back at me to see my struggle though, and nor should she. Instead, she takes the coffee upstairs to her mate, smiling slightly as she climbs further up the stairs. I wish her all the happiness. I need to know that, no matter how badly we failed her, she still has a life worth living.

Clay is sitting upright and watching me when I re-enter the living room. "How much of that did you hear?" I ask him.

"How much of that did you want me to hear?"

"None of it," I snap.

"Then I heard none of it. You're freaked out. Why are you freaked out?"

Of course Clay would notice. Fucking Clay. When did we cross this line, where he can see that in my eyes?

I'm trying to make some excuse when he asks, "Does this have something to do with the vampires?"

"What makes you think—"

He shrugs. "You get all shifty-eyed. You were watching the blond one like he might bite you. What's the deal?"

Of course. Of course Clay noticed, of course he—I need to distance myself from him. How is it he can see this, can know? How am I letting him just walk right past every wall I ever made?

"So, is it? What's the issue with them? Because if they hurt you, tell me now so we can—well, I don't know what I'll do. Get another poisoned knife? Do I need another poisoned knife?"

"Not here," I hiss, looking at the door. Callum told us to be gone by morning, so I'll take his advice and get out. I'm not having this conversation in this house.

I drag him by the arm, barely stopping to pull on shoes, and tug him outside, continuing to walk until we're in the forest.

He wrinkles his nose. "Ugh. Nature."

"It's beautiful," I retort automatically, my heart not even truly in it.

"C'mon. You like the finer things in life just as much as I do. Don't pretend."

"You can like both. You weren't complaining about nature last night."

"No, last night I had—I thought we weren't talking about that. And don't think you can distract me. I asked you about the vampires and you freaked out. Explain."

"There's nothing to explain," I say, walking deeper into the forest like I really am interested in all the nature.

"Bullshit. Don't lie to me, Estrid."

I lie to everyone, I almost say. And I do; I lie as easily as breathing. But while I've kept things from Clay, I've never lied to him.

And fuck it, I don't want to start now.

"The things you didn't hear this morning..." I begin.

"Mhm. What might I have not heard that I should remember now?"

"What I said about us, and being taught to let go of any children that aren't like us—it's not just an excuse. It's very real. And we can be punished for messing with creatures of Earth. Even if they're our children."

"Because of the worship thing," Clay says, nodding as he pieces it together.

"Yeah. Except once, I didn't want to let my child go. So I didn't."

"You have children?" he blurts out, then shakes his head. "I don't know why I'm surprised, you've been alive a long time, and—"

"One," I interrupt him, because if I'm going to tell this for the first time ever, I can't stop. If I don't say it, it'll stay inside forever. "His name was Lionel. My little Lion. His father was a vampire. I forgot him as soon as it was over, but he was irrelevant. I wouldn't abandon my son. And because I couldn't do anything by halves, I did something foolish. I put Lionel on a throne, made him an empire. I laid the world at his feet because I wanted the best for him. And Lionel had a daughter, and that daughter had a daughter, and that daughter has a son now. Just one son."

"Silas," he says. "The vampire prince."

I nod. "I stayed. I watched over them, lived in their household. My son called me mother, even when he'd grown old, when a thousand years passed. And it was fine. It was a quiet life, and I had my family, and it was happy. No one bothered me and I didn't bother them. Back then, the vampires weren't one kingdom under one king. There were many little kingdoms, and mine was just one of them. But then the current king rose to power. And he is a powerful vampire. Maybe fate did decree him to be king, I don't know; fate is above even the divine. He started attacking other kingdoms, taking over their land and their people."

"And you fought back?" Clay guesses.

If only. "I tried. A vampire army doesn't stand a chance against a properly motivated divine being. There is a reason we're not supposed to interfere, and it's not just the worship. We're just so different—we can sway a war without trying."

"And you did."

"And people noticed. Creatures like me noticed. I was called away, chastised, punished, and by the time I was released, the war was over. My little Mina—my great-granddaughter—had grown and been traded off in a marriage to the very king who attacked her people so the war could be over."

"What happened to you, Es?" he asks quietly.

"I told you; I am made of stardust. And my sisters, they were afraid someone would see what I did and blame all of us. That they'd say I was—well, trying to do what Andreas did. I didn't want to be a god. I just wanted my family. But they couldn't risk it, so with their combined magic, they turned me back into stardust, and kept me that way until the war was over."

I don't think back on those days if I can help it. I've never known if my sisters always intended to return me to my current form, or if they just got bored with punishing me. When I was free again, Lionel was dead, my granddaughter stripped of her rightful title and land—and dead not long after—and my great-granddaughter, who I'd barely gotten to know, was sent away from her home to be some man's wife.

Mina's made a life for herself. Her husband trusts her beyond almost all others, and she seems to like him, in her own way. She's a stalwart politician, a strategic force, and she raised a clever and noble prince and has helped train the crown princess to boot. Mina would likely tell me she doesn't regret her life. But I can't help seeing what was lost.

I blink when I feel pressure around me. Clay is holding me, rocking me gently. "I'm sorry," he murmurs into my hair. "I'm sorry, Estrid."

I fight his hold a bit, but not enough to truly get free. "It's in the past," I say shortly. "It doesn't change anything. It—"

"You should tell them."

"Haven't you been listening? The whole point is there are rules."

"Rules set by gods and divine who won't help us? Who won't even listen to us?" he asks, and I stop moving. Stop breathing for a second, listening to what he has the nerve to imply.

I haven't dared to think about it. I've dared to bend the rules, just a little, here and there. I've enjoyed life on Earth, watching over my descendants. But Clay—my Clay, my greedy, selfless, fascinating witch—says what I haven't even allowed myself to think.

Maybe it's the punishment still doing its job. Maybe I've just had tunnel vision. But he's not wrong.

The gods have abandoned us. Everyone has abandoned us, too content in their lives. Maybe they don't see the creatures here as family, but I do. This is my family—Mina and Silas and the people they chose, Marielle and her chosen family, every halfling who they protected last night—they're all mine.

Clay squeezes me again. "I get we don't measure up to you," he says seriously. "But don't shut us all out. That's not how things get done." His lip twitches sardonically. "Believe me. I've learned that the hard way."

I open my mouth to argue, to say something—he's too hard on himself—but then my mind starts turning. He's not wrong.

Not just about telling Silas and Mina, although he's right that it seems a little ridiculous not to. But no, Clay's right about it all.

"You're smarter than you seem," I tell him.

"Gee, thanks."

"I just mean—"

"I know what you mean," he interrupts, squeezing me slightly. "Are you going to be okay?"

Right, because we're out here in the middle of the forest just after dawn, and I'm about to propose a plan that's liable to get me killed. Because I told him we're just a distraction, but I held him most of the night and am letting him hold me now.

But all my reasons for that don't hold true anymore, do they? If I'm going to tell Silas and Mina, if I'm going to have this conversation with everyone, if I'm going to say *fuck it* to all the rules I was ever taught, then testing the waters of whatever this is with Clay seems small by comparison.

I kiss his cheek, gentle and barely a brush. He's so surprised that he lets me go, and I take the opportunity to tug him into a proper kiss, tasting him, knowing him. Remembering him.

He takes a moment to kiss me back, but when he does, he does it with enthusiasm, grabbing me and tracing his hands up my back, finding my hair and grabbing it to tilt my head.

"What was that for?" he asks, voice a breath against my lips.

I grin, nip at his lip once, and break out of his hold, walking back toward the house. "We'll find out."

CHAPTER TWENTY-SEVEN

ESTRID

C lay looks at me with wide eyes, but I ignore him. We're all sitting in Callum and Marielle's living room. Chairs have been dragged in from the kitchen so everyone can sit, but we're still all squished rather close.

I keep looking at Silas and Mina, who should not be here. I haven't known Mina to leave her home in decades, but here she is, sitting in the middle of a werewolf village planning war like she does this every day.

I want to demand to know what she's doing here, but she hasn't let on that she knows me, and that's probably the right move. Generations of family secrets shouldn't be exposed just because I'm nervous about them. There's a way to do that privately.

"Are all the halflings safe?" I ask.

"As safe as they can be," Celia says.

"We need a plan. What do we do about Andreas?" Ryder demands.

I've been thinking about it all night, and there are very few options. Really, if I'm going at this alone, there are *no* options. But what Clay said struck a nerve. There's an entire group of people I haven't considered yet. A group of people I've been taught to ignore, but might have enough magic to give me a fighting chance.

Of course, this is a big ask. A monumental one, even.

"Andreas is essentially a god," I remind them, still stalling. "And we don't have any gods on our side. They won't answer my calls. None of my sisters will come."

"Yes, yes, we're fucked," Hannah agrees. "So, what's next?"

I like her. She's practical like that, and I can see how she survived as a mercenary for so long.

I hesitate one more second, but it's not going to start sounding better if I wait. I need to just *say* it. "I think halflings could help make the difference."

The room is completely silent. "Like, a spell?" Silas asks lowly, and I nearly flinch that he'd think that of me, that I'd start ripping apart my kin just for spell ingredients.

Marielle clears her throat. She's gone pale, but her eyes look resolute. "What do you need from me?"

"Marielle, no," Callum growls, holding her hand even tighter in his.

Lorne rocks forward, looking like she's on death's door again.

"If it ends this—"

"I'll do it instead—" Hannah interrupts.

"You will *not*," Ryder hisses, his voice deadly serious.

She turns on him. "So you'd rather Marielle have to do it? Again?"

I save him from needing to find a response to that, to him balancing his desire to protect his mate with basic decency. "Neither of you need to do anything of the sort," I interrupt. "That's not the type of help I'm talking about."

"Then what do you mean?" Celia asks, trying to get us all back on track.

"We've spent so long pretending you weren't like us. And you aren't, but I think you all know that you aren't entirely like your other parents either."

"Yeah," Hannah mutters. "Other. I know." Ryder squeezes her hand, and she squeezes back.

"You have more magic than you know. More magic than we ever let you know."

"I don't have any magic," Hannah says, shaking her head. "Magic that baby demons pull off is beyond me."

"You don't need magic—" Ryder begins.

"I'm aware," Hannah says dryly, clearly having heard it before. "But she doesn't seem to be."

"You have magic," I tell her. "I can feel it."

"Then explain why I'm like *this*," she says, gesturing to herself with her free hand. "I don't. I just don't feel it. When other demons talk about pulling energy from the source, shaping it, I just can't. I don't feel it."

That is a little trickier. From what I can tell, Marielle got her magic from both parents, mixing divine magic with druidic spells. Hannah's two sides seem to have been incompatible. "You're trying magic like a demon, trying to channel spells through living creatures. For obvious reasons, that won't work for a divine."

"Then how do I do it?" she asks, leaning forward in her seat. She drops Ryder's hand and clasps her own hands together, and Ryder moves to rub her back.

"Your father is one of the sons of the earth. My guess? You channel through that."

"Like I do?" Marielle asks.

Oh, if only she knew. "Think less *plants* and more *stone*," I suggest.

"How do you know who my father is?"

"I told you; it's magic. I can feel it even if you can't. But it's true. Besides, haven't you noticed that you're physically stronger than most other demons?"

She shrugs. "Just thought that was a by-product of being a halfling."

"It is, to some extent. But not like you have. That's being of the earth. Trust me."

"I want to try," she says, bouncing up to her feet. "Do I need to touch the earth or something?"

"It can't hurt."

Before anyone can say anything else, she's moving to the door, Ryder hot on her heels, and the rest of us follow along.

"How exciting," Silas says drolly.

Theo shoves his arm. "Shut up."

"What? I'm being honest."

"You're a nuisance, that's what you are."

Hannah has kicked off her boots and is standing barefoot in the grass, toes in the dirt. "Like this?"

I nod, and Ryder steps up behind her. "If it still works anything like demon magic," he murmurs to her, so low I can barely catch it, "feel the energy. And then direct it at what you want."

She closes her eyes, and Ryder wraps one arm around her, hand on her stomach. "You got this," he tells her, kissing the back of her head as she breathes in deep.

She exhales and the two of them disappear, re-appearing on the other side of the big tree growing in the yard.

"Whoo!" Mae cheers, clapping for them. "Go, girl. Love the magic."

Hannah looks like she's going to pass out, leaning forward and breathing deep. Ryder immediately goes to his knees, supporting her and trying to look up into her face. The rest of us rush over.

"Hannah?" Marielle demands, voice tight as she pushes closer.

"That was *awful*," Hannah mutters, eyes closed and still breathing deep. "That felt *so bad*." She opens her eyes to look at me, a little lost. "Did I do something wrong?"

"Not that I can see," I tell her, a little bewildered. I hadn't expected that. Her magic is perfectly natural and normal, as far as I can tell.

"It's alright, love," Ryder tells her, hands cupping her face. "You don't like how it feels, then you don't have to do it. I told you; it's never been a problem that you don't have magic. And it never will be."

"But Estrid said she needs my magic!" Hannah nearly whines, and everyone freezes and looks at her. I get the feeling that this isn't how she usually sounds.

"Hannah," Ryder says slowly, "You wouldn't be able to do what she's asking anyway. You're not supposed to go into battle. I let you insist these last few days, but this is too much."

"I can handle myself," she snaps. "And you don't go into battle without me."

"I know, love," he says, voice soothing again. "I'm well aware which one of us actually keeps the both of us alive. But from the sounds of it, Estrid doesn't need me, so you don't need to worry about me."

"No," I say slowly, hating to interrupt a moment, but needing to redirect the conversation back to our purpose. "I don't need you. But Hannah's right; I do need her. I'm sorry you don't like magic, but I need you to do it just once."

"No," Ryder says firmly.

Heath shifts. "Ryder—"

"*No,*" he says again, then takes a deep breath. "Hannah's pregnant."

It's absolutely silent for a minute, and then the yard erupts with congratulations.

"We weren't going to tell anyone yet," Hannah says, glaring at him.

He shrugs. "Circumstances changed. And you're four months along; the biggest risk is over, right?" He turns to all of us. "I know my mate is the fiercest warrior out there. But she's not going to fight a *god*." He stands and holds her, like she's somehow going to disappear from his arms if he lets go.

His hands cradle her belly, still not really showing, but he holds her like he's personally holding the baby right this second.

Hannah puts her hand over his. "If the world is in danger..." she begins hesitantly.

"We have been trying for this baby for three centuries, Hannah," he says desperately. "We've gotten our hopes up and been let down again and again. And now that it's real—don't ask me to give them up. Or worse, risk both of you."

"Hannah," I tell her firmly, because I see the war in her eyes. I know she wants her baby, wants her mate and her home. I know she wants to fight, too. "I can keep you from the front lines. Keep you safer."

Ryder's mouth tightens like that's not an acceptable compromise to him, but Hannah's eyes shine with relief. She's a warrior through and through.

"Well, that explains the magic," Mae offers. "Some witches go on and off magic during pregnancy. Kind of like a food craving, I think. Don't know if demons are the same, but it'd make sense. You might find it more tolerable later. Or not; obviously, it's fine if you just don't ever like doing magic."

Clay turns to look at his cousin like she said something vital, and something prickles at the back of my neck. He's studying her like she knows a secret, and I'll have to ask him about that later.

Ryder kisses her temple. "It doesn't matter either way."

Hannah's mouth goes thin, but she's rubbing her belly longingly. "I'm not used to sitting out wars. I fight them; that's kind of my thing. Magic or no magic."

"I'll help," Lorne volunteers. Callum clears his throat, and she turns to glare at him. "What? You said I'd know when the time is right."

"And this isn't it yet, kid. Trust me; you'll know. Wait until you're sure you're an asset, not a deficit."

I expect her to lash back at him, but whatever conversations happened between them when I was out seem to have done a lot. She nods and steps back.

"The world will need you someday," I tell the girl.

"Oh, how the tables have turned," Celia mutters to her mate, who elbows her in the side.

"So that leaves me," Marielle surmises.

Mina steps forward. "And me."

Silas turns like he's not actually sure she's the one who spoke. "Mother?"

But Mina doesn't look at him. She just looks at me and I look at her. "How long have you known?" I ask her. So much for not having this discussion in public.

"A long, long time. I've suspected. Grandfather told stories, you know. And I didn't remember you outside of the stories, but when you came back—I knew they were true."

She's known this whole time and kept her mouth shut. Was she protecting my secret, or protecting herself?

"Mother?" Silas asks again, voice getting more urgent.

When Mina doesn't answer him, still staring me down, I turn to him. "You are my great-great grandson," I tell him. "And your mother is my great-granddaughter. But you're far more vampire than divine. There's a spark there, perhaps, but that's it. I'm only able to tell because I *know*. Because I was there."

Silas just gapes at me. Mina's mouth twists. "It was worth a try," she says.

"I never wanted to abandon you," I say abruptly, like anyone asked. But if I don't say it now, then I'll explode. I need her to know. "But I'd already tipped the balance of the war, and I couldn't—they wouldn't let me—" I clear my throat. "What they did to me—I can't describe it. But suffice to say, they ensured I couldn't meddle in your family ever again."

I'd been angry when I first re-formed after the punishment, and then guilty. I'd let them make me believe that I'd deserved it, that I was lucky to get a second chance to please our father. But they'd robbed me of my child, all on the words of gods who no longer talk to any of us. And then they'd told me I wasn't allowed to mourn those lost years. They'd stolen it all, and the grief nearly knocks me over now when I look at Mina.

She smiles softly. "Everything happens for a reason. I'm content with my life."

Maybe she is content. Maybe she doesn't regret her life. But we've lost so many years.

"So, that leaves me," Marielle says quietly. "Am I enough?"

"You are more than enough," I promise her. "And you always have been. Have you noticed your power is stronger at night? Under the moon, perhaps?"

I'd taunted her once, saying she had an affinity for the moon, but I need to know how true it is. Her cheeks pinken as she nods. "Good. Then yes, you have everything I need. I'll prove it to you, too."

It took a god to form me out of starlight and six divine beings to turn me back into dust. Will I be able to do it with just myself and Marielle's power? I don't know, but it's our best chance.

Celia clears her throat. "After we eat. Some people here need food, and if we're planning a war—even an unconventional one—we need all our strength. And a plan."

I nod at her. She's right. We need to take care of our forces.

I look around the yard. These are our forces. I never thought I'd be facing down a *god* without my sisters. Hell, I never thought I'd go to war with anyone but them. Even when Lionel was still a king, I'd fought his battles alone. I hadn't needed an army.

But here I am, with this motley collection of creatures, and it somehow feels right.

CHAPTER TWENTY-EIGHT

CLAY

E strid looks like a fucking goddess, confident and in command, and we're all agreeing to follow her. Two queens, a king, four princes, a princess, warriors—all fall in line to follow Estrid.

As she deserves. Estrid's cool confidence makes me half-hard in my pants, and I know this is a wildly inappropriate time, but I can't help it. Not since our kiss this morning. Not when she looks like that.

I know I'm all but useless in her war. I barely have magic anymore, and I definitely don't have what she's looking for. I'm not meant to fight gods. But if she'll kiss me like that again, then I'll wait for her on the sidelines. I'll be whatever she wants, wherever she wants me.

My cousin drags me from my thoughts by stepping in my line of sight, crossing her arms. "You can go now."

"Go?" I echo uselessly, a dumb parrot unable to parse her meaning. Where the fuck am I supposed to go?

"You did your job, right? Got Lorne here? We have her now. Even got the other halflings safe. Your job is over. So go back to whatever hole you crawled out of and leave us alone."

I look around. No one is paying attention to us except Estrid and Bryce. I nod at Estrid, letting her know I have this, and she nods back, turning away. Bryce continues to watch, and I'm reminded of when he beat the shit out of me on the floor of Greta's shop.

Not that I didn't deserve it then, but I'd like to think that I don't deserve a repeat performance now.

"My job is at Estrid's side," I tell her. "Wherever she sends me. And right now, that job is here. Sorry, but I'm sticking this out."

"Do you do this just to get to me?" she demands. "I moved on, Clay. I have a life here. Family, not that you'd know what that means." I can't hide my flinch from her. She sneers, mean and cruel in a way I know Mae isn't. This is my fault; this is what I did to her, what my actions made her. "What's the matter? Don't like the reminder that Greta would be ashamed of you?"

"Have you talked to her?" I ask her quietly.

"No. She left, and—"

"She had a baby," I tell her abruptly. "I wondered if that's how you knew that pregnant witches can have issues with magic."

Mae physically stumbles. "What the fuck? No."

"Yes."

"Why didn't she tell us?" she demands, then stops. "Tell me?"

"She didn't tell me either," I assure her, because the last thing I want is to convince her that Greta didn't love her. "I found out because when things got bad, I went to look for her." I laugh at myself. "Wanting Greta to solve my problems again."

"And she did?" she guesses.

I shake my head. "She was pregnant. Like hugely, obviously pregnant. I didn't even try to approach her. Wouldn't bring the things that were chasing me to her door."

Mae's silent for a moment, then grudgingly admits, "That's good of you."

"Good gods, Mae, it's a baby. Our niece or nephew. I know I haven't presented myself in the best light, but I'm not a monster."

"They're our cousin, I think."

"What the fuck ever. I watched her for a few days. She gave it all up. Our whole community. Our way of life, really. She's not living some glamorous, magical high life like she said, Mae. Her husband is *human*. And they were having a baby."

"Is the baby a witch?" Mae asks.

"I didn't go back to find out. Too dangerous."

"Fuck," Mae whispers, running her hand through her hair. She half turns away. "I can't—why wouldn't she tell us?"

I have no more answers than she does. I know Greta, though, and I'm sure she thought it was best for everyone.

Mae knows the same. Mae loves Greta, was her prodigy and her success, and I was her screw-up. But I genuinely think Greta loved us both.

I'd love to live through this and meet our niece or nephew or cousin or whatever. I'd love to be worthy of meeting them. I don't know if Greta will ever let us. Maybe she never told her husband about the magic at all, and she'll need us to stay away. But there's a baby out there, and that baby is part Greta, and I want to know them so badly it hurts.

Mae should meet them. Mae isn't a threat to them like I might be.

"I'm sorry," I tell her, because I can't become worthy of that future if I can't start here. "I'm so damn sorry. I know I hurt you and scared you. I know I betrayed you."

"You betrayed Greta," she whispers, like that's the bigger crime.

"I did," I agree. I could list my crimes alphabetically and be here all day.

"Why did you do it? Why throw everything back in her face to go to *them*?" she asks, saying *them* like it's poisonous. "You were willing to give Greta's store to them. She worked so damn hard on it."

"I'm not like you and her," I admit. "I've made fun of you for years because you don't do big magic. I made fun of your stupid jobs and your little magic, but the truth is—I'm not much better."

She raises an eyebrow. "Don't try to flatter me. I know what you can do."

"Sure. When I have a spell book, I had a fuck-ton of magic to make it happen. I could do big spells, spells that took a lot of power. But you and Greta had a talent, and that one skipped me."

"What could I possibly do that you can't?"

"You can *create* spells. I've watched you do it for years."

"Small spells," she says, waving her hand like she can just dismiss that. I frown, because that's probably my fault. Mae still thinks her magic is insignificant when it's actually just beautiful.

"Magic. You *invent* magic. I could never do that. If I don't have a spell book, I'm powerless. I collected as many as I could. I was hungry for magic. Needed more. Needed to know I had as much as possible. And when March offered me—what he did—I, well…"

"Sold your soul," she finishes.

"Yes," I admit, and it still hurts, but it's like lancing a wound, I think. Painful and necessary. "Power, money—all things I craved. And the cost was only my soul. And my power."

Her mouth twists. "I thought something was wrong. You don't look right. You don't feel right, either. What the fuck did you do?"

"You know those spells Andreas does?"

"The ones that he used pieces of my friend for?"

"Yeah," I wince. "Those. They take a lot of power."

"You *have* a lot of power."

"It's not like doing a big spell, Mae. I'm not channeling my magic to do the spell. I *am* the spell. My magic is a component."

She looks a little queasy at the thought. "Will it come back?"

At this point, who knows? A little came back when Estrid made me rest, but not a lot. I have as strong a relationship with my magic as Hannah does right now. I shrug.

"I'm sorry," she murmurs.

"No you're not. I deserve the consequences of my actions. And you have to see the irony here."

Witch is willing to overlook scruples to chase power. Witch loses power in the process. It's a perfect punishment, so perfect that it has to have been crafted by fate just for me.

"I can still be sorry you're hurting," she says. "It sucks to not have magic."

Mae has never not had magic, but I appreciate the gentleness anyway, even if I don't deserve it. I nod.

"I don't forgive you," Mae says quietly.

"I know," I tell her. I never expected her to.

"I forgive you for scaring me. And for what you said. But I don't forgive you for going to them. For needing to be *better* than us so badly that you couldn't even talk to us. I grew up just like you did. Just as poor, and just as bad at magic. Even worse, really. So. Fuck you for that. We could have been teammates, not enemies."

It's a fair condemnation, and I just nod.

"When this is over, when we survive—" She says it with an insistence I'm not used to from her—"And we go see Greta. If she forgives you, then I do too."

That's a big ask, but I don't argue it. It's fair for Mae to set the terms, and I nod. "Alright. But just to be clear, I'm not leaving until this is over. This is my fight too."

She nods. "Alright. Fine. If you can help in any way—we'll take all the help we can get." And then she walks away, going over to her mate who takes her in his arms, kissing her forehead and cupping her ass before the two of them walk back to their house.

When I join the others inside Callum and Marielle's house for breakfast, Estrid sidles up next to me, despite clearly not needing to wait in line for food. "Alright?"

She asks it like she's genuinely concerned, and that's not the action of someone talking to a person who was just a distraction. I don't know what we are, and I have to figure it out soon. I should probably wait until this is over, but I can't. I'll explode if I don't find out soon.

"It's fine," I tell her, and when she smiles at me, quick and then gone, I'm surprised to find out that I actually mean it.

CHAPTER TWENTY-NINE

ESTRID

"Feel it around you," I instruct, watching Marielle stand in her yard at twilight. "Stop grounding into the earth—feel *upward*."

"But all the magic is down here," she protests, wiggling her feet in the grass. Flowers bloom right out of the soil and snake up her legs.

That's a lot of magic on its own, but it's not what we need. "No, the magic is everywhere," I correct. "That's the point. Each god is the embodiment of a different facet, and their divine children can tap into that facet. The cold of night, the darkness—your mother can channel the power and light of the moon." Her face darkens when I mention her mother, so I move on. "You're just used to feeling the magic in the plants. Let that go; that's not the magic that will help me. Try sensing something else."

She doesn't complain, just closes her eyes to try again. She holds up her hands like she physically needs them to feel the sky, an amateur move, but I'm not going to stop her. "There's something..." she murmurs.

"Keep feeling," I instruct, looking around to see if she's latched onto anything.

The shadows under the tree get longer, although that might just be the sun setting.

"Keep going," I murmur. "Feel for it. Reach, if you need to."

"I found something," she says. Her hand turns, and she points, eyes still closed as she furiously tries to hold on to whatever it is. I follow the trail, seeing the moon low on the horizon.

Like mother, like daughter. I don't dare mention it. "Good. Hold that. Now—"

She doesn't need any more instruction from me. The shadows cloak her, wrapping her up in a layer of comforting darkness. Callum grunts from where he sits on their front step, but Marielle doesn't stop.

"Now send it my way," I instruct. "Let me feel it, Marielle."

She takes another moment, but the darkness pushes toward me, a rush of night embracing me. I close my eyes, sinking into the comforting feeling of them, even if I know they're not *mine*. They're Marielle's.

They still feel like home, a balm to my soul when I thought I might never feel that again. "That's it," I croak, fighting tears. Good gods, I'm crying more than Hannah lately, and at least she has the excuse of being pregnant.

"Let go now, Marielle," I coach, and like a string is cut, she does. I take in her shadows, absorbing them into my own. It's just like when my sisters turned me to stardust, except instead of incredible power being forced on me to the point of destroying me, this is just a little extra, a warm boost.

Her body sags the moment she lets go of the magic, and Callum rushes forward, too late to catch her but cradling her in the grass. He glares at me. "You said this was safe for her."

I catch my breath, watching flowers blossom around Marielle as she rests in the grass. "Marielle has an exceptional amount of power," I tell them both. "But she's never trained this side. It makes sense that it's hard at first."

"But that's it?" Marielle asks, looking no worse for wear. "That's what you want from me?"

"That's it," I confirm. That's more than I thought I'd have. It's nowhere near the strength of two divine beings, but Marielle lending me her night-soaked power will be something at least.

Is it enough to beat an almost-god?

That's the question none of us dare ask. I don't have a backup plan, and if this doesn't work, I know full well that everybody who comes with me will die.

I've talked to Ryder, told him his job is to protect his wife and take anyone else he can with him. I've told Chase to get his family away. I've told my family—and now I'm allowed to call them mine, even though I always stop myself, unable to overcome the fear without prompting—that they shouldn't come. But they will anyway, and I know it.

I need Marielle, and Callum won't let her go alone. And because of that, none of the wolves will let her go alone, determined to protect her. I need Hannah too, even if I don't need her the same way I need Marielle. And that, of course, means Ryder will be there. The vampires have no business being there, though. At first I thought it was for Marielle, because Theo is attached to her. But Mina told me it's because of *me*. Because we're *family*.

I don't know what to do with that.

I worry I could be leading them straight to their death, but then again, if I fail, what chance do they have? Andreas won't stop until he's the only god this realm has, and he won't care who he hurts along the way.

"Again?" Marielle asks, and Callum grips her tighter, but he doesn't stop her.

"Again," I agree, because what else can we do?

***

Lorne stalks around as Hannah and I run through what I'm asking of her. She doesn't need to be anywhere near the fighting, and I won't do anything to risk that baby. But if she's the daughter of one of the sons of earth, and Andreas is a son of earth, perhaps with some training, she can counteract his magic.

Hannah frowns. "This is damn weird. Like like fingernails down your spine when you don't expect them."

I refrain from mentioning that, as we've been doing this for two hours, she should start *expecting* it by now. It's not the point anyway, and Ryder has been watching from the shadows, and I know one unkind comment and he'll whisk Hannah away.

"You've got it, though," I promise her. Technically, without having someone for her to work against, we can't guarantee that she can hold the Earth for any amount of time. And maybe Andreas' magic will so deeply out-class her own it won't even matter. But every second counts, and if she can hold the Earth from him for even a moment, it'll be an advantage.

"Great," Ryder says shortly. "Can I take her to rest now?"

Hannah flips him off. "I'm not an invalid, Ryder."

"You're tired," he protests, and yes, even I can see she is.

"Go rest," I say. "We're done here."

Besides, Lorne has been skulking around, and I doubt she wants an audience when she says whatever she has to say.

Ryder disappears with his mate, and I don't bother turning. "Say what you need to say, Lorne."

"When this is done, where are you going?" she asks.

"I have no idea." I have no idea if this will be *done,* at least not with me alive. But I'm not going to tell the girl that. "Why?"

"I want to come with you. I want you to teach me like you're doing for them."

I raise an eyebrow. I didn't expect that answer. I expected at best for Lorne to take Silas and Mina up on their offer of a home. At worst, I thought she'd slink off and vow revenge, and become a problem for someone to hunt down and rescue in the near future.

"You're aware I'm not your family," I say carefully.

"I know my mother," she says quietly. "You're not her."

"What I mean is, your magic isn't mine. I don't know it."

"You didn't know Hannah's either."

Fair point. "Alright kid, I'll tell you what. When this is over, wherever I end up—I won't forget you. And I'll teach you whatever I can." I leave *if I survive* unsaid.

"And you won't make me go back to my mom," she adds hurriedly, like she's stating the terms and conditions of this.

"That one's just a given." Like I'd send her back there. "I promise, kid. But you have to live to get there. Which means no messing around with things too big for you yet, alright?"

She rolls her eyes at me. "You don't all have to keep saying it. I get it, alright?"

"Good. Now—have you eaten?"

She bites her lip and shakes her head. "Theo said he'd go out with me."

"Then take him up on it. Shoo."

She gives me one long last look, like she can force me to keep my word with just her stare, and then moves off.

"You're good with her," Clay says.

I jump. "Fucking hell, since when are you sneaky?" I gripe.

"You were distracted. By the kid. Who you are good with."

"I am not. I think I just offered to teach her magic."

"Mhm," he agrees, walking the rest of the way over. "And you taught Hannah and Marielle. Estrid's Magic School for Wayward Halflings."

I point a finger at him. "Don't even joke."

He just laughs. Me pointing my finger at someone has been enough to be considered a threat many times in the past, but for Clay, he just *laughs*.

And I like it. I like that he's not scared of me anymore.

He sobers up, looking me over. "I think we need to talk," he says.

He's not wrong. I feel a little bad, having kissed him and then run off. I thought we'd talk. I thought we'd sort it out. But instead, I've been training with Marielle and Hannah for days, leaving Clay waiting for answers.

"We do," I agree, and I impulsively extend a hand to him. "Come with me?"

He takes my hand without question. "Where are you bringing me?"

Fuck, he's trusting. "For a walk?"

"Estrid, queen of the shadows, taking a walk like us normal people?" he teases, smiling and squeezing my hand. "Sounds good. Lead the way."

So he follows me without question, and I'm starting to think he always will. That's both heady and terrifying. What do I have to offer him that makes him trust me like that? What do I possibly have to give?

Like a mind-reader, Clay leans closer and brushes a kiss across my hair. "Relax," he murmurs. "You think too much."

"And what should I do instead?"

"Feel," he says simply. "Just feel. But let me feel it with you, Estrid. Please. I'm begging."

CHAPTER THIRTY

CLAY

She's cute when she looks at me like that, all flustered and confused. It's not a look I imagine I'll see on her often, so I'll relish it while I have the chance.

She's so thrown by what I said that I take pity and give her a moment to get her thoughts together.

I suppose she could be finding a way to let me down gently, but I doubt it. Estrid doesn't let people down gently. More to the point, she'd already let me down gently before she kissed me. I'm not the instigator here. This has been her show all along, and I'm just an eager player in it.

"Leave it to you to drag us out to the woods," I tease, waiting for her to get her bearings. "What is your obsession with the outside?"

"Do you want to go somewhere else?" she asks. "I could take us wherever you wanted to go."

I'm definitely not used to Estrid being so accommodating. I look up at the darkening sky, watching night spill into the valley. It's peaceful here. Not that I'm planning on staying; I have no desire to live in the middle of absolutely nowhere, and Mae and I might have come to a tentative truce, but I don't think I'll be invited for family dinner at any point. But it is peaceful, and I know Estrid feels something under the night sky.

"Here's fine," I tell her. "Do you want to start, or should I?"

"I am a poor bet, Clay," she tells me, eyes wide and imploring. "I need you to see that. I am something *else*."

"I'm going to live forever too, Estrid," I say mildly.

She bites her lip. "You'll live a very long time. But not forever. How old is the oldest person you know?"

"You."

"A woman doesn't like being called old," she says almost automatically. "Beside me?"

I think it over, because I don't actually have a quick answer. "A few thousand, maybe?"

"Exactly. Eventually, you all die. And I was here before you. If all goes well, I'll be here after you too."

If I think about that too long, then my head will spin. "What's it matter?" I ask. "I thought your kind doesn't do long-term." It hurts to say it, which is ridiculous. I'm not exactly known for long-term relationships either. My life has been my own, and I haven't wanted to share more than a night or two from it with anyone.

But Estrid looks at me with anguished eyes. "You aren't like that," she says hoarsely. "I'm not saying I'm tying you to me for eternity, but you have to know you're not like that, Clay."

"I'm not a distraction?" I dare to ask.

She kissed me, I remind myself. I don't need to hold my breath waiting for this answer.

"You are the worst type of distraction," she grumbles. "You are the person I keep looking for in a crowded room. You're the one I think of talking to whenever I think of something. You're the one I let hold me when I cried,

Clay. I don't let people do that. Not even my sisters—it's you, Clay. And you don't have to feel the same, I'd get it—I am a bad bet, but—"

I can't listen to her be down on herself for a moment longer. I'm actually fundamentally incapable of listening to that, because Estrid deserves so much better. She needs to think the world of herself. I need her to be as arrogant and self-assured as she pretends to be, and I need her to stop believing this nonsense about herself.

I step forward, take her in my arms, and kiss her until she can't think anymore. Until there's absolutely no room in her mind for any of the things she's been thinking. Until there's only room for us.

She takes a moment to respond, but then her sharp little claws grab my shirt, digging into my skin underneath and sending little pinpricks of pleasure through me. When I finally pull back, she's tilted her head back to watch me with hooded eyes, and I can't resist her for another second.

"Fuck, you're beautiful," I tell her, because I need her to know. She's *beautiful*, with her eyes that remind me of stars in the night, that dark hair, the way she's pierced her pointed ears more times than I've bothered to count just so they glitter in the fading light. "I want you, Estrid," I tell her, because I won't have there be any more confusion. "Any objections?"

She bites her lip. "And if I die, Clay? I don't want you to get attached just to die on you. Maybe it's better if we wait—"

"I'm already attached," I interrupt her, because this is foolish. "Estrid, I am so attached. You have to know. You *saved* me. You gave me another chance when everyone else had long since given up on me. You saw something worthwhile in me."

"I threatened to kill you," she protests.

"And I deserved it. And you didn't do it." I don't know, maybe that's fucked up. But Estrid gave me the kick in the ass I needed, the chance to turn things around and be more than just a pawn to Andreas.

I'd rather be her pawn any day of the week, but I don't even feel like that anymore. I'm one of her team. I belong here, at her side, and I'll stay as long as she lets me.

"And what the fuck do you mean you might *die*?" I demand. "You're supposed to live another ten thousand years or whatever. Estrid, what do you know that I don't?" She bites her lip and half turns away, but I keep holding her, sliding my hands so I'm gripping her arms lightly. I don't want her to walk away, but I'm not so stupid as to think I should restrain someone like Estrid.

"Andreas is practically a god, Clay," she says, like I need the reminder. "And Marielle and Hannah are *helping*, but they don't make me a god."

"Then we need a new plan," I say immediately, but she's already shaking her head.

"There is no other plan. It's this or let him do what he wants, and I won't stand for that. Not when he crosses every fundamental rule and hurts people the way he does. I won't have Andreas be a god with more power than any other. I'm willing to die to take him down. I've accepted it."

"Well I haven't," I snarl, not recognizing my own voice. "Gods, Estrid, were you going to say something?"

"No," she admits, and there is some of her fierceness. She glares me down, confident in her decision even as it devastates me. "What's the point? What happens, happens, Clay. No one else needs to suffer for it."

"I'll suffer for it either way!" I let her go, taking a step back, needing to pace. But she takes a step back too, and I immediately know I made the wrong call. "Fuck, Es, come here, please, I—" She doesn't move, and I almost lose it. "You're the reason I'm like this," I croak, my voice breaking. I can feel a tear sliding down my cheek, but I ignore it, because if I stop talking, then she might walk away and never understand. "*Better.*"

"You wanted to be better all on your own," she disagrees. "You wouldn't have done all this otherwise."

Estrid doesn't understand. I'm a coward, and she's not, and how do I make her understand I'd already looked for a way out, decided it was too hard, and given up? That she's the only reason I ever felt like I had a chance, and she's the one who made this happen?

"I couldn't have done it without you," I say. "And I won't. So you better plan to survive this, Es. I'm not doing this alone."

"You sound like the wolves," she huffs. "You barely know me, Clay. We're not fated to be together forever."

I try not to take offense to the comparison. When it comes to love, the wolves have a few good ideas. "Witches don't have fated mates," I tell her. "But I know that I am *yours*, for as long as you'll have me." There's no other option, not a single other possibility. Estrid took a dead man walking and brought him back to life. Not only that, she made him want to live again.

And I want that life with her.

"But what if I can't give you very long?" she asks.

Fuck that. I will not live in a world without Estrid. I won't let her go, and I won't let her give up on herself. "Then become a goddess," I say.

She scoffs. "Oh, such an easy plan. Why didn't I think of that?"

"I'm serious." The idea is fleshing out in my mind, pulling pieces of every conversation we've ever had. "If you need to be a goddess to beat Andreas, then do it. You say that gods require worship? That direct worship from us makes them even more powerful? Done."

"I can't—that's not how it works. I can't just go and get worshippers."

I privately think that Estrid is underestimating how loyal everyone here is. Mina spent her whole life believing in Estrid, after all. Marielle, Hannah, and Lorne are looking to her for instruction. We're all hanging on her every word. But that's not what's going to convince her. "You have a worshipper. Right here."

She looks me over like she's waiting for the punchline, so I advance on her, boxing her in against a tree. She lets me, looking up at me with eyes that look closer to lost than I'm ever comfortable seeing on Estrid.

"I worship you," I say, bringing my mouth to her ear. "Completely, totally, and willingly."

"Clay—" she moans my name, and that just spurs me higher.

"I worship you," I repeat. "Let me prove it to you."

"You don't—" I don't want to hear any more protests. I lean in and kiss her, trying to pour everything I feel into that kiss.

Estrid is mine and Estrid is a goddess, and I'll worship her happily for the rest of my days. I need her to know it, and the only way I know to convince her it's true is to prove it.

I kiss down her neck, bending my knees so I can reach her collarbones. "Have I told you how fucking beautiful you are?" I murmur into the dip of her throat. Estrid knows she's beautiful, I have no doubt about it, but I need her to know *how* beautiful. Show-stoppingly beautiful. Overwhelmingly beautiful. Life-changingly beautiful.

"Clay—"

"Shh," I reprimand. "Let me worship."

And then I slide to my knees, pushing up the dress she's wearing. Only Estrid would insist she likes walking around in the woods at night while wearing a designer dress.

Her panties are jet-black, lace, and look expensive. I admire the view, playing with the band for a moment before I work them down her legs. She kicks them off for me, leaving them who-knows-where, and, in gratitude, I pick up her leg and put it over my shoulder.

"Let me worship," I say. I can't even recognize my own voice between the rasp and the need. I *need* this woman like I need air, and I finally understand the meaning of devotion.

I wait for her nod, a tiny little jerk of her head, and then I show her what it means to be worshipped.

I tease over her clit, just a little lick, an introduction really, and then familiarize myself with the rest of her cunt. I want to taste her, drown in her, so I reach for her hips and pull her a little further against me, needing to be as close as possible.

With one leg over my shoulder, she huffs when I pull, losing her balance until my face is the only thing keeping her upright. I suck her clit, a little thank you for giving me what I want, and set to making her come.

She tastes like a goddess, pure and sweet, and I think I could stay here for hours. But I need her to come. I need her to soak me, anoint me with her taste. And I need her to indisputably know how I feel about her.

She gets her fingers in my hair, using me in one more way to anchor her. I feel honored, needed, and beloved. *I* am the one here, between her legs. I'm the one holding her upright. I'm the one who she trusts with her pleasure.

"I'm going to—" she moans it like she's surprised.

I suck her clit, teasing with my tongue. I hope she feels powerful right now, worshipped and strong. I feel more powerful than I ever have, being the man who gets to see her like this.

Estrid soaks my face with her come, and I nearly howl with pleasure, lapping her up. Her hand in my hair gets gentler, and soon enough she's stroking instead of pulling. I can't stop licking at her, chasing another orgasm.

She finally tugs again, tilting my head back. I go willingly, staring up at her. I can feel her come soaking my face, and I take in her flushed cheeks, blown pupils, and still gently opened mouth. I feel delirious, watching her watch me, and for a moment I swear there's a golden light around her. "Clay," she murmurs, and her voice sounds angelic. "Let me down, Clay."

I do, albeit unwillingly. I help her get her leg off my shoulder and find her balance again, but all I want to do is make her come again.

Her dress falls back into place, to my immense disappointment. I don't get off my knees, unable to find the strength.

Like she can read my mind, her hand traces through my hair again. I lean into it, letting my eyes slip closed. "Clay, will you fuck me? Fill me?"

My eyes fly open, staring up at her as she watches me intently. I nod, and then my hands find her thighs and that dress, pushing it back up.

She lets me, helping me when it gets high enough, and then the dress is gone. She evidently wasn't wearing a bra, so she's left bare beneath the trees, and I watch, spellbound. I watch her in the twilight, the darkness embracing her skin beautifully.

"I should ask—I don't have a condom," I murmur stupidly.

She smiles fondly. "I got the shot, Clay. Don't worry—we're not bringing any children into this mess. Now—your turn," she says, and I clamber to my feet so I can strip off my clothes, not giving a fuck and throwing them any which way. I need to be naked with her. Need to hold her, touch her.

When we're both naked, I gently take her to the ground, laying her out in the leaves. A part of me thinks this is disgraceful, that Estrid deserves the nicest bed I can get her, with luxurious sheets and soft pillows. But there's something magical about this too. Estrid looks great in the dying light, like she belongs here.

She guides her hands overhead, laying them out so I can see her body stretched out and waiting for me. There's a slight look of uncertainty in her eyes, and I know that she's not used to putting herself in positions at anyone else's mercy. I need to show her it's worth it.

I start with kissing her wicked little mouth. She pushes up against me, searching for more, but I just move away, kissing down her neck, making my way to her pretty tits. At the same time, I trace up her hip, feather-light touches I hope make her feel as on-edge as I do.

"Clay," she gasps, moving one hand to reach for me.

210

I reach up and firmly put it back. "Shush," I scold her. "I'm worshipping here." I lave attention on her breasts, sucking first one nipple and then the other, kissing the valley between them before starting all over. I need her. It's like my whole body exists only to need her. There's no before, no after. There's just *her*.

"If you don't get inside me—" she threatens, but then trails off with a groan when I kiss around her belly button.

"I'm surprised you don't have this pierced, considering how much you like jewelry," I say, licking into her belly button to feel her stomach contract beneath my tongue.

"Clay." She's getting sterner now, but the effect is kind of ruined with her sprawled out beneath me, body desperately reaching for more.

"Hush," I tell her again. "I'm going to kiss every inch of you, alright? So let me."

"I will pin you down and ride you myself," she threatens.

"You like it." I kiss her hip bones, reluctantly skipping her cunt. I want to taste her again, but I also need to stretch this out. I need her to get out of her head and just feel.

I kiss her thighs, her knees, her calves. She tries to draw her legs back, but I just press lingering kisses, hoping she understands what I'm trying to say. Hoping she feels even a fraction of it.

"Clay," Estrid murmurs. "I need *you*." The emphasis she puts on *you* gets me moving. She doesn't just need to be fucked, she doesn't just need to come. She needs *me* and what I can provide for her.

"How do you want me, Es?" I ask, kissing back up her body, hands moving ahead of my lips. "Tell me how to make you feel good."

"You fucking know," she practically growls. "Fuck me, Clay. Make me feel it."

The directness does something to me. I hook one of her legs over my hip, taking a moment to stroke lightly over her calf and thigh, feeling the soft skin there. "Whatever you want."

She moves her hands from above her head, and I'm about to try to scold her again, tell her to let me take care of it, but then she slides her hands down my chest, scraping lightly with her sharp nails, and I shiver under her touch. Fuck, I hope she leaves marks.

"Now," she whispers, like she has to cajole me, and I can't hold out anymore, sliding inside. She's so hot and tight, a perfect heat around me, and I want *more*. Want to live here, want to die here, want this to be my entire reality.

"Estrid," I murmur, voice a fervent prayer. She needs worship? I'm here, worshipping every twitch of her pussy, every flicker of her eyelashes, every whisper from her mouth. She kisses me, and it feels like she knows. Like I'm her devoted disciple, and she's rewarding me for my dedication.

"Fuck me," she whispers against my mouth, and I'm helpless to resist. I withdraw slowly, then push back into her in one thrust, giving her the fucking she's looking for.

She groans, and her nails dig into my chest before her hands fall away entirely and land on the ground once more, letting me drive her where she needs to be.

"Fucking beautiful," I tell her, watching the way her eyes flutter with pleasure, enraptured by her lips, her mouth just slightly open as she enjoys what I'm doing to her.

"Clay..." she whispers.

I fuck her even harder as a reward. *Me*. She wants me. I've never felt more powerful in my entire life. There is no magic, no wealth, no power worth more than Estrid and the way she's squeezing around me right now.

I'm going to fucking come. I can't help it; Estrid squeezes my cock so perfectly, and she's a dream come true beneath me. But I refuse to come until she does again.

"I'm close," she murmurs, rocking her hips furiously against me. "Clay, please, I—"

"I've got you," I promise her. "I've got you, Es, I'll get you there."

Her eyes, which have been sliding closed with pleasure, open completely and lock onto mine. "I know you will."

Fuck.

I grit my teeth, determined to get her there before I fall over that edge. Her eyes flutter again when my cock brushes against that spot inside her, and I reach to stroke her clit, rubbing my thumb over it.

When she comes, her cunt squeezes me like a vise. I groan, the perfect pleasure sending me right over the edge. "*Fuuck.*" It's like ascending to a higher state of being. It's *more* in a way I can't quite describe, just know I'll be chasing it for the rest of my life.

I can't stay upright, not after my soul has somehow been reformed through sex. I am *hers* now in a way I never even knew was possible, and as such, I need to be so close to her that daylight won't pass between us. I lay my head on her soft tits, breathing her in.

Estrid scratches her nails through my hair, humming softly in my ear. I trace the sweat on her temple, marveling at the moment.

"Do you feel like a goddess yet?" I ask her, barely recognizing my own voice.

She smiles tremulously at me. "You know what? I do."

Chapter Thirty-One

Estrid

I lay there in the dirt, trying to get my breath back, blinking up at the star-flecked sky above us.

I just let Clay fuck me again—and what is *with* us fucking outside?—and I don't regret it. No, if anything, I feel more alive than I ever have. I can't find it in me to give a single fuck about the rules, about keeping distance, about the fact that I could very well die soon.

Clay somehow makes me feel like anything is possible. Like we're going to survive this and go start a life together.

I don't even know if he wants that. He talks a good game, but he wouldn't be the first man to tell a partner all those things and not intend anything longer than a night.

His lips press against my neck, like he already knows what I'm thinking and is determined to convince me otherwise. I tilt my head, letting him kiss me, relaxed and satiated under his touch.

I've never felt like this before. Cherished, *worshipped*, even—but safe. More importantly, most astonishingly, safe.

I don't think I've ever felt safe before.

And now I'm going to ruin it. "It's going to be tomorrow," I tell him.

He sits up abruptly, and I feel a cold tingle on my neck, where his lips should be. "Tomorrow?" he repeats, like I've suddenly started speaking a language he doesn't know.

"Mhm. Tomorrow."

"Why tomorrow?"

Because if I let us get any more attached to each other, I won't do it. Because Marielle and Hannah don't need more practice, and they're not going to get any more skilled than they already have. Because Andreas shouldn't get any more time to gain more strength. Pick a reason, any reason. They're all true.

"It's time," I tell him.

"When were you going to tell us all this?"

"First thing in the morning. And then in the evening..." As soon as I can feel the night, we'll do this.

It's uncomfortable to be lying down while he stares at me, so I sit up too, drawing my legs up close to me. Clay takes one of my hands, already playing with my fingers and watching them more than my face like he needs a distraction.

"You're going to survive it." It's not a question. "You're going to beat him, and then I'll follow you wherever you're going next. Or wait for you, whatever."

I raise an eyebrow. He's talking about a future, and a real one. Ignoring whether or not I survive tomorrow, Clay is talking like this between us will last.

The flutter of butterflies in my stomach tells me I like the idea too. More than I ever have.

"I promised I'd teach Lorne about her magic," I say abruptly.

"So you're coming back here?"

Hardly likely. I'm not deluded enough to think anyone but Clay actually likes me here. "How do you feel about castles?" I dare to ask.

He raises an eyebrow. "You *would* live in a castle." It sounds like a compliment when he says it. "Not the one you brought me to before?"

"Yes. That one." Lionel's castle. More accurately, the castle I won, raised him in, and set him on the throne in. Once my home, ripped away from me by my sisters insisting I couldn't exist among the creatures of Earth.

But no more. If I want to have a fucking castle here on Earth, I will. And if I want Clay in that castle, want to fuck him stupid night after night—well, as long as he'll agree, then I'll have it.

"It needs some fixing up," I admit, because I'm not ignorant of the nearly thousand years between when I left my home and when I returned. "And probably some government is claiming it as a national landmark or something."

"I wouldn't be so sure. Castles are a dime a dozen over there," he muses. "And a lot of them just go to ruin. So, you might be able to legally reclaim it easily."

"I have money."

"Oh, I know."

"Do you like that?" I ask, because I've watched him watch me, watch the places I take him.

He grins. "You going to spoil me, Estrid? Have me as your sugar baby?"

I roll my eyes. "What, put you on an allowance? Show you off at nice parties?"

He shrugs. "If you want. I wouldn't complain."

No, he doesn't look like he would. And I don't think I'd mind either. For however long he wants to let me spoil him, I want it too.

"I meant, I could pay to buy back my castle. And fix it. You saw the kind of condition it was in, though. It'll probably take a while."

Clay just looks at me for a moment, then reaches out and brushes his fingertips along my cheek. "I've got plenty of time, Es. I'm not worried about it."

I swallow, my heart beating unnaturally fast. "Are you sure?" I ask tentatively.

I don't even know if I have time. Clay can do everything in his power to distract me, but that doesn't change the reality. But if I make it out of this, if we all do—

He wants to be there. He wants to rebuild a godsdamn castle with me.

"I'm so sure, Es," he promises me. He rakes his free hand through his disastrous mess of hair. "You think you can save me like you did and not fundamentally re-write my brain? I am obsessed. I have been obsessed. And it won't go away. And I wouldn't change a fucking thing about it. I want this with you."

No ambiguity, no uncertainty. My heart swells.

I might be lying, but I don't care. I need to tell him, need him to know—"Then let's have that future," I say, and kiss him once more, just to seal the deal.

***

I'd like to say Clay and I fucked the night away, distracted ourselves, but there's too much to do, and as good a distraction as Clay is, even he can't get tonight off my mind.

When Clay and the others went to retrieve the list of halflings, they stole everything in Andreas' safe. I go over it all once more, studying the pile of spells in there.

"I recognize that one," Clay murmurs, chin hooked over my shoulder. "March used to have me do this one all the time."

I suck in a breath, disgusted. "Alone?"

"Yeah?" he asks, now nipping at my ear like he can distract me from what I'm reading.

The amount of magic Clay would need to dump into this spell—even if all his ingredients were powerful, like, say, from Marielle—well, no wonder he had almost no magic left to give when I met him, and hasn't recovered a ton since.

"They really just used you, huh?"

He shifts, uncomfortable now. "I mean, yeah. When I failed to get them Greta's shop, it was like I became persona non grata. Only the shittiest jobs."

He mentioned that before. "What the fuck did Andreas want with that store?" I muse, because I can't fathom why a man who wants to be a god would want a shop.

"A good place to sell from? Greta had a loyal customer base."

But I'm already shaking my head. "Sure, some of them might convert, but not enough of them to make it worth his while. You were sent to threaten your cousin for that store. You drew a lot of attention to yourself; a werewolf prince still looks at you like he might kill you with one wrong move."

"Yeah, thanks for the reminder that I'm not exactly welcome at the family reunion," he mutters.

"Why would Andreas care so much?" I press. "He's not hurting for business." I pick up another sheet of paper, one filled with names of clients, for emphasis. "I don't get it, Clay."

He shrugs. "Greta was a powerful witch."

"Not as powerful as Andreas."

"She liked to invent spells?" he offers. "She's where Mae learned it from. I, unfortunately, didn't get that particular talent. We always said the place hummed with magic. She left spell books lying around. Mae found a few of them, but I'd bet real money that there were more."

Everything about this feels weird, like there's something I'm missing. "I want to go to the shop," I tell him.

"Yeah, I can't do that."

"Your cousin isn't there anymore, so it's not like you'll have to face her."

"No, I literally can't go there. Greta spelled it against me. And then when I finally found a way around it, Mae re-did her spell. It's effective." He grimaces, and I decide not to ask how many times he ran himself against that barrier.

Then his eyes go wide. "Wait. You got us into the werewolf village."

"I did," I agree, not seeing where this is going.

"It's the same spell. Mae does the barrier spell they love so much here. And it's the same spell she and Greta used to protect the shop."

Interesting. "We're going for a ride."

He sighs, but pushes himself upright. "I hate your stupid shadows."

"No, you don't."

"No, I don't," he reluctantly agrees, extending a hand to me. I take it, and a second later, the shadows engulf us, bringing us to a magic shop cloaked in darkness.

"Fuck, that still feels weird," Clay mumbles, looking around. "Feel anything here?"

Yes. There's a tingling prickle along my neck, like the shadows aren't as deep or as strong as I'd expect. There's a vibrant energy that makes my hair stand on end.

"Hey Clay, know much about your cousin's parents?" I ask as casually as I can.

"I mean, our moms were all sisters. And they took the witchy 'don't touch what's mine' to an extreme, all three of them. Not like they had much to protect, but they'd barely share it with us. My dad wasn't in my life much, and neither was Mae's. Greta's dad left before I was born, I don't know exactly when. Why?"

Because a lot of pieces are falling into place.

"I know you're here," I say as calmly as I can.

"Shh," Clay hisses. "Pretty sure Mae's little assistant lives here. Violet or something."

Violet is here, the shadows inform me, asleep upstairs in their bed. But that's not who I'm talking to.

A faint glow steps out of the back room. "Was wondering when I'd see you."

Clay's jaw practically hits the floor. "What the fuck are you doing here?"

"That's what you say when we haven't seen each other in years?"

The woman who stands in front of us looks like she has a halo. She smiles beatifically at us, and I know I've just met Greta.

Chapter Thirty-Two

Clay

"What the fuck are you doing here?" I repeat. "You're supposed to be on a quiet suburban street in *Jersey* or something."

She raises an eyebrow. "You found out more than I expected."

That is *not the point* right now. "You left," I say, "and yet you just *happen* to pop in for a visit on the night we show up?"

"She's not real," Estrid murmurs beside me. "Look at the edges."

I instinctively look down, and, sure enough, around Greta's hands is a little fuzzy, like a pixelated image. She shrugs. "Even I haven't successfully made a spell for teleportation yet," she admits. "But astral projection? Perfectly doable, especially since it's all about bending light."

"You never told your cousins you're a halfling," Estrid says.

Greta's smile doesn't flicker. "They never asked. And I'm very much a witch, so, I really didn't need to say anything."

"But this light bending you're doing..."

"Oh, I assume that comes from Dad. Any guesses who he is?"

Estrid waves a hand, calling some shadows to dance through her fingers. "Light is not my forte, as you can see. But you definitely belong to the day, Greta."

My mind is absolutely spinning. Fucking hell, my cousin is godsdamn powerful. She's literally bending light to project an image of herself across nearly a hundred miles. I always knew she was powerful, but this is an entirely new ballgame.

Greta looks over her shoulder, responding to something we can't hear. After a moment, she relaxes. "Think Jeffrey is going back to sleep."

"That's the baby's name?" I croak out, all I'm able to say. It's ridiculous, and not at all the point right now, but I feel like I'm desperate for information. That's my nephew, or cousin, or whatever. That baby is half Greta. Thinking about him makes me choke up a bit.

"Jeffrey is two and a half," she tells me, smiling slightly. "And he still sleeps like shit."

I try to process that. "Is he like us?"

"Definitely a witch, and driving his father crazy."

"So he knows?"

"I told him."

"He knows you're... this?" I check.

"Given he has no basis to know what *this* is, he's less impressed by it than you are."

Good fucking gods. I cannot wrap my mind around this conversation.

"I'm sorry," I say, because it seems like the logical place to start, and I owe her a lot of apologies. "I'm so sorry, Greta. I know you raised me to do better. I let you down. I threatened Mae, I went against your wishes. I hurt people and I was a selfish bastard. And I'm apologizing too late, but I'm sorry." I feel like I've run a marathon when I finish. Estrid reaches out and grabs my hand.

It's a move that doesn't escape projection-Greta's notice. "Interesting," she muses. "So, you're not here to steal my spells?"

"So there are spells," Estrid surmises, eyes lighting up.

"Can't you feel them?"

"The magic of this place is intense," Estrid agrees, which is an understatement. Greta's always been a powerful witch—and now, it's obvious why—and we felt the magic baked into these walls even as kids. And Andreas clearly knows it's here too.

"I put up protections years and years ago, the minute I felt that lowlife and his minions skulking around. It should never have needed to extend to my own flesh and blood," she says, with a hard look at me that makes me want to wither away. "I can check in whenever I wish. I saw Mae, and then Violet. But when my barrier is crossed, I know."

"It's Mae's barrier now," I say automatically, because it's kind of impressive that she managed to duplicate Greta's spell.

"Oh, now you're defending your cousin?"

"I'm trying."

Estrid squeezes my hand again. "He is trying. And he's doing. Clay almost died to save a child like you, Greta. He became my spy, knowing the risks. And tomorrow night, he's following me to finish this." I can't describe the warm feeling inside me when Estrid defends me like this, but I know I want more of it.

"So, tomorrow night then," Greta muses. "It'll be over?"

"It will be," Estrid agrees. "How much do you know about it?"

"I know Andreas is an asshole. He approached me years ago. Heard about some of the magic I was doing."

"Like what?"

"Barrier spells. Of a more permanent kind."

Greta's always been powerful, more powerful than the average witch should be. Now it makes more sense. And her magic must've been catnip to someone like Andreas.

"But he didn't go after you when you disappeared," I muse.

She shrugs. "I have some tricks up my sleeve. And I had a baby to protect."

"And," Estrid says slowly, "whatever he wants—it's here."

"What?" I ask.

"He didn't have you chase down Greta. He told you to get this place. Which means he doesn't actually care about her, which makes sense—Andreas would never respect a halfling enough to think they could be his partner. Plus—you must feel it. The magic here is—well, I can feel it through my whole body."

It's always felt like that. I look at Greta, who shrugs. "Mae found some spell-books behind the refrigerator, I heard," she says. "But she didn't open up the walls."

"The walls?"

"Might as well hide them where no one looks."

"There are *mice* in the walls here," I point out, because I used to help set traps when I was still welcome here.

She rolls her eyes. "Give me more credit than that."

"And these spells will help us?" Estrid asks, studying my cousin's too-bright face.

Greta grows serious. "Maybe. As much as I can, at any rate. I'd be there tomorrow, but the baby—"

Estrid waves her off. "Night and day are not compatible. Your presence wouldn't help me do what I need to. But the spells might."

"If we start tearing out walls, Violet will wake up," I caution them, because I seem to be the only one here with a single bit of logic left.

Estrid has the gall to roll her eyes at me. "Oh, ye of little faith." She closes her eyes and concentrates for a minute, and then a beat up book appears in her hand, surrounded by shadows.

"Not that one," Greta says.

Estrid sighs and tries again, and on the third try, she produces a book that Greta nods at. "Boundary spells. Look toward the end—that was a lot of experimenting."

I look over Estrid's shoulder. The spell is written in a hodge-podge of languages, only some of which I can read. I vaguely remember making fun of Mae for not being able to read ancient spells. Should I buy her flowers? Is that the type of apology she likes?

But, come on. Greta's like two hundred years old. Why the fuck is she writing in so many languages, half of which I'm positive are extinct?

Estrid doesn't seem to have the same problem I do. She looks up at Greta. "You sure?"

She shakes her head. "No. It's just a theory. The amount of magic involved is too much to imagine. Maybe if I had a hundred halflings."

"Maybe not even then," Estrid murmurs, tracing the letters on the page. "This might be it."

"Might be what?" I complain, wanting them to remember I'm here.

"A way to end this safely," Estrid says softly. "I can't win in a straight-up fight. But this..."

Greta looks over her shoulder again. "He's awake now," she complains. "I swear, I think our mothers enchanted our sippy cups to make us sleep, and I might've been ethically against that before, but it's becoming a grayer and grayer area..." She shakes her head and turns back to us. "Good luck," she says, and her face is grave. "And one more thing."

"Mhm?" Estrid asks, half her attention still on the damn book.

"Hurt my cousin, and I'll hurt you," she promises, and then the light fades away and the image of Greta disappears.

I stare at where she once was. "Was that fucking real?" I ask.

There's a creak above us, and Estrid grabs my hand, and before I can say anything, the shadows take us once more.

***

We land back in the hotel room Estrid took me to one time, the first day I saw her anything less than perfectly put together. "You never checked out of this place?" I ask, which is a stupid question, but it's the first thing that comes to mind.

She looks around. "Why would I?"

Right. Because she has more money than she knows what to do with.

She's already moving to the couch, flipping through the book, one finger trailing down the page as she reads.

Meanwhile, I fall into an armchair, trying to wrap my brain around the past half hour.

Greta is a halfling. She's always been exceptional, but this blows my mind.

"Her ears," I blurt out. "How the fuck did I never notice her ears?"

But no. I think back, and even tonight I didn't see pointed ears.

Estrid looks up and rolls her eyes. "You're a witch, Clay. You're telling me you've never cast a glamor spell?"

I sputter. "Since she was a kid? That's one hell of a spell."

She hefts up the book. "Trust me, she could do it. Now, let me read. Take a bath or something."

"You saying I smell?"

"I'm saying that you like nice things. Behold, a nice thing I can give you. And I need to memorize this, so it's a win-win for both of us."

Well, when she puts it like that... do I feel like a useless child she's placating with a prize? A little bit. Do I want a nice bath in a big tub? Also yes.

This hotel has even softer robes than the one she dumped me at for a week, so I take full advantage of that, shedding my clothes. They are *covered* in dirt, no doubt from leaving them on a forest floor. Could Greta see that? Is she aware of what Estrid and I did?

Probably. She was always observant.

The bath is huge. It's a claw-foot tub, but definitely not an antique; I'm pretty sure this thing is big enough to fit half a dozen werewolves, and the back shelf is lined with products that I already know would wipe out my meager bank account multiple times over. Did the hotel leave them there, or did Estrid buy them?

Either way, I'm planning to take full advantage.

I get the water steaming hot and step in, closing my eyes and leaning back, letting the water ease out the tension in my muscles.

Turns out, this tub is so fancy it has a sensor that tells it when the water is getting cool, so it can drain a little and add more hot water. I didn't even know things like that exist.

Maybe Estrid wasn't kidding when we joked about her being my sugar momma. I could get used to this life.

I have no idea how much time has passed. The tub has refilled at least once, but it could have been five minutes or five hours for all I know. The bathroom doesn't have any windows, and I'm barely opening my eyes, anyway. But eventually, there's a disturbance in the water, and when I open my eyes, a beautiful, naked Estrid is climbing into the tub with me.

"Done?" I ask, opening my arms so she can settle back against my chest.

"Done," she agrees, snuggling into me.

Chapter Thirty-Three

Estrid

He presses kisses against my neck, and I let him. I know I should get us out of this tub and go to bed. It's almost four in the morning, and if I'm really going to fight an almost god tonight, then I shouldn't do it sleep-deprived.

But I don't want that. I want—*need*—Clay.

His hands find my breasts, brushing his thumbs lightly over my nipples. I shiver, arching up to him, silently asking for more.

But then his hands fall away. "No," he says, and I freeze for a minute, but then he adds, "I'm going to fuck you in a bed this time, dammit."

I laugh, standing back up. "Well, then, let's find the bed."

He follows me eagerly, splashing half the water on the floor in his haste. I throw a towel at him, and he catches it while still walking toward me with a hungry look in his eyes.

"I'm going to worship you," he practically growls, stalking toward me as I back out of the bathroom.

And *I* am going to be selfish and take this, because if this is my last chance, if today doesn't go like I want it to—I refuse to let myself think about it right now. I have Clay here and now, and that has to be enough.

"Oh, pretty boy," I croon, smirking as I watch him miss a step. "If you think you're running this show, then you have another thing coming."

He holds out his wrists like he's waiting for cuffs. "Take me then," he says. "Fucking have me, Estrid."

Since he's offering, I wrap the shadows around his wrist, the touch so gentle, more a suggestion than an order. But then I tug, pulling him to me.

He grins salaciously when I draw him into my space. "Hello, goddess."

"Clay," I scold, but he ignores me.

"Is this what I can look forward to for the rest of our lives? Because sign me up."

"You've already signed up," I remind him. "We have a castle to restore, remember? Or did you change your mind?"

"Never."

"Good." I push him back onto the bed, which is still covered with the haphazard pile of clothes I'd ordered when I first got here. He reclines, smirking as he settles into the very expensive mess, and places his still-bound hands over his head.

I straddle his hips, looking down to take him all in. For a brief moment, I see a flash of the future I wish we could get, just like this forever. I run my fingertips from his shoulders down his chest, circling his nipple.

He pushes up into my hand. "I—*fuck*—I need *more*, Estrid."

I make my finger as cold as ice and trail it over his nipple in retaliation, making him hiss. "Don't rush me."

He pouts. "That was mean."

"I'm sorry," I croon, all fake sympathy as I lean down and suck his nipple into my warm mouth, tracing it with my tongue. He sighs under me.

I give the opposite nipple the same attention, then kiss up to his neck, sucking a bruise there.

"You leave the best marks," he murmurs.

"You like when I mark you?" I pull back, looking at the spot where my mouth just was.

"My pretty goddess wants to leave her mark on me, how could I not love it?" he asks, grinning dopily. I kiss him, then release his hands.

I'm not his goddess. Tonight I'm just Estrid, in bed with a man who makes me feel things I never expected to feel.

He takes a moment to realize I've dropped the bindings, but then his hand is in my hair, tilting my head to deepen our kiss. I let him, sinking into it, and it's like the rest of the world falls away, just for a minute.

"I want you to fuck me," I tell him, pulling back enough to talk. "Face-to-face. Slow. Just like this."

"Anything you want," he promises, then moves to sit up without displacing me.

He uses one hand on my hip to urge me up, then positions his cock at my entrance. I sink down onto it, not breaking our kiss as I rock him into my body fully. There. Just like this. Just him and me, one being with no beginning and ending.

He grounds me to Earth even when I feel like I'm a million miles away. I cling to him, rocking slowly together, letting him fill me and anchor me *here*, letting his eager, assuring kisses guide me home.

My orgasm doesn't punch through me like the last times we fucked. Instead, it creeps up on me slowly, then rushes through me, all-consuming and deep, a full-body experience that has me throwing my head back, unable to do anything but ride it out.

I'm floating. I'm floating away and only Clay grounds me, keeps me here with him as he rocks into me a few more times, then comes in me, his hot come filling me so entirely, proof this is real and we're *here*.

I hope I can feel this tomorrow. I hope when I walk I'm reminded of him, of us, of what we have. I hope I can't forget it, not even for a single second.

We rest there against each other, and I let him hold me like that, still inside me until at last his soft cock slips out and I know we have to face the morning light.

***

We haven't slept, but Clay doesn't complain. He puts on the clothes I ordered for the two of us before I joined him in the bath, a dark, all-black ensemble, and willingly takes my hand so I can bring us back to the wolf village.

Knowing more about the boundary spell protecting this village now, I have a new sense of appreciation for Greta's magic. And Mae, who apparently maintains the boundary spell to this day, despite proclaiming that she doesn't have a lot of magic.

"Where have you been?" Bryce asks, eyebrow raised.

We're standing in front of their house like we're just coming for a casual visit, about to knock on the door. I wish I could maintain that image. I wish I could let Clay and Mae talk about Greta. But I have to ruin it for everyone. "Getting ready," I tell him. "It's going to be tonight."

He just stares at me for a moment, and I stare right back. He looks away first, then nods. "I'll tell the others."

***

All these people barely fit in Celia and Bethany's living room, a fact that has not escaped Bethany. "Should we buy more couches?" she asks, setting a plate of sliced vegetables on the low coffee table.

Celia grabs her mate by the hips and pulls her onto her lap, forcing her to sit. "As much as I like everyone here," she drawls, "I could do with not having to have a three-species-wide war council in my home ever again."

"Five," Mae corrects. "You got werewolf, vampire, demon, witch, and halfling."

"Druid," Marielle says. "Halflings aren't our own species."

"Damn right," Hannah mutters. "It'd get lonely."

They've felt the othering that I have my entire life, I realize. Not quite a god, forbidden from going near humans. They're not quite one species, cast out from the divine. It's a shitty way to live.

It seems like all the halflings I know have found a family, at least. And Clay, still sitting beside me, hip to knee due to the tight quarters, might be mine.

"I want to thank you all for coming this far," I say after I tell them what we learned last night. "If anyone doesn't want to come along, I'd understand." I look over at Hannah when I say this, trying not to be too obvious about it, but wanting her to have a way out.

Hannah doesn't say anything, just flattens her mouth and waits me out. Ryder looks like he will say something for a moment, but thinks better of it.

Lorne, thankfully, stays quiet.

"No one's backing out," Callum says, voice deep. "You'll need us there." I open my mouth to say that I definitely don't need all of them, but he beats me to it, saying, "What if he brings backup, hm? He has a cult, Estrid. I know we've all killed a few of them, but there's probably more."

That is unfortunately a good point. I never considered that, falling into the same trap as Andreas, discounting anyone with less than my amount of power.

I suppose I should be thankful I'm surrounded by war generals who can fill in the gaps of my mistakes.

"Speaking of—I know you can probably find him with your weird shadow-thing," Heath says, "but what about civilians? Two near-gods going at it, that's going to cause a lot of damage."

"We need to lure him away, obviously." And I have the perfect place in mind.

"And how do we do that?" Heath presses.

Clay moves, drawing all eyes to him. "I can do that," he says, looking only at me. "I can get his attention."

I hate the idea of that. But Clay isn't wrong; he's the most qualified to tempt Andreas right now, the only one beside me who knows him personally.

So I nod and look out the window. It's well after mid-day now. Only a few hours left.

***

The plan isn't really that complicated.

Clay complains about freezing his balls off, but really, the northernmost point on Earth, with its near-eternal night this time of year, is my best bet. And I warned him. It's not my fault that he didn't think to get a warmer coat.

He's only been here a few minutes, anyway. I'd used my shadows to find Andreas, and then Chase had brought Clay there to yell our challenge and get out fast. Now, we wait.

"Think it worked?" I ask.

He smirks, temporarily forgetting the cold. "I told him there was only one divine turning into a god, and it wasn't him, and you were a thousand times the god he'd ever be, and you were prepared to challenge him for control of Earth. So, you know. Probably."

Good gods, that is *not* what I'd imagined. "Control of Earth?" I manage to ask.

He shrugs. "Mostly, I was just thinking of the ability to stay here and be with whoever you wanted. But if you want to become an evil dictator, I'll sign up as your first evil minion."

I roll my eyes. Of course. "I'll keep that in mind." I look around. "You should get back." Marielle and Callum are standing a dozen yards back from me, but everyone else is much further away, giving us a wide circle.

Clay kisses me, grabbing my shirt as if I'm going to disappear. "Not a fucking chance," he says. "If you're here, I'm here."

"That's all well and good, but you are *breakable*."

"Way to hurt my ego."

"Clay."

"I know what I am, Estrid," he says, suddenly serious. "And I know I'm yours. This is what it's all been for. I have to believe—I did so much wrong."

"You've fixed it," I argue.

"No," he says, smiling sadly. "I haven't. I know I haven't. I can't, not really. But being here, doing this, being what you need—that's a step."

"I need you to live through this," I tell him. I need him to live so I can convince him he's forgiven. That he's not a bad person.

"Same here. And I'm not leaving."

Fucking insufferable man. But before I can argue, the ground rumbles. It's time.

I can't call for Hannah from here, so I just have to hope she's ready. I look back at Marielle, giving her a small nod that she returns. Her mate, while hardier than Clay, really shouldn't be here either, but I know better than to argue with a wolf about protecting their mate.

Andreas rises out of the rocks and snow like some warped flower, standing tall and proud before me. "I heard you think you're a goddess now," he says.

I shrug. "Thought that, since the position was up for grabs, I was the one qualified to take it."

He laughs. "You? You never disobeyed the gods in your life. Patient little puppet, got punished for wanting a baby too bad. You don't have what it takes to take this world and *mean it*."

If I actually wanted to become a god, I might take offense to that. But I have no intentions of being a god, and that alone makes me better than him.

I take a deep breath, then step forward so Clay's behind me. I can't have Andreas think about him. I need this fight to be about just me and Andreas.

"Let's see, then," I offer him. "You, and me. The strongest divine wins godhood. Won't this make a wonderful story to convince your little worshipers that you're the god they always dreamed of?" I mock.

"You have no idea what you're saying," he rumbles. "I am the Earth, Estrid, and now, I am all living creatures. They feed me, the Earth feeds me. You're no match for me."

"We'll see."

His grin drips malice. "We will. But it's only fair, if you bring an audience—so will I."

Creatures pop out of the ground, surging through the crust of the Earth. Sorcerers, witches, demons, even a few fae—Andreas brought an army with him.

"This is about you and me," I tell him, shifting my weight.

"Oh, it will be. But we can let the rabble entertain each other." Like that's the signal they need, his small army moves, locking onto my people.

I can't turn, can't look. I can't take my eyes off the god in front of me.

"We have this," Clay says behind me, voice firm. "We knew what we were getting into. You do what you have to—we'll take care of this."

I force myself to take a deep breath, then another. I feel the night around me, the shadows dancing under my fingertips, the icy cold of the snow. I feel the people I care about and then let them go. This is it.

I can feel when Andreas reaches for his magic, trying to bring the rocks up to crush us once more, but more importantly, I can feel when he doesn't get what he wants. His eyes flash, and I feel a swell of pride for Hannah, holding the very Earth against Andreas.

She won't be able to do it for long. Even if she'd been practicing her magic since birth, she just doesn't have the strength to hold out against Andreas. But I just need a chance.

"What—"

I could tell him that this is his problem; Andreas has never considered anyone but himself. He's never thought about the children we abandoned, and he never considered the creatures of Earth as anything but pawns. But if he doesn't know the truth by now, then it's far too late for him.

I bring my darkness around me like a cloak, soaking in its protection, and ready to use it to kill. I send shadows to reach for Andreas, but he dodges out of the way, confusion still clear across his face as he reaches for the Earth. The already frigid air crystallizes around him, and he has to move fast so I don't encase him in a solid block of ice.

I try again and again, but he continuously dodges my attempts. When he starts throwing rocks at me, boulders as big as houses, I know Hannah's lost her hold. I spare a thought to hope that Ryder got her out of here, that the people Andreas sent after them never reached them, but I can't think about it too long, too busy trying to keep boulders from crushing me.

"You can dodge as long as you want, Estrid," Andreas taunts, stepping closer while neatly ducking out of my shadows. A bolder as big as a car almost hits me, and I have to grab it with my shadows, launching it back toward Andreas. He crumples it to dust, moving in on me in the split second my shadows are too busy protecting me to attack him. I try to freeze his feet to the ground, but it doesn't work; he breaks the snow with earth, and keeps walking toward me, a path of snow clearing for him. "I am the Earth. It is literally my destiny to rule this world. You can never hope to live up to that."

Energy crackles through the air. There. Marielle's found her source, and I can feel her gathering the magic.

It hits me all at once, a warm, bracing swath of night. I welcome it, dragging it into my own darkness, and close my eyes, letting it fill me.

The last time this trick was used on me, it hurt. It was alienating, isolating, taking the thing that is supposed to unite us and using it to punish me. But here, Marielle's darkness is like an embrace, like the greatest gift she could possibly give me. Whatever energy she pulls out of the night sky just fuels me, until I'm somehow *more* than I ever have been. I am the moon and stars, the cold of the night, and the warmest night breeze. I am peace and dreams and fear; I am everything, suddenly more than just my body can contain.

"I am literally made of starlight," I say, and my voice has a strange echo in it. "You have no idea what I can do."

And then I burst apart.

Chapter Thirty-Four

Clay

The darkness is all-consuming. I couldn't see six inches in front of my face if my life depended on it. I can hear steel clashing against steel, but I hold still, hoping to stay mostly unnoticed, holding my breath and waiting for Estrid.

And then stars emerge everywhere.

It's not like distant points of light on a clear night, though. It's closer, so much closer, and this is what it must be like to witness a star being born up close.

It's blinding. I duck my head, needing to look away even if I can't stand doing it. I need to watch Estrid, need to know she's okay—

But she's stardust right now. She's the light blinding us, powerful and beyond our comprehension, something more than the mere body she inhabits.

She *is* a goddess, whether or not she wants to accept that title. I keep thinking it, keep thinking that she's my goddess, that I worship her. I don't know if she can feel it, but if Andreas is stronger because he has worshipers, than for-fucking-sure is Estrid going to have some too.

Sound dies around us. It's not just quiet; it's unnaturally, deathly silent. I hold my breath.

C'mon, Estrid. C'mon.

She promised Lorne she'd teach her about her magic. I think Marielle has forgiven her enough that there's a future there for the two of them. And I need her at my side. I want to rebuild a godsdamn castle with her and live in the middle of nowhere.

I picture that future. We'll fix the castle up. We'll put in a bathtub like the one in the hotel last night, and we'll build a walk-in closet big enough for all the clothes Estrid has. She'll teach Lorne magic, and I'll work with mine until I recover it. Estrid will be at my side as I try to mend things with Greta and Mae. She'll hang out with her vampire family, and we'll have awkward family reunions.

And we'll travel, and we'll spend nights together, and, yes, go outside and sit in the woods because she enjoys that for some damn reason. Anything and everything, just as long as we have our future together.

There's a scream piercing the air, terrible and like nails on a chalkboard, sending shivers up my spine. I dare to look up, only to see a burning star falling toward me.

Chapter Thirty-Five

Estrid

I am the night.

It's hard to explain the feeling, the distance from what I am and the real me. I'm not me, but at the same time, I can't be anything else. This is the very essence of my being, the stardust I was born from.

Last time I was turned into my pure components, I'd fought it every step of the way. I'd screamed and cursed and clawed to return to myself until at last my sisters let me go. But now, I lean into it, letting myself be *more*.

My presence is effusive, spreading. Like liquid, like darkness, I take up all the space available to me, enveloping the world in my grasp.

Andreas panics and tries to sink into the Earth, but he's not fast enough. No longer bound by my body or the confines of the magic I've always known, I grab him, lifting him into the night sky with me.

"You were never going to win," I tell him, my voice coming from everywhere and nowhere. We're so much higher now, way above everyone that I so badly need to protect. If I look, I can see my way home, my way back to my sisters.

But no. It's not home anymore, and it never will be again. I won't go crawling back. I won't pretend I want to sit there and wait and wait and *wait* anymore. I won't live in a cage like the long-forgotten songbird.

Blood streams from Andreas' nose from the pressure of my grasp. I wonder absently if he's ever bled before. "And you think a little star can kill me?"

I think that this man doesn't know what a supernova is. The massive, incredible energy housed in a star, pure potential just waiting for its moment. But what I tell him is, "I have bigger problems than you."

Andreas is a symptom of a problem, and Greta gave me the last piece of the puzzle last night.

"Get off my home," I tell him. "You're each other's problem now, and I don't give a fuck what you all do to each other. If the gods show back up and take an interest in Earth again, you give them a message from me that they're not welcome either. You all can keep them entertained."

And then I push him away, letting the darkness hold him, and recite the spell I memorized last night.

I can feel it tugging at me, pulling on every molecule of my magic. It's good that Greta never tried this, because I have no doubt it would have killed her instantly. I'm relatively sure it's going to kill me. But my home, and all the people in it, will be safe, and that's what matters.

I close my eyes, watching the darkness grow thicker, an impenetrable barrier between us and them they can never cross again. Whatever they choose to do, it can't affect Earth anymore.

And then I fall.

CHAPTER THIRTY-SIX

CLAY

I move without thinking, positioning myself to catch that falling star.

I can barely look at her, bright as she is, but that doesn't matter.

As she gets closer, the burning heat from her singes the hair on my arms. At first, it's a prickle, and then a roaring inferno consumes me, setting me ablaze. I bite back a scream and force myself to hold steady. When she lands, both of us are driven into the blessedly cool snow, then down into the Earth.

My flesh sizzles with the contact, but I grit my teeth and hang on. The pain eases, but that might be because my nerves are destroyed. But the shape in my arms gets more solid, more real. "Estrid?" I croak. "Can you hear me?"

"Fuck!" I hear from above us. I ignore them, because they don't matter as much as the woman in my arms, the star whose light is slowly fading, and I can't decide if that's a good sign or a bad one.

"I'm here," Estrid murmurs, voice faint. "It's done."

I couldn't give less of a fuck right now. Suddenly, the two of us move, being thrown out of the ice and snow and onto the surface.

There's so many people standing like a shield around us. Hannah, presumably the one who threw us out of the ground, is panting, hands on her knees while Ryder fusses over her. Everyone else watches us with poorly hidden trepidation, blood splattered on their clothes and faces, but no one looks seriously hurt.

Estrid's glow fades entirely, until I'm looking at normal, beautiful her.

"Estrid?" Marielle asks, stepping forward.

I pull Estrid back into me. I can't help it; it's irrational and stupid. Marielle is a damned healer, and she's Estrid's niece. She's not going to hurt her.

I have to repeat that to myself five or six times before I can convince myself to let her close.

"How do you feel?" Marielle asks, kneeling in the dirt. All the ice melted from Estrid's heat, leaving a little circle around us.

Estrid opens her eyes. "Check Clay. I burned him."

I look down and see the raw, red skin and blisters on my now-bare arms, my jacket and shirt burned clean through. It doesn't even hurt anymore, which is probably a bad sign. "Huh."

Marielle reaches into her bag and pulls out a bunch of loose plants. Presumably, there's more logic behind it than I understand. She holds out her free hand to me, and I realize they're shaking. "You alright?" I ask.

"She exhausted herself, then tried to do more magic to slow Estrid down," her mate says shortly, voice more growly than I think I personally deserve in this case. His eyes keep flicking around like he expects more combatants to pop up out of the snow. A distant part of my mind is glad someone, at least, is taking the initiative to ensure we're safe.

"And I'll survive a little more," she says firmly. "Let me see your arm?"

I give her my arm, and it's like a warm, wet cloth when the magic rushes through me. When I pull back, my skin is clean and blister-free, and Marielle is swaying.

Callum grabs her before she collapses completely, sitting down in the dirt with her on his lap. He wraps around her like he needs to shield her, and I look away just as Mina sits next to us.

"You alright?" Estrid asks her. She doesn't turn her head, doesn't seem able to yet, but even her quiet voice carries the urgency of the question.

"You underestimate us if you think this crowd can't handle a few cultists," Mina says. She's got blood on her, and it doesn't escape my notice that a fair bit of it is concentrated around her mouth. "Is it done?" she asks Estrid gently.

"Done," Estrid confirms. I watch her, looking at the slow, listless movements, the way she doesn't make eye contact with any of us. She hasn't even tried to move from my arms.

"So he's dead?"

"No. He's their problem now. And none of them can come to Earth ever again."

There's silence for a minute, and then realization dawns on me. "The boundary spell."

"Yeah," she agrees. "I'm the boundary."

"Fuck," Heath mutters, a low whistle between his teeth. "That's crazy magic, right?"

"Way, way out of my realm," Chase agrees.

"Mine too," Ryder agrees, barely looking up from Hannah.

"I'm the only one who could do it. So I did," Estrid says firmly. Or as firmly as she can, at any rate. She still sounds a little like a kitten with a cold. "My magic, the darkness—it's in the boundary now. That's an entire star's worth of power, and no one else here could duplicate it. With the magic Marielle gave me—it was more than he expected, and now it's too late for him. I don't give a fuck what they do. I don't care if they punish Andreas or make him their new god or what. Just as long as they stay over there, and we stay over here."

"And this is one of Greta's boundary spells?" Mae asks.

"Mhm."

"You should be the one to go tell her she's safe now," I offer. Mae's eyes flicker to me, then away before she gives a curt nod.

Estrid closes her eyes, and my attention is immediately drawn back to her. "Are you okay? Are you hurt?"

She shakes her head, but I'm not very reassured when I see a tear slip out. "I can feel it," she whispers. "All of it."

"Does it hurt?" I press.

"No," she murmurs, and she opens her eyes to look directly at me and smiles, even though she's still crying a bit. "It feels safe now."

***

Ryder and Chase take turns teleporting us all back to Crae Village. Estrid frowns when she has to let someone else bring her somewhere, but she's in no condition to be spending so much magic right now.

As soon as we're back, Ryder nods his head and disappears with his mate. Callum stares at us a moment and then takes Marielle upstairs, carrying her as if she can't walk. And then Lorne bounds down the stairs, a look of stark relief crossing her face. "You all made it?" she checks.

"All in one piece." Mostly. We'll heal, at any rate.

"And you killed Andreas?"

"Banished," Estrid corrects, raising her head from the back of the couch, looking over at the kid. "It's done. You're safe. He'll never touch you again, Lorne."

Something in her relaxes completely. Her shoulders drop and her eyes brighten. "So, you're going to teach me magic now, right?" she checks.

Estrid chuckles, then raises a still-shaky hand to show the tremors off for the kid. "I spent a shit ton of magic doing what I did, and it's tied up now forever. I won't ever be as powerful as I was. Sure you want to learn from me?"

Lorne crosses her arms, looking very unimpressed. "What, did you have to give up your ability to teach too?"

"Not as far as I know."

"Then don't be an idiot," Lorne says, and she turns away.

Estrid pauses for a minute and then gives me a wry smile. "Well, I've been told, I guess. How do you feel about having the kid with us in the castle?"

I pull her back into my side and kiss her temple, because right now, nothing in the entire world sounds better.

CHAPTER THIRTY-SEVEN

ESTRID

If I could, I'd get us out of here in a heartbeat, but I can barely make the shadows reach out to me right now. My whole body starts physically shaking every time I try.

Mina has been more than helpful, trying to check in if there's anything I need every five minutes. Marielle wandered back downstairs an hour ago, seeming in better shape even if her werewolf follows a foot behind her at all times, and she offers any healing I might need. I should feel love, should feel a warmth that these people care about me enough to want to check on me, but I just feel stifled.

I don't need anything they're offering. At best, I need time. At worst, I need to accept the new reality that I have far less magic than I'm used to.

Clay notices first. "Hey, Chase."

"Yeah?"

"Can you do that thing? Where I picture something and you bring us there?"

"It'll cost you," he says blithely, shrugging.

"Clay doesn't pay for things," I mutter, nudging him with my foot. "That's my job."

Clay's hand lands on my ankle, squeezing lightly. "I'll pay this time," he says firmly. "I don't think you're quite up to giving up any more energy, Es. We need to go to bed anyway. You'll take us?" His thumb strokes over my ankle bone, and he reaches his other hand out toward Chase.

"Sure thing." And before I can so much as protest, or muster up the manners to say goodbye, we're gone.

We reappear in our hotel room, looking exactly the same as when we left it. The bed is still a mess with my clothes everywhere, and there's a bath towel balled up by the foot of the bed. Was that just this morning? Less than twenty-four hours ago? It feels like a million years ago.

"I'll leave you to it," Chase says, dusting off his hands. "I'm sure you'll hear from us soon, but for now, thank you. You kept my family safe, and we don't forget that." Then he disappears before I can say anything back.

"Let's get you to the couch," Clay murmurs, then stops. "Unless you'd prefer the bed?"

I roll my eyes. "I'm not actually sick, you know. I don't get sick."

"You're exhausted, basically. So, you should sit down."

I let him lead me to the couch. But when I get seated, I grab his wrist and refuse to let go until he sits with me. He doesn't put up much of a fight.

"You're free of whatever you think you owe me, you know," I murmur. I don't look at him, but I need to say it. Need to make this clear.

"Alright. Great, I guess. And what does that mean?"

"You did what I asked." I power through, because if I stop, I won't force myself to start again. "You're a hero, Clay. You were a part of this. You don't owe me or anyone else anything. So, if you don't want to stick around, I'd understand."

"Did you change your mind about the castle and all that?" he asks. "Because that's the future I've been planning on."

"What if I never get my magic back all the way?" I demand. "What if I'm just average? Normal. What if this is the most magic I ever have?"

He shrugs. "I'm probably never getting my magic back fully either. It's been a while, and I still don't feel like I used to. I think we need to accept it and move on. Doesn't change how I feel."

I finally allow myself to look at him, seeing how serious he is. "Even if I can't offer you power?"

"Yup."

"Even if I can't whisk you off to whatever thing you want to see?"

"First of all, you've never worried about what *I* want to see, don't pretend to start now. And second, planes exist. I hear first class is nice."

"Even if we have to rebuild a castle the old-fashioned way?"

"Like first class tickets, skilled workers can be hired with enough money."

"Oh, I see," I say, forcing levity into my voice even if I don't fully feel it yet. "So, as long as I still have money..."

"We're all set, yeah. I'll be a happy sugar baby and you'll hear no complaints from me." He kisses the side of my head, and I can feel the smile against my skin.

But I have to ask him one more question. "You liked the magic," I say. "You liked how powerful I was. You called me a goddess."

"If you think you are any less of a goddess because you have less magic at hand, then you're sorely mistaken." He takes my chin between two fingers and tugs me to look at him, and I let him. "You impressed me with your skills the first time we met, alright? You're powerful. You can kill me with a look. I already got it long ago, and I don't need a reminder to keep worshipping you. You are stunning exactly the way you are." He leans in and kisses my forehead. "And if you never have any magic at all, ever again, then that's fine. Besides, you're a hero, Es. You lost your magic protecting the entire world. I won't ever forget that."

I sigh, close my eyes, and lean in to kiss him. He greedily returns it, and soon enough, he's reclined on the couch and I'm straddling his hips.

"You can barely stand," he says, hands holding my hips as he pulls his mouth away from my searching kisses.

"If you think I don't have enough strength for this—"

He rolls his eyes. "Yes, yes, I get it. You're big and bad. Is this what it's going to be like with you forever?" It doesn't sound like a complaint, though.

I pause for a moment, pulling back so I can just look down at him. "Want to buy a castle with me?" I double-check.

He squeezes my hips. "Crumbling stone work and all." He tries to tug me down in another kiss.

But I have one more question. "Want to spend forever with me?"

He sits up, careful not to displace me, and leans in for another kiss. "I'd like nothing else," he promises, and then I kiss him, and as our lips collide, I finally believe it.

EPILOGUE: ESTRID

I wipe off my brow as discreetly as I can. I can't have the kid know that every damn one of our lessons puts me through my paces.

Lorne's magic grows in leaps and bounds, and she has years left to grow. As it is, I have to work my ass off to stay one step ahead of the kid. My sense of my magic has returned slowly, and I can feel it all now—but a lot of it's tied up in the spell I cast. I can feel the barrier spell, strong and impenetrable, protecting us all. It's there in the back of my mind, a constant itch almost, but that doesn't mean I can touch the magic.

"Alright, kid, you're done for the day," I tell her, studying the warm effusion of air around us now. Fascinating. I could put it out with a thought, and I have confidence that my chill will beat out her warmth. But maybe not forever.

Lorne rolls her eyes at me, a habit no amount of goodwill seems to break. "I'm going to town."

"Don't get arrested again." A seventeen-year-old wandering around the nearby town alone in the middle of the night and reporting she lived at the supposedly haunted castle on top of the hill did not go over well. Clay had to pick her up from holding.

She doesn't deign to give a response, flashing a peace sign and walking off.

She's young, and perhaps we should worry about her more. But she always comes home, and she knows how to take care of herself.

Lorne has also been instrumental in recruiting other halflings to come here. She didn't ask my permission first, but I'm learning that's Lorne's way. She does what she wants, and we all learn to work around her.

Lorne and Clay have started calling this place the "Estrid Night School for Wayward Halflings," which is both ridiculous and catching on. I have five halflings living in the repaired west wing right now, and Lorne promises me there will be more.

They're mostly adults, at least. At seventeen, Lorne is the youngest, and while I don't doubt we'll find some halflings younger than her, at least we know there's only so many years of that left.

One day, the only halflings will be old halflings. There will be no more abandoned children on Earth.

And while there are questions about what Greta's son or Hannah's newborn girl will grow up to be like, at least I know for sure they'll both be loved and wanted. Being loved means a lot more than being powerful.

Speaking of being loved, Clay wraps his arms around me from behind, leaning down to nip at my ear, teasing by tugging gently on my dangling earring with his teeth.

"Long day?"

"She runs me ragged," I admit, but only to him.

"Time to relax, then. Come see what I finished?"

I'm not sure I want to know.

Clay has gotten very *handy* since we took back ownership of the castle. Far from just spending my money on construction crews, Clay has apparently needed something to spend his time on, and half that time is spent on various experimental projects, claiming YouTube taught him how to fix whatever his target of the day is. His success rate is mediocre, and the construction crews I've hired have spent more than enough time fixing the messes he makes.

But he's happy, and that's all I can ask for.

When Clay isn't breaking my house, he's emailing my great-great-grandson. Silas' love for research has collided with Clay's desire to collect spells, and they've built quite a little library between them. I think one day Clay might even work up the nerve to share it with others, even if he's still hoarding it pretty hard.

Who knows? Maybe one day this place will be the Estrid Night and Clay Sparks School for Wayward Halflings and Witches. I wouldn't mind that.

We'll need to fix up another wing before that could even be possible, though.

"Well, let's see it, then," I agree, bracing myself for the disaster.

"Where's the kid?" he double-checks.

"Headed into town. I'm assuming she's looking for a meal."

"Perfect. And the others are making their own dinners."

"Did you eat?" I check.

"No. But I'm starving. Let's go get me a meal right now." He squeezes around my middle as he says it, rocking against me, and I know exactly what type of meal he's after.

I lightly hit his arm. "You know exactly what I meant, Clay."

"I ate an hour or so ago, promise. Now let's go."

Rolling my eyes, I wait for him to let me go and take my hand so he can drag me where he wants me. Judging by his comment, I assume he's dragging me to bed, and I am definitely not opposed. Finishing a hard day's work with some vigorous sex? Yes, please.

Only when I go to the west wing, Clay tugs on my arm and steers me east. "Not there," he says.

I frown. The whole east wing is a dilapidated mess and includes the room where I held Clay hostage the first time I brought him here. There's not even a functioning stairwell, which had been the point when I'd tried to trap Clay here.

Except now there is a staircase. It's not quite done yet, the wood needing to be stained and polished, but I raise an eyebrow anyway, impressed. "You've been busy."

"Don't give me all the credit. I had help."

No shit. The stairs don't feel like they might fall down under us, so that was my first clue that this isn't just Clay's work.

The upstairs hallway looks better. It's not back to its former grandeur by any means, but it doesn't look like a health hazard. I'm wondering exactly how long I've avoided looking in this wing, because this isn't just an afternoon's worth of work.

"Yeah, I know it's not all pretty yet," Clay murmurs, misinterpreting my stunned silence. "We had to prioritize some things. Consider this a work in progress."

If this isn't what they prioritized, then what the hell did they do?

The answer becomes apparent when Clay leads me into the bedroom. Not the one I imprisoned him in, thankfully, but a grand room that once was beautiful.

I walked the whole castle when I re-claimed it, and I can tell you with confidence that this room was filled with rubble and animal remains then. But now it looks like something out of a fairy tale.

Perhaps not a fairy tale. That's a flat-screen on the wall, and that's a decidedly modern mattress. But the luxurious finishings and beautiful touches make me tear up.

"Knocked out the next room on either side to make closets and a bathroom to die for," Clay murmurs, as if he knows I need a moment. "Tub is more than big enough for two, if you're interested."

And oh, am I interested. But not right now. Right now, I'm more interested in the giant bed in the middle of the room and the man beside me.

Wordlessly, I grab him by the front of the t-shirt he's wearing, and that should have been my first clue. He was so excited that he didn't change before coming to see me.

Huh. I should maybe consider that bath. If he didn't change, he certainly didn't shower.

But no. I need him and I need him right now. Nothing fancy, nothing dramatic. Just me and him, me and this witch who can still barely do magic, but nonetheless, has me entirely under his spell.

He grins as I tug him toward the bed. "You like it?" he asks, like that question even needs answering.

"I like it." It feels like *home*. Not like it's meant to replace my old home, whether that be this castle in its former grandeur or my home with my sisters. I've described both to Clay in varying amounts of detail over the last six or so months, but he didn't try to emulate them. No, this home is ours, a place for us. A place for our future.

"I figured it was time we had space away from everyone else," Clay says. "It's not like they need us to look after them, and we're reasonably assured we're not getting younger ones, and—"

"And you needed a place where we could be loud?" I ask, pushing him onto the bed and crawling over him.

His grin widens, sexy and deadly. "You get me."

I do. And he gets me.

His hands find my hips, trying to tug me to sit on his cock, but I stay leaning over him, just making him wait. "How much do you want me?" I ask.

"I built you this entire bedroom. Doesn't that tell you?"

"It tells me you want to fuck."

"I *do* want to fuck," he mutters, but he rolls us so he's hovering over me, my legs around his hips. "I want you forever, Estrid. You have to know that. I want an eternity of re-building this damn castle, and learning what it means to be a teacher, and being at your side. I want that. All of it."

I let him stay on top of me, something warm and satisfied coursing through me. I lean up to take his mouth in another kiss, biting at his lower lip when I pull away. "Then have me," I murmur. And, just so there's no confusion, I add, "Forever."

He rolls his still-clothed hips against my core before stepping back, shedding his clothes in record time. I get my shirt unbuttoned before he comes back and removes my leggings so decisively I think a seam might have ripped.

"Fuck me," he mutters. "You were wearing this all day?"

I preen, running a hand from the edge of my breast down to just above my panties. The silk and lace set in a deep emerald had looked stunning in the store, but it looks even better on me. "Mhm."

"Fuck me," he mutters again, and then makes a sucking sort of noise when I sit up to remove my bra. He sounds more like a man gasping for his last breath than my lover, and I just raise an eyebrow. "You've seen tits before."

"Still fucking beautiful," he murmurs. His cock, half-hard from rubbing against me in bed, is now completely ready for me. I want him inside me, want to tug him down and roll him over and take him, make this good for both of us, make us—

No. I take a deep breath, spreading my thighs. Seduction. Clay built me a bedroom worthy of this place, of the life we're going to build. The least we can do is break it in properly.

Clay falls to his knees between my spread thighs, looking up at me with an expression that's more tease than devotion. His hands move like feathers over my thighs, spreading them slightly wider. "Still feel worshipped?" he checks.

I don't need his or anyone else's worship. I don't need more magic than I currently have. I don't need a palace of night or goddesshood or even the approval of my father. I just need this. Us. Here.

The way Clay looks at me, touches me, loves me. That's all I need.

"Come here," I whisper, tugging him up to me, and he does.

LOOKING FOR MORE?

Check out an exclusive bonus epilogue for newsletter subscribers featuring Clay and Estrid joining the mile-high club. You can subscribe at addyjames writer.com, and be the first to receive updates on future stories.

WHAT TO READ NEXT?

Looking for more supernatural creatures, obsessive, adoring mates, and tension? Check out the Supernatural Christmas series, which starts with Max and Casey's story.

A Werewolf for Christmas contains tropes such as: he's only good for her, obsessed mmc, touch her and die, werewolf shifter, and secret identity. It has plenty of steamy scenes and also some light violence.

***

When I drive, I force myself to let go of the version of me that exists only when I'm in our house. Another version of me exists in the outside world, and that's the version Luc and the others expect to see.

I'm not a good man, never have been, and don't pretend to be except when I'm with Casey. Even then, I'm not really a good man—I can't ever pretend I wouldn't do horrible, horrible things if I needed to keep her happy and healthy and alive—but at least I'm a good husband.

I'm not technically her husband, no matter how much I want to be, but it doesn't stop me thinking about myself like that. I'll be the best damn husband for Casey.

In the entire time I've known her, there's only been four things she's wanted that I've denied her, and each one hurts me bitterly. I want to give her the world, and each of these things is something I ache to give her, but just can't.

One, a pet. Casey has never flat-out asked if we could get a pet at our place, but I'd have to be blind to not see the way she coos at cute animals. She strikes me as a cat person—or perhaps I just want to be the only canine in her life—and I could see her working from home with a cute little cat curled up on her lap.

I'd take her to the shelter this afternoon to adopt one, but animals don't like me much. They're much more astute than humans at sensing the predator inside me. And how would I explain that to Casey? A whole shelter going quiet when I walk in, all the animals too afraid to be near me, and then whatever fluffy little creature she adopts spending its life hiding away from me, terrified to be in my presence. I can't do that to her.

Two, a vacation. I travel plenty on Luc's orders, but I've never taken Casey away for more than a night or two. I've had wet dreams of her and me at some tropical resort, her in some little string bikini that shows off her tits, me rubbing sunblock into her skin. But if Luc needs me, I need to be here. That's the deal I made, and I can't see that debt being discharged in this lifetime.

Three, a tattoo. Casey has a whole body full of them, beautiful artwork she takes so much pride in. And she knows I love them and can spend hours touching and licking them. There's a crescent moon on her upper thigh that I can get hard at just the barest sight of, like some Pavlovian reaction.

She knows I have a few tattoos, too, so she doesn't understand why I won't go meet her favorite artist—a nice woman named Jack who I did a very thorough background check on the first time I learned she was going to be putting her hands on my wife—but how do I explain that, in order for a tattoo to stick in my skin for more than a day or so, the ink needs to be infused with silver dust? And that the tattoos I have are more than six centuries old?

Four is the hardest, though. I know Casey wants to be married. We've even talked about it a bit, and in the last six months or so she's started to say things like when we're married, which makes me feel simultaneously like I'm fifteen feet tall and like I'm shit on her shoe.

I can't marry her. Not when I can't give her the truth. And I can't give her the truth until I can give her a solution. What, am I supposed to say hey, I'm a supernatural creature, I turn into a great big dog sometimes, I strike fear into the hearts of nearly everyone, I can lift a car one-handed, and, oh yeah, I stopped aging when Roman legions were still in style?

Worse, though, is I know what's expected after a marriage. Children. I suppose I could pretend that I don't want them, but Casey would know I was a liar. A baby that's half her sounds like the best thing in the world, but I just know it would be like me. A baby like me could kill her. It'd be like having a wild animal in the house.

So I can't marry her. Not until I can promise us both that I have a solution to that little problem.

Either a solution that makes me mortal like her, or one that makes her like me. I'm not going to be picky about it, although I won't lie; I'd prefer to make her immortal. For one thing, I think this world could use someone like Casey sticking around a lot longer than one measly human lifetime. For another, I'm not sure if I believe in any sort of specific afterlife, but if I did, I'd be an idiot to think people like Casey and people like me go to the same one. And I can't find it in me to be satisfied with just a few decades of her.

And that's why I have to go see Luc, even if it's two days until Christmas and there's nothing I want more than to do whatever is on Casey's honey-do list for this party tomorrow night.

I owe Luc my life. I owe Luc my soul, really, because the compound we'd been raised in, bred and trained as soldiers, caged until it was time to fight, was no life at all. Luc had been the only one smart enough to find a way out, and he'd chosen to take me with him. In return, he'd asked for just one little thing; my protection and dedication to his rise to power.

It had taken just about two millennia, but I'd done it. I'd helped him secure a metaphorical crown, been the muscle behind his empire. I'd intimidated, threatened, stalked, and murdered on his behalf.

I'd even fucking hammered in lawn signs when he decided he needed to run for governor, just to have that one extra layer of political power. Because it wasn't enough to rule creatures like us from the shadows; he'd needed to have the real, tangible power that even the humans can see.

Lucius Lawson is going to be President of the United States one day, a hilarious fate for a man who is not technically a US citizen and is far, far older than the country in question. And for a while, that hadn't bothered me at all, because I'd assumed I'd be out. I'd have facilitated his rise to power, given him the control he needed, and I'd either be working for him of my own free will, or else moving on.

Until I'd met Casey.

I'd just cleared one debt to Luc when I already knew I'd need to enter into another one; I needed whatever magic there was to make our lifespans match. I didn't care what it would take, or who I'd need to kill. I just needed it. And I know I'm not smart enough to find it for myself. But Luc is.

So yeah, I'm not a good man. Luc's orders have permanently stained my hands red, and I won't pretend I could ever be clean of them. I won't pretend I care that much, either. But for Casey? I'll be whatever she fucking needs. I'll be Luc's killer to the rest of the world, and the husband who adores her whenever we're together.

ALSO BY ADDISON JAMES

Supernatural Christmas

A Werewolf for Christmas

A Recipe for Love

Crae Romance

Callum

Bryce

Heath

Celia

Silas

Estrid

Standalones

The Heat Cure

Dragon's Treasure

ABOUT THE AUTHOR

Addison James is a romance book author from New England. They are obsessed with all things mythical, mystical, and magical. A lifelong fantasy reader, that evolved to fantasy romance as they grew up. Addison always has a story to tell and is excited to introduce you to their world of fantasy romance.

www.ingramcontent.com/pod-product-compliance
Lightning Source LLC
Chambersburg PA
CBHW020718130726
47899CB00011B/401